W9-ATZ-752

Praise for the
Mothers & Daughters
collection, also available
from Signet . . .

"Wonderful! . . . an inspiring anthology guaranteed to touch the heart and lift the spirits of mothers and daughters everywhere."   —*Romantic Times*

"If your daughter doesn't give you *Mothers & Daughters* for Mother's Day, bestow a copy on her."   —*Good Housekeeping*

"Poignant tales that celebrate the love and bonds between mothers and daughters."
     —*Publishers Weekly*

Mothers & Sons

*A Celebration
in Memoirs, Stories,
and Photographs*

Edited by Jill Morgan

A SIGNET BOOK

SIGNET
Published by New American Library, a division of
Penguin Putnam Inc., 375 Hudson Street,
New York, New York 10014, U.S.A.
Penguin Books Ltd, 27 Wrights Lane,
London W8 5TZ, England
Penguin Books Australia Ltd, Ringwood,
Victoria, Australia
Penguin Books Canada Ltd, 10 Alcorn Avenue,
Toronto, Ontario, Canada M4V 3B2
Penguin Books (N.Z.) Ltd, 182–190 Wairau Road,
Auckland 10, New Zealand

Penguin Books Ltd, Registered Offices:
Harmondsworth, Middlesex, England

Published by Signet, an imprint of New American Library, a division of
Penguin Putnam Inc. Previously published in a New American Library
hardcover edition.

First Signet Printing, April 2001
10 9 8 7 6 5 4 3 2 1

PUBLISHER'S NOTE
Some of the selections in this book are works of fiction. Names, characters,
places, and incidents either are the product of the author's imagination or are
used fictitiously, and any resemblance to actual persons, living or dead,
events, business establishments, or locales is entirely coincidental.

CONTENTS

Jill Morgan

With Love

AN INTRODUCTION

Family gatherings are a time for reflection on relationships. Recently, I attended my younger son's wedding. Chris looked handsome and a little nervous as he stood at the altar waiting for his bride to walk down the aisle. Beside him, also looking handsome and nervous, stood his best man and brother, Terry, my older son. My husband John and I glanced from our sons to the back of the church where our daughter, Lisa, would join the maid of honor and other bridesmaids in the bridal procession to the altar. The bridesmaids had not arrived at the church doorway yet. I turned my attention back to my sons. Swept up in all the joys of this day, memories flooded my mind as I saw both of my sons, their childhood and adulthood mingling through the loving vision of a mother's eyes.

Years passed in an instant, and once again my sons were two small boys, noisy, playful, smart as whips, and always the light of my life. Highlights of that time connected one by one as events, big and small, replayed in my mind. There is Terry, beside me on the sofa in our tiny one-bedroom apartment. He is eighteen months old, an adorable baby with impish green eyes, boyish bangs that fall across his forehead, and a happy contagious laugh. He is turning pages in a copy of *TV Guide*, as if he could read.

"Channel Two," he says, pointing to the page. "*I Love Lucy*." I am amazed that he is right. Then he points to *Sesame Street*, another favorite show of his, and I realize that he really *can* read. He has taught himself to recognize letters and numbers. I look at my year-and-a-half-old baby, thrilled by this achievement of my bright little boy. Yet, late that night when everyone else is asleep, I lie awake and think about the fact that my son is growing away from me. He has not needed me for this. I feel the loss keenly. He will grow and change and become a strong, independent person. It is what I want, and what I know must be, but in my heart I grieve a little for the mother and child bond that must be stretched in order to give him room to grow.

When Terry is nearly four, his brother is born. Christopher comes into my world, and the mother and child bond that had seemed so full, stretches and grows again, enfolding the love of two sons. Chris is an absolute charmer, with an angelic smile and a mischievous twinkle in his eyes. His hair is blond and full of baby curls, and his little bare toes turn up as he laughs in peals of delight.

Each milestone in their lives—Christopher at a year old and learning to walk out of my arms and race after his big brother; Terry at two and a half, going to his first day of nursery school and reading for the teacher a handwritten note taped to the door of her classroom—is noted with tremendous maternal pride . . . and with a tiny pang of regret that the circle of our love is ever widening, expanding, and moving away from the oneness at the center. Once, they were part of me, children I carried beneath my heart. Each day, they wander from me a little farther. I know this is how it should be. "Go, little birds," I want to say to them. "Try your wings. Fly. But always come back home to me."

And how they flew!

Over the years I watched my sons change from little boys to young men, saw them graduate from elementary school, intermediary school, high school, and college. With each of these ceremonies I stood back a little farther. *Wow*, I thought, seeing them in turn, *look how far he's come.* The circle seems very wide now, holding all that each of my sons had become, and it is still stretching and growing.

When my first novel sold, I was on vacation with my husband in Carmel. It was Terry who called and told me that my agent had sold the book. I remember the sound of his voice, how excited he was for me. He knew how much this meant to me. And later, when my book was published, it was Terry who sent a telegram from London, where he was attending a summer university semester, congratulating me on my achievement. Terry has read every published book and story of mine, and some that never sold. I have no illusions that he does this because I am his favorite author, but because I am his mother and he loves me. I hope he knows how much I love him for it.

Each of my sons has shown me his love in many ways. Six years ago, when my mother died and I thought I would break into pieces from grief, it was then twenty-two-year-old Chris who volunteered to go to Texas with me for her funeral. He stood beside me at the graveside service. I remember asking him to stay close, and he did. He was gentle, strong, and supportive for me, at a time when I truly needed these things. At Chris's suggestion, instead of flying back to Los Angeles as we'd planned, we rented a U-Haul trailer and loaded it with a few boxes of my mother's dishes, precious photographs and letters, and an antique Victrola I'd inherited from her. Chris drove the whole way from Austin to L.A., listening sympathetically while grief made me talk endlessly about my mother, the pain I felt at losing her, and compulsively list in detail all of the legal documents I still had to file as executrix of her estate. He comforted me when I wept, and was there for me when I needed him most. I will never forget it, and want him to know that it is sealed in my heart forever.

Each time my sons have gone away, leaving home for college, or a graduation trip to Europe, I know that one door has closed and another has opened. We are moving into a larger space. I was the one who sent them, insisting that they have the experience of living away from home during their college years, and that they travel to other parts of the world, still testing their wings and learning to fly. I knew one day they would have to fly away, and I wanted them to be strong and ready. And if I let them go again and again and again, they would always remember where home was.

My heart has many rooms, and memories that fill them to overflowing . . . of Terry and his puppet shows and haunted houses, of Chris climbing the hallways of our house as *Spiderman*, of Cub Scouts and Cotillion, of a thin boy in an Indiana Jones hat, cracking a bullwhip in our front yard, of my sons and their little sister racing through the sprinklers on hot summer afternoons, of four-year-old Chris and two-year-old Lisa sharing tea parties with their stuffed animals on the lawn . . . all the sweet days of their childhood.

The music plays, and we turn to see the bridal party entering the church. This is Chris's wedding day, and I am back in the present. Terry stands beside his brother as best man. Their sister, Lisa, a bridesmaid, walks down the aisle toward us. There are tears of joy in her eyes, tears in her brothers' eyes, her father's, and in mine.

It is a day of letting go.

We stand to honor the bride as Michelle walks down the aisle on the arm of her father. She is so beautiful. I glance back at Chris and see the look of complete love for this woman shining from his eyes . . . and know that he is already gone.

It is the way it should be.

In this anthology of twelve original stories and tributes on the theme of relationships between mothers and sons, you will find memoirs so poignant the images will stay with you forever. There are stories by high-profile women authors, written in collaboration with their sons, a memoir written by mother and son, and loving tributes to their mothers written by best-selling male authors.

I imagine that behind each story, memoir, and tribute, there is a mother-and-son bond, strong and enduring, that stretched and grew to enfold and encompass all the memories found within these pages. This book is our gift to mothers and sons everywhere.

With love.

Eileen Goudge

Looking After Lulu

Michael and Eileen Goudge at her wedding.

"Why should I listen to you?" Eric slouches against the refrigerator, arms crossed over his scrawny chest.

Despite the anger coming to a boil inside her, Nan hesitates. The standard responses come to mind: *Because I'm your mother!* or her personal favorite, guaranteed to get her son's eyes rolling, *Twelve-year-olds don't get a vote in this house!* But under the present circumstances, neither seems to apply. Or maybe she's just too tired to think of the right thing to say, exhausted to the bone from moving three thousand miles to what might as well be another planet. If you took a poll, she wonders, how many of her neighbors on Avenue J and East Fourteenth in Brooklyn would know that the Pacific Ocean isn't just one shade of blue, but a thousand different ones that shift, like moods, from day to day?

Like the mood she's in now: a combustible brew of exasperation, anxiety, and being stretched to her absolute limits. All of it focused at this moment on her son.

"Because," she snaps. "Because you don't have a choice." Sucking in a deep breath of the sluggish July air that creeps through the open window to sit like an uninvited cat on the sill, air redolent of curry and exhaust fumes and wet laundry strung out on clotheslines (even the smells here are like a foreign language she must struggle to interpret), Nan reminds him, *"None* of us has a choice. Don't you think we'd be living in a nice apartment in Greenwich Village if I could afford it?"

"It was your choice to move out here, wasn't it? We were just fine in Montecito." Even Eric's body language is insolent somehow. In baggy Levi's that puddle about his preposterously huge Nikes, he begins to rock back and forth, propelling himself forward with twisting thrusts and thumping back against the fridge on bony shoulder blades that stick out like dorsal fins.

Ready tears spring to Nan's eyes, but she blinks them back. "We were fine until your dad walked out on us, you mean." She watches Eric bounce to a stop and swallow hard. His Adam's apple bobbing in his skinny neck reminds her of his favorite toy when he was little: a clown that rode up a stick when you pulled a string. She knows he's hurting, too—a severe case of arrested hero worship—but it doesn't stop her from adding, "One thing's for sure, he wasn't thinking of us, or how I was supposed to support you and your sister."

Eric casts a scornful eye about the dingy kitchen with its plywood cabinets and beige linoleum curling away from the walls like an old Band-Aid. "Like you're doing such a great job."

She itches to smack his smart mouth, but their gazes lock in a deadly staring match instead. From the living room drifts the low mutter of the TV and the chirping of her five-year-old playing contentedly with her Barbie dolls. "Ooohhh, Marcy, you look so preeeetttty," Lulu mimics in a high singsong voice. The same voice in a slightly lower register replies, "Why, thank you, Darla. I bought it from Home Shopping Network, all for the super-low price of ninety-ninety dollars, avail-bubble in four easy payments." An uncomfortable reminder of how much TV the children have been watching lately. Lulu, for reasons known only to her, is entranced by the Home Shopping Network, with its sparkling zircons and once-in-a-lifetime offers.

"I'm doing the best I can." Nan speaks in a low, tightly furled voice. "Which is more than I can say for you. It's not enough just to walk your sister home from school. I expect you to treat her the way a big brother should, not hit her for going too slow."

Eric drops his gaze. "I didn't hit her that hard. And she was dragging her feet on purpose, making me look stupid in front of my friends."

What have your friends got to do with it? she almost shouts before remembering what it was like to be Eric's age, when every little thing was viewed under the magnifying glass of peer approval. More gently, she points out, "A lot of your friends have little sisters, too. I'm sure they won't think less of you just because they happen to see you with Lulu."

Her son stalks over to the cupboard by the stove. Rummaging around—he's so tall, he doesn't need to stand on tiptoe anymore—he pulls out a box of Saltines, griping, "How come you never buy Goldfish anymore? This stuff sucks."

"Because I can't afford Pepperidge Farm, and you

know it. Give me that"—she snatches the box of crackers out of his hands—"and go apologize to your sister. *March.*"

He glares at her, stubbornly rooted to the spot. "I don't see why. She's over it by now. Playing with her stupid Barbies. That's all she ever does."

Lately, Eric has begun to object to everything about his sister, including her nickname, Lulu, short for Liesel—the legacy of her Austrian grandmother on Russ's side. He says it makes her sound like a dog, one of those fluffy French poodles like the one the old lady next door to them in Montecito used to carry around in her purse. Why couldn't she have a *real* name, like Tiffany or Heather or Chloe? And why did she have to wear that stupid pink My Little Pony backpack to school every day when everyone knows they don't give homework to kindergarteners?

Nan is suddenly too tired to argue. Sinking down at the kitchen table, a leftover from the former tenant, a Pakistani grocer and his family, she stares at the whorls in the yellow Formica. If she stares long enough maybe they'll reveal something, like cloudy mists evaporating in a crystal ball to show a bright sparkling future.

Six months ago when Russ moved out, her friend Carole from high school stated emphatically that it was the best thing that had ever happened to Nan. Carole had done the smart thing herself by skipping marriage and motherhood and proceeding directly to Go. Now, fifteen years later, she is a senior vice-president at Random House. She insisted Nan pull up stakes and move to New York like she'd always talked about doing, adding slyly that there was a job open-

ing in her department for which Nan, who'd majored
in English Lit at UCSB, would be perfect.

It had seemed like a good idea at the time. Like
Katharine Hepburn in *Desk Set*. A fresh start, a whole
new life. And if she had two kids to support on a piti-
ful starting salary, well, they'd simply make an adventure of it.

Not until she and the children had arrived, entering
the strange and forbidding territory of two-fare zones
and CLOSED FOR SHABBOS signs and public schools
barred and fenced in like prisons, did she begin to
wonder if perhaps she'd made a hasty decision. But
it's too late for regrets, she tells herself, determined to
look on the bright side. Their apartment, the top floor
of a two-family house, is sunny at least. And while
the streets in their neighborhood are a cross between
New Delhi and Tel Aviv, she reasons that it will be a
good cultural experience for kids whose only real lesson in racial tolerance has been Kermit the Frog war-
bling, "It's Not Easy Being Green."

Even so, she frets. About Eric mostly. He was never
a problem before this. He used to love playing big
shot to his baby sister. In Montecito, he would occasionally read to her. And when he was in a goofy
mood, entertain Lulu with monkey faces or armpit
farts that would send her into peals of laughter. On
long trips in the car, he would sometimes let her crawl
into his lap.

Nowadays he can't look at Lulu without scowling.
Nan fears he'll turn out like Russ, who has little use
for females except when they're waiting on him. Or
worse, that Eric's anger at his father for leaving them,
coupled with being uprooted from the only home

he'd known, has damaged him in some fundamental way. What if one day he gets mad enough to stalk off and leave Lulu stranded on the sidewalk? If Nan can't trust Eric to walk his sister home from school, she doesn't know how she'll manage.

Below, she can hear the faint sound of the klezmer music Rabbi Scheiner plays on his stereo—the only music allowed in their home. The Scheiners' six children, ranging in age from two to fourteen, are amazingly well behaved. The older ones cheerfully look after the younger ones, and seldom fight with one another. Ezra, the oldest boy, is the same age as Eric, but the two have about as much in common as aliens from separate planets who happen to be thrown together under one roof. Just the other day, Eric reported to Nan with disgust that Ezra even changed his baby sister's diapers.

Despair rises up in Nan, thick and hot as the summer heat that isn't so much dispelled as pushed from side to side by their ancient window fan. She never should have moved out here. She'd imagined publishing to be glamorous: women in high heels and men in coats and ties exchanging witty remarks and offering cogent criticisms to the Virginia Woolfs and Truman Capotes of tomorrow. Instead, it's mostly slogging through dog-eared manuscripts and sitting through endless meetings for less money than she would have made as a secretary in Montecito. And for what? So she can pretend she's fulfilling her dream of a career while her children more or less fend for themselves— under the watchful eye of Mrs. Scheiner downstairs— and her son grows to resent his sister more with each passing day?

In the next room, the TV channel is switched to something noisy and no doubt mindless, with Eric shouting over Lulu's protest, "You've seen enough of that junk. The Home Shopping Network isn't even a real show, dufus."

Lulu lets out a high-pitched wail that brings Nan to her feet with a dizzying lurch. She rushes into the living room and instead of merely switching off the TV, reaches around to yank the plug out of its socket. Eric, sprawled on the hideous blue shag carpet in front of the screen, tilts his shaggy blond head up to fix a wary eye on her.

"That's it! I've had just about as much of you as I can take, young man," she scolds. "Go to your room this instant. And don't you dare set one foot out that door without my permission."

He takes his sweet time dragging himself to his feet, glowering darkly at Lulu as if it were all her fault, while his little sister watches teary-eyed from the sofa, like an injured flower girl in her ruffled gingham dress, Barbie outfits, and tiny plastic pink accessories strewn about the cushions like rose petals.

Even so, Lulu sniffles back her tears, piping, "It's okay, Mommy. Eric can stay. I promise I won't be a crybaby."

As he trudges past, Eric mutters under his breath, "I hate you."

Nan isn't sure who it's directed at, her or Lulu. And right now she's too angry to care. If one of Esther Scheiner's sons were to talk to his mother that way, there would be no end to the repercussions, she's sure.

She plops down wearily on the sofa next to Lulu.

"Mrs. Scheiner said you were crying when you got home. She said you told her Eric hit you really hard. Is that true?"

Lulu nods so hard, her flaxen pigtails bob up and down. Nan notices the part in her hair is crooked; she should have done a better job of combing it this morning—*would* have, if she hadn't been so rushed. "It wasn't my fault," Lulu insists.

"What wasn't your fault?" Nan coaxes.

"My shoe. It gotted a rock."

"Did you explain that to Eric?"

Another emphatic nod. "He yelled at me to hurry up. Eric was mad 'cause Bobby wanted to play, but he had to take me to Miss Susie's instead."

Every Thursday after school, Eric walks Lulu to her ballet class on East Sixteenth and picks her up an hour later. The rest of the time, until Nan gets home from work, Esther Scheiner keeps an eye out. Nan feels bad about taking advantage of a woman with six children of her own, but since she can't afford a baby-sitter she has no other choice. And Esther is nice enough not to rub it in, claiming she isn't really doing much more than leaving the door to the stairwell ajar. And what's an extra helping or two of *kugel* when she's already feeding so many?

Lulu hops off the sofa to twirl about, arms steepled over her head. "Look at me, Mommy. I'm a fairy!" Her first recital is in two weeks, and all Nan can think of is how relieved she is that it's taking place on a Saturday.

"The only fairy I know with Play-Doh stuck to her fanny," she laughs.

Lulu spins to a halt, and starts to giggle. The sight

of her chubby daughter attempting to peer over her shoulder at her backside while trying to hold her wobbly balance causes Nan to giggle, too, in spite of herself. She jumps up, scooping Lulu into her arms just as she's about to topple over.

"Hey, how about dinner? I brought home those Chinese dumplings you like."

"Some for Eric, too?" Lulu asks hopefully. Despite how he treats her, she worships the ground her big brother walks on.

"You bet." Nan wonders how long she ought to leave him to sulk in his room. It's quarter past seven. Downstairs, the Scheiners are probably already washing up. She sighs. Ten more minutes, she decides.

But when she knocks on the door to Eric's room, there's no answer. Easing it open, she peers inside to find her twelve-year-old son fast asleep, one stocking foot dangling over the edge of the mattress and his face mashed into his pillow in a way that makes him appear to be scowling. The dried tears on his cheeks cause Nan's throat to catch. She doesn't have the heart to wake him. She'll leave something in the fridge in case he gets hungry later on.

Hours later, though, it isn't the sound of Eric prowling about that startles her from a sound sleep. Nan wakes to the sight of Lulu standing beside her bed with her thumb plugged securely in her mouth and her eyes pooled with shadow.

"Sweetie, what's the matter?" Lulu has been having bad dreams lately, but this one must have been *really* scary—she hasn't sucked her thumb in months.

Lulu uncorks her thumb with a soft wet plop. "Mommy, Eric's not in his bed," she whispers loudly.

Nan drags herself into a sitting position. "He's probably in the bathroom. Or in the kitchen getting something to eat."

In her wrinkled Winnie-the-Pooh nightgown, Lulu looks small and defenseless. Since Russ moved out, she's fallen into the habit of conducting bed checks in the middle of the night. The psychologist Nan consulted had said not to worry too much, Lulu is just making sure no one else deserts her.

Lulu shakes her head. "I looked *everywhere*."

A flicker of alarm propels Nan to her feet. The thought creeps in: *What if he's run away?*

"Eric?" She waits a moment, calling out even louder, *"Eric!"*

No answer.

Her bare feet shuffle frantically over the cold floorboards in the darkness in search of the battered Weejuns parked by the bed. Her head, stuffed with cobwebs just moments before, is as achingly clear as if she'd dived into the unheated swimming pool they'd left behind in Montecito. Charging into the hallway, she races from room to room like a mad scientist in those *Goosebumps* books Eric can't seem to get enough of.

It's four blocks to the subway station. Eric knows where she keeps extra tokens: in a chipped coffee mug on the counter next to the toaster. He's also clever enough to navigate the subway system; he often plots their route for Nan when she takes him and Lulu into the city on weekends to visit museums.

Her heart begins to pound in earnest as she yanks on jeans and T-shirt then hoists Lulu into her arms. Much as she hates the idea, she'll have to wake the

Scheiners; there's simply no other way. Lulu would slow her down too much. And she can't leave a five-year-old alone in an empty apartment.

It seems an eternity before her frantic hammering brings Esther Scheiner to the door, blinking sleepily and clutching a robe to her plump nightgowned bosom. Something about her short dark hair strikes Nan as odd until she remembers that it's usually covered with a marriage wig. As she explains what happened, stumbling over her words in her haste, Esther merely holds her arms out for Lulu, murmuring, "Ah, poor little scheinenke." It isn't clear whether she means Eric or Lulu; all Nan knows is that she will be eternally grateful to this woman for not judging her, for not making her feel like a worse mother than she already does.

The temperature outside isn't much cooler. As Nan races along the sidewalk in search of her son, she feels as if she's swimming in warm, murky water. Swimming against the current. Her eyes fill with tears, and the shabby row houses on either side of her melt into a dark blur. Does Eric have any money of his own saved up? Is he planning to run away for good . . . or, please, God, just long enough to scare the holy bejesus out of her?

At the corner, she heads right. Three blocks away, the elevated subway tracks loom. Her heart is hammering so hard she can feel it pulsing behind her eyes with each beat. She casts about frantically, her gaze searching the sidewalk for her son.

It's close to midnight, but Avenue J is far from deserted. A handful of pedestrians straggle past. Some of the stores are still open, too, like the Hot Spot bagel shop, its cold fluorescent light making her think of the hospital delivery room where Eric was born. Times had changed by the time Lulu made her entrance into the world, in a cozy birthing room surrounded by pastel prints and a quilt stitched by Nan's grandmother.

In her panic, she recalls how scared she was those first few weeks after bringing Eric home from the hospital. He was small, only five pounds, too weak to nurse properly. Her swollen breasts leaked constantly, and as she'd cradled him, tickling his feet to coax him to nurse—unsuccessfully, for the most part—tears would pour down her cheeks. Russ had jokingly nicknamed her the Fountain of Lourdes.

It seems a miracle now, equal to that of Lourdes, when she spots a familiar figure trudging along the sidewalk a block ahead of her. Eric. He's clutching a blanket about his hunched shoulders, and below the filthy hem dragging along the pavement, she can see that he's still in his stocking feet. Her heart stops, then in a single mighty bound seems to catapult her to the next corner.

"Eric!" she calls out breathlessly, oblivious to the people passing by who glance at her curiously.

But he's not turning around. He doesn't seem to hear her. And something about his slow, stumbling gait and the way his head droops from the pale wilted stem of his neck sends a jolt of comprehension through her: Eric is sleepwalking. It's been so long, she'd forgotten how she used to bolt both front and back doors at night, and keep one ear cocked even in sleep for the padding of his feet along the carpeted hallway. She'd been fearful that he would hurt himself. Trip and fall, or step on something sharp. Luckily, the episodes of sleepwalking had stopped when he was around Lulu's age.

Nan catches up with him as he's turning onto Sixteenth. Where does he imagine he's going in his dream? Back to Montecito? She won't think about how he might have been hit by a car. That's for later, when she can allow herself the luxury of melting down, safe in the knowledge that her children are fast asleep in the next room. Nor will she think about the fact that Eric is so homesick, so fed up with their new life here, that even in sleep he's like a compass pointing west.

Nan seizes him gently by the shoulders. "Eric? Come on, honey, let's get you home." She knows from talking to psychologists that a rude awakening can be harmful. She also wants to spare him the sight of her face right now—he'd think he was seeing a ghost.

Eric mumbles something she can't hear. Something about Lulu. In the same moment she catches sight of a familiar brick building—Miss Susie's Dance School. It hits her then: Eric isn't running away. In his dream he's going to pick Lulu up from her dance class.

The realization is crushing, and at the same time it is as if something heavy is being lifted from her heart. Tears fill her eyes. She'd misunderstood. Eric doesn't hate his little sister. However much he might resent looking after her, he would never leave her stranded. What chafes at him isn't Lulu herself, but the burden of so much responsibility, of being the man of the family now that Russ is out of the picture. Nan understands, too, with a rush of love that causes her to pull her son tightly against her and tilt her face up to stars that right now seem to be the only things salvaged from their old life, that she's been looking at the situation from the wrong perspective as well: that of an abandoned wife, not the mother of a boy who is twelve going on forty.

By the time they reach their house, Eric is half awake but still too groggy to be very aware of what's happening. She guides him up the stairs and into bed, taking the time to pull off his filthy socks and tuck him in before going to fetch Lulu. Kneeling beside him in the dark, she kisses his sweaty forehead.

Eric smiles, and with his eyes closed mutters, "Mom?" just that, as if to make sure she's still there.

"I'm here," she whispers, smoothing his hair back from one temple. With the hard defiance gone from his face, she sees that he's not like Russ at all. The line of his jaw, the way he holds one fist tucked under his chin like Rodin's Thinker, that's her dad all over again—a sweet, somewhat absentminded man who believed there was no such thing as spoiling your children with too much attention.

They will get through this difficult time—she doesn't know it so much as sense it, like a new taste or smell she can't quite place. There will be days like this one when Eric will hate her, and looking after his sister will seem like a punishment. But they'll manage. Not because they have no choice, but because they do.

AFTERWORD

In the winter of 1984, I moved to Brooklyn from California with my two children, Michael and Mary, who

at the time were twelve and six, respectively. Though
their father hadn't abandoned us—that part of the
story was fictionalized—it's true I was a divorced single mom struggling to get by on precious little. I had a
few thousand dollars saved up, not enough to send
for my furniture in Santa Cruz (which didn't warrant
the expense, in any event), so we lived in a mostly
barren apartment, on the second floor of a two-family
house owned by a rabbi and his wife. Michael and his
friends played Frisbee and Nerf ball in the living
room. They didn't have to worry about breaking anything; there was nothing to break. We slept on beds
that were our only furniture, along with a kitchen
table and chairs and a desk for my typewriter. During
my frequent trips into the city by subway, where I
was working overtime to help launch the *Sweet Valley
High* series, Michael looked after Mary. Supper was
often a meat and a potato knish split into two, half of
each equaling what I hoped was a fairly balanced
meal.

During that time, we struggled not only to survive
but to redefine the boundaries of our new single-
parent family. I relied on Michael a great deal, more
than I'm sure is advisable, for chores such as baby-sit-
ting, laundry, and walking his sister to and from
school. They bickered as a result, and I'm sure
Michael grew resentful. To this day, Mary's nickname
for him is "Mr. Master."

Whether or not that played a part in a memorable
incident that occurred one evening, in which he wandered outside in his sleep, wearing nothing on his feet
but socks and dragging a sleeping bag, I can't be sure.
What I *do* know is that it left a lasting impression, not

just due to the sheer terror I felt racing down the sidewalk in search of my son, but because of what it seemed to imply: that even in an unconscious state, we are driven by a deep sense of responsibility for those we love.

Many years later, when my son and I discussed the incident in preparation for the writing of this story, Michael, now twenty-eight, said what he remembered best about that day was being tired. Not mad at his sister, or resentful of the burden I'd placed on him, but being "so tired I could have walked all the way to the subway, and nothing would have woken me." I didn't have the heart to tell him he'd merely gotten an early taste of what being a parent is like. But in retrospect, I don't think there's any need. He already knows.

Joe R. Lansdale

O'Reta, Snapshot Memories

O'Reta and Joe Lansdale at five months, 1952.

Her maiden name was O'Reta Wood. Most everyone called her Reta, or Reeter, with the exception of my dad. He called her O'Reeter, which, akin to Reeter, is one of those rural Southern peculiarities I never have figured out. It's like Cinderella becoming Cindereller. Who added the er, and why was it added? But I loved to hear my daddy call her name, and I think she did too.

My first memory of my mother is her sitting in a chair beside me, before a long row of curtainless windows, looking out at the night.

I guess I was three or four years old. We were in the first house I remember, and below us was a honky-tonk, and beyond that, across the highway, a drive-in theater.

On the huge drive-in screen were cartoon figures (most likely Warner Brothers), and sometimes actors going through their paces, and from that distance cartoons and humans were about the size they would be on a television screen, which we didn't have.

Since we couldn't hear what the characters were saying, my mother translated their silence to words. I had no idea then she was making it up; I thought she was omniscient. What I do know is I enjoyed it. It was my introduction to storytelling.

When I think of my mother, this is most often the first memory that comes to mind. That and her reading me Uncle Remus, and of course, the tornado.

One day, while my father was off at work, which was a lot of the time, the birds went quiet and the sky turned greenish, and my mother suddenly grew agitated. She threw open the windows and the doors, and from those same windows where we had watched the drive-in theater, we saw something else.

In the distance, beyond the drive-in, trees leaped up and swirled in a cone, and the cone danced. It was a tornado, a Texas cyclone, a twister, looking not too unlike the tornado I would see later on television (when we finally got one) while watching *The Wizard of Oz*.

Mom scooped me up and ran to the next-door neighbor's house. He had a storm shelter. Once inside with the neighbor's family, we found ourselves at least a foot deep in water. There were jars of canned food on shelves, and the man who owned the shelter, a person I barely remember, stood with flashlight and club. As we watched, he killed a water moccasin that had crawled in down there. Above us the storm hollered and stomped and tugged at the latched double wooden doors like a maniac with a knife. My mother stood in the water and held me in a death grip.

I don't remember being afraid of the storm, just excited. But the snake, my first, had scared me. Never have liked them since. Maybe I got that from my mother. She was scared of snakes, water, drinking alcohol, and electricity. So am I.

The storm was over almost as fast as it happened. All I remember is that when we came out into the light, our house was untouched, as were the handful of houses in the immediate area, but the drive-in screen was gone and partly in our yard, and some of the honky-tonk's roof had been taken away. It had all seemed like a dream.

Later, I remember it being said that a house some distance behind us had the tornado drop in, as if for a visit, only to leave the place in shambles. We were lucky. The damn thing had jumped over us and gone on.

Other memories of that time: Wandering bums. They call them homeless now, but they called them bums then. They were sometimes men down on their luck, more often than not lost souls who claimed to be preachers. They'd come to our door and ask for food. My mother nearly always fixed them something. Sometimes they did a little work around the house in return. Sometimes they preached, or gave us a little story of how they had come to where they now stood, or wobbled, as was the case with some.

If my mother smelled alcohol on their breath, they not only didn't get fed, she ran them off by locking the screen door and lecturing at them through it about the depravities of drink. They usually took hat in hand (as everyone seemed to wear hats then) and slunk off apologetically.

None of this sympathetic twelve-step stuff. These guys were drunks. Mom was a fanatic teetotaler and viewed 1920's prohibition exponent and saloon smasher, Carrie Nation, as a kind of saint. My father viewed her as an annoying busybody who might have served more good if she had been hit by a truck.

Looking back, seeing a number of friends of mine who took to the bottle, fell in and didn't come out, the number of social drunks I've been around, I'm glad Mom scolded me at an early age. I don't see the occasional drink as quite the resident evil my mother did, but drunkenness I've never liked and have never been drunk myself. A legacy from my mother: have no respect for the bottle, because it has none for you.

My mother was pulled into this century as if by a tornado of technology. Future shock. And she never quite adjusted to it.

My mother's Scotch-Irish mother, my grandmother, Óle, was born in the 1880s in Oklahoma Territory. It didn't become a state until a few years later. She traveled by covered wagon and actually saw Buffalo Bill's Wild West Show. I remember her telling me about it. White horses. Stagecoaches being chased by wild Indians, gunfire, sharpshooters (maybe Annie Oakley), and the old man himself, white-bearded, handsome, magnificent. Wild Bill Hickok had only been dead about ten years when she was born.

She told me of seeing Indian encampments as a child. Of attempting to homestead land (most likely Oklahoma during the land rush), where snakes tried to climb in the wagon all night and were fought off by her family. But the snakes were so thick and persistent, the very next day they abandoned their homesteading adventure and departed.

She told me Irish ghost stories about birds that appeared before the death of loved ones. Family stories, like how her brother, George, an older man, fought in the Civil War in place of his son, George, Jr., who had deserted. George Sr., however, was later shot and killed for stealing horses.

Óle saw a number of her children buried. She lived to be ninety-eight years old, and in pretty good health until the end. She loved the modern world and thought the good old days weren't all that damn good. I think she adjusted to the changing times better than my parents, who were born in this century.

At the beginning of the twentieth century, shortly after the death of the Wild West, my parents were born. My father in 1909, my mother in 1916. Buffalo Bill was still alive, as was Wyatt Earp, Bat Masterson, and Emmett Dalton, the lone survivor of the Dalton gang's last raid. Frank James died a year before my mother was born. My father was approximately six years old at the time.

My mother's family moved to Texas, where she met and grew up with the man who was to become my father. She and A. B. Lansdale were married in 1933. My father wanted to be a mechanic. Mom bought Dad a Model T with some money she had earned from berry picking. She told him to take it apart and put it back together until he could do it without thinking. He took her advice, and that was how he learned his trade.

My brother was born in 1935. Emmett Dalton was still alive and writing for the movies. Wyatt Earp had only been dead six years. Pretty Boy Floyd was about to meet his end. It was the middle of the Great Depression.

Sixteen years later, in 1951, I was born. World War II was but six years gone. It was the Eisenhower generation. The nuclear age. The baby boom. Hank Williams and Ernest Tubb were on the radio. The birth of rock and roll was on the very near horizon. Prosperity ruled the nation, if not East Texas. Some dumb ass was going to invent the hula hoop.

This to me is the most amazing thing about my family. That they had a foot in so many different generations. The Wild West, the Great Depression, the nuclear age. I think this was part of what made them who they were.

My mother and father were very close, and very different. They argued a lot. My father was uneducated. He had begun helping raise his family at eight years old when his mother died. His father was a mean-spirited jackass who was quick with the whip, and my father had scars to prove it. As well as brawling scars, snakebite scars, and smallpox scars. He never so much as spanked me.

My mother had come from a family that wasn't overly educated, but had a respect for education—especially her father. Her father, my grandfather, was her hero. She adored him, told me stories of him, and praised him. He was no saint, however. Besides her four brothers and one sister, her two half brothers from a previous marriage, there was a simultaneous marriage to a woman on the other side of the Ozarks. The result of that second union was a half sister. When we found out about her, met her years later, there was no denying she was kin. She was the spitting image of my mother.

When I was growing up, the Depression was constantly in our house, even if it was supposedly long over. We pinched pennies. We ate what was on our plates. We saved bits of cloth, paper, damn near anything we could get our hands on. My mom ran the coffee grounds through twice, sometimes three times. We saved the grease from frying and made soap out of it with lye.

My mother never could get hold of the idea that times were better. For her the wolf was always at the door. She had a terrible fear of going hungry. She was absolutely paranoid about it. And it wasn't something my father took lightly either. I remember Dad hunting squirrels, and it wasn't just for recreation. My mother made meals from polk salad and wild dandelions, made jelly out of wild grapes and persimmons, tea from sassafras. We raised a garden, hogs, and chickens a lot of the time.

There was never a moment in my mother's life when the future was secure, and because of this, I think it was hard for her to plan too far ahead for herself. For her family, yes, but she and my father constantly denied themselves things to make sure it was there for the family.

In spite of this, my parents probably did better during the early fifties than at any other time in their lives, and it's the only time I remember living in a close neighborhood with a house immediately next door. Then my mother was a full-time housewife, and my father worked at Wanda Petroleum, a butane company. He was a mechanic troubleshooter, on the road a lot of the time fixing broken-down trucks. Sometimes he'd work in horrible weather and be out late and far away, have to lie in puddles of water on freezing nights working on a motor. I've seen him come in the door with freezing chills and icicles in his hair. Next morning, he'd be up and gone before daylight, back to work.

My mother was a great lover of books, especially nonfiction. She was interested in comparative religion, and it's my belief she wrestled with her views on religion all her life. There were times when her views were strictly hard-shell Baptist, and times when she was somewhat agnostic. Most of the time she was what I would call a liberal Baptist. An oxymoron to many, but the truth is they did and do exist. My mother loved reading the Bible, and she hooked me on the habit. I'm not religious, but I still read the Bible. Great stories. Great lessons for life. Lots of sex, murder, and perversion.

She loved William Faulkner, more for what he accomplished than for his books, which to my knowledge, she had never read. Faulkner, for some reason, reminded her of her father, a conclusion I presume she gleaned from reading about his life. I doubt she knew Faulkner was a notorious drunk.

My mother had a natural knack for color. She loved to paint, often did her painting with her fingers, using boards, squares of plywood for her canvases.

She would just suddenly have the urge, and she would paint. Perhaps for days on end. When she was finished, occasionally these paintings would find their way on our walls, or she would give them away, or sell them, and sometimes, she would just toss them. Usually the paintings were of flowers. My mother loved flowers. Sometimes they were just colorful, and not obviously anything but fine displays of color.

The paintings, no matter what they were of, always had a kind of, well, fuzzy weirdness about them. They were art, and they were unique, but they weren't at all traditional. Later, when I saw Van Gogh's work, I realized that it had much the same appearance. Not on the same level, but the same sort of technique. My mother had never taken an art lesson, and had never even heard of Vincent Van Gogh. Maybe part of the result was due to the weakness of her eyes, but I tend to think she painted what she saw. A world bright and beautiful, but fuzzy around the edges.

She was great at making something out of nothing. From food to throw rugs to coffee tables to flower arrangements, she could take nothing—which is mostly what she had to work with—and turn it into something.

When I was young, she was very optimistic. Always looking for a better day. She instilled that in me. Unfortunately for her, this wasn't her true nature. She was subject to tremendous ups and downs. I think now she would most likely be diagnosed as a manic depressive. In later years, it got worse.

Growing up, my mother was always there to read to me, tell me she loved me, impress on me how intelligent and special I was, but how I should keep in mind that others didn't have all the advantages I had, and that I should respect every human being, no matter their race, color, religion, or financial station in life. Do unto others as you would have them do unto you.

It never occurred to me that we were poor. We

thought of ourselves as broke. It wasn't until years later that I realized it.

There was no reason I should have felt poor. When I was young my mother made my shirts and even jackets, sewed them on a pedal Singer sewing machine.

She always found money for me to buy comic books and the occasional paperback book. At Christmas I always received a book or two, because I was a fanatic for the stuff. At the time I loved D.C. comics especially, and some offbeat comics like Black Cat, which starred a female crime fighter who had Judo tips in the back of her comics. But Batman, he was my main man.

My mother made me a Batman uniform with ears I was never quite satisfied with. They tended to droop. She solved this to some degree by placing cardboard inside the ears. She made my nephew, who is only a few years younger than me, a Robin outfit. I wish I still had mine.

My nephew and I had plans to solve crimes in Mt. Enterprise, but the place seemed short on the stuff. Nonexistent, in fact. And besides, we had to be in the house at a certain time and go to bed early enough to be up for school. My bedroom may have been the Bat Cave, but it was still in my parents' house.

But Bat Cave it was. With chemistry sets, insect and mineral collections, finger-printing materials, and books on all these subjects.

In my Bat Cave, it was my plan to also include mementos of cases to come, but, alas, the most I ever did was run around with my cape flapping. To remedy this, I began to think of adventures to write and draw about, my own comics. Mom always took time out from whatever she was doing to hear me read my comics and show her the pictures. In time, I preferred the stories to the pictures, possibly because I was better at it.

Mom introduced me to Tarzan movies on television, perhaps to get me out of her hair. Every Saturday morning there was a jungle theater with Tarzan, Jungle Jim, Bomba the Jungle boy, that sort of thing, and every Saturday morning I was glued to the tube. I looked forward to it all week. Later, I discovered Edgar Rice Burroughs, the author of the Tarzan books, and my life was absolutely turned around. I had always wanted to be a writer, but when I started reading Burroughs, I knew I had to be.

Again, I owe it all to Mom.

When I was young, though people find this hard to believe, I was shy. My mother sent me around the corner to a lady who taught what was then called Expression. It was taught at her home, and I learned to memorize poetry and sections from books, and to give recitations. I discovered an unusual knack. I was a pretty good public speaker, a good reader, and could memorize entire poems and pages of books rapidly. I loved it. I didn't know it at the time, and neither did my mother, at least not directly, but she was further grooming me for my future career as writer and public speaker.

When we moved back to Gladewater, we moved there with considerably less money. My father quit Wanda Petroleum and struck out on his own. My cousin made him a wallet card that read: HAVE TOOLS, WILL TRAVEL.

My father loved the independence, and never gave it up again, but it was hard sledding as a freelance mechanic, and it took time for him to get his own garage and build up a clientele. In the meantime, we ate a lot of pinto beans and cornbread. It wasn't until years later I realized we did that because they were cheap. I just thought we liked them.

My mother sold encyclopedias door-to-door, bought things from swap meets and refurbished them, resold them at a higher price and made money for me to join the Boy Scouts, have uniforms and equipment, and to attend Scout camps. One year she raised enough for me to go to Philmont, a prestigious Scout camp in New Mexico. I still remember my Scouting days with great fondness.

Later, Mom worked odd jobs so that I was able to go to the Y.M.C.A. in Tyler, Texas, and take a variety of martial arts. We had to drive thirty miles every Saturday, and eventually several times a week when I discovered the variety of martial arts offered at night.

I became a fanatic.

Mom even let me try the wrist locks and arm bars on her when my dad wasn't around. She held pillows for me to kick and helped me build punching bags and other simple training devices.

My mother and I were very close until I reached the age of sixteen. That's not unusual. Teenagers strike off on their own for a while, but this was during the turbulent sixties, and though my mother supported much of the change that was going on, civil rights, women's rights, she disliked the long hair, the slovenly clothes, and the antiestablishment mood that the sixties, and now I, represented.

We never became enemies, my mother and I, but we didn't see eye to eye on much. I was troublesome at school, was often expelled, my grades dropped, and I just skimmed through till graduation. I'm sure Mom must have wondered what all the lessons in Expression, Boy Scouts, and martial arts had done for me.

I married when I was eighteen and began attending Tyler Jr. College, and then I was off to the University of Texas. My marriage fell apart during that second year of studies, and I came home.

It was really pretty wonderful, and for about a year or so, kind of like a second childhood. At the time I was very much interested in Thoreau. My mother loved him too. She and I read Walden a lot and talked. The closeness returned.

It wasn't until my father's death some years later that things went haywire. From the moment he died, she was lost. She didn't pull in and give up, but she seemed frantic all the time. She had never had the ability to stick to any one thing, even the things she loved, like sales, flower arranging, painting. She dipped into these like a bee at a flower, then moved on. The moment something became a bit difficult, she was out of there. She wanted to keep that high of discovery all the time, and therefore sacrificed the greater high of really becoming good and successful at something.

Finally she remarried. A nice enough fella. Shortly thereafter she was in a wreck that caused her to be thrown through the windshield. She never would wear a seat belt, fearing being trapped, often commenting that she would rather be thrown free. And she was. Right through the windshield that banged her brain and put her in the hospital.

She was operated on, and my brother and I and our families went to see her daily. Her husband, Cecil, received only minor injuries and was soon up and around.

But for mother, it was strange. Even when she was allowed to go home, she didn't know where she was. She couldn't get out of bed. She couldn't care for herself. She didn't know who her family members were. Those same eyes that had looked at me with love, and even frustration, were now more like the eyes of a frightened animal.

Slowly, her memory came back, but though she could remember her past, and me, she had lost the ability to show emotion. It was akin to the novel *The Invasion of the Body Snatchers*, or the movie made from it. She looked like my mother, talked like my mother, but something—a lot—was missing.

Eventually her husband became too ill to take care of her, and my brother tried to keep her in his home, but her injuries resulted in twenty-four-hour-a-day specialized care, and it was a care that working people weren't easily available to do.

We did what we had vowed never to do. We put her in a nursing home near my brother. By this time her memories were not only back, but a lot of her personality. Her emotions returned, but she was never quite the same.

She had periods where she seemed absolutely lost. One time when I visited her she would be fine, lucid, the next confused. She asked for paints, and I bought them for her, and so did my brother, but she never

used them. She would give them away, ask for more.
The old urges were still there, but not the ability. She
would become so frustrated with the fact that she
could no longer paint, didn't even know how, that
she would rid herself of the kits.

She couldn't do what she loved most. Read. Her
mind wouldn't follow the prose; she couldn't visual-
ize the words. She couldn't watch and keep up with a
simple television show. She misunderstood the news.
During the Gulf War she called to tell me that Iraqis
were invading a small Texas community of about two
hundred, making terroristic attacks on the gas lines.

She had heard that certain publishing companies
were in league with the Mafia, and it became stuck in
her mind that I was working for the Mafia by writing
for the publishing companies they owned. I often
wondered if in her mind she put my martial arts
training in league with this and saw me as some sort
of freelance hit man for the publishing field.

Having come from the Great Depression, she never
could understand how I made as much money as I
did. Well, it was a lot by her standards. Not all that
special, really, but for someone who every day had to
plan their existence down to the penny, she was in
awe of the money I made and thought it must come
from illegal sources.

Also, the kind of fiction I wrote sometimes led her
to believe that I might be crazy, or going crazy. It was
all very strange and frustrating, for me as well as her.

On one of her doctor visits, the doctor told me that
the X rays revealed she had a cancer on her lung.
Here was a woman that had never smoked in her life,
who had had nothing but hardship, was badly injured

due to a stupid automobile accident, and now she had a cancer on her lung.

Mom refused to have it operated on. She was adamant about that. She had had too many operations due to her injuries, and now in her late seventies, feeling horrible, she felt it was better just to let time take its course. Her belief was she had lived long enough, and that even without the cancer, she didn't have that much time ahead of her anyway, and if she did, who the hell wanted it?

I pursued her having the operation for a time, but finally dropped it. Her mind was made up. About mid-May of 1993 she had a sudden and continued period of lucidness. We began to talk about old times, relive them. My Batman suit. The comics I read by the tons. My room fixed up like the Bat Cave. The martial arts. And my dad. We talked about it all, and it was wonderful.

One night, late May, I got a call from Mom asking if I would come over to see her. Since my family and I lived about a hundred miles away, I told her I would, but I would be there in the morning. She said that was all right.

Early the next morning I got a call from a nurse saying I should come over and see my mother. I told her that was my plan. The nurse didn't indicate that the situation was vital, and Mom and I often went through this. On any morning I was to come see her, she might call two times before I left, two or three times to talk to my wife, Karen, before I arrived, as well as ask the nurses to call while I was in route.

This morning I got ready as usual, and was going out the door when the phone rang.

It was the nurse. My mother was gone.

*   *   *

She was buried beside my father. Later I bought them a double tombstone. It was a large funeral. Friends and relatives turned out and told stories of her generosity. I knew she was kind and generous, but I was amazed to learn of the many selfless things she had done, the lives she had changed.

She was an amazing woman who played the hard hand life dealt her. Played it with courage and with a kind of crazy style.

I miss her.

I'm smart, I adjust to their idiosyncrasies and everyone's happy.

Jesse has always been a boy's boy. His favorite activities as a young child were, in preferential order, crashing into hard objects, pulverizing things, and jumping off high ledges—mainly the top of his bunk bed. Once, dressed as Superman, he pedaled his trike out of a window to see if he could fly. Luckily, at that time, we lived in a one-and-a-half-story house. He landed in the bushes below, brushed away the dirt and leaves, and continued his caped crusade without missing a beat. It was a miracle he survived childhood without broken bones.

His penchant for smashing his body into solid matter was evident at an early age. As a babe-in-arms as young as five months, whenever we walked through doorways, he'd leap up from my grasp, and hit his head against the doorframe. The first time he did this, I was appalled at my negligence as a mother. How could I be so careless as to bump my child's noggin? After the third time, I realized that this baby was actually cracking his skull *on purpose*. And don't think it didn't hurt him. It did. Every time he'd knock his bean, he'd break into tears. But the pain was obviously not a deterrent as he kept on head-banging. So it came to pass that whenever we walked through doors, I restrained his head with my hand.

Believe me, it was a struggle. The child was twenty-five pounds at a year. I'm five-three and slight. We had a little wrestling match going on. At that time, Mom prevailed. Later on, when the wrestling matches turned into debates and word repartee, I knew that "prevailing" over my progeny was a thing of the past.

My kids are so much smarter than me, I can't even get up to the plate much less take a swing.

Jesse is one of the smartest people I have ever met. I often wonder how truly gifted his genetic endowment was at birth. Because I figure he dropped at least twenty IQ points by impacting his bone-sheathed cerebral cortex against dense objects.

When he was older—preschool age—his favorite game with his father was belly-bucking. This involved Jesse running toward my kneeling spouse, and colliding into his stomach full force. My son was a compact, muscular child and walked away from the encounter with a smile on his face. My husband, Jonathan, on the other hand, felt as if he had been punched in the solar plexus with a medicine ball.

As he got older, Jess decided that walloping Dad wasn't enough of a challenge. He graduated to careening into impenetrable items such as thick walls. Bouncing off these inanimate structures, he'd flop to the ground with a thud. Every time, I found myself asking, "Jess, are you okay?" And every time, he'd shake himself off and say something like, "Gee, that was cool." Jess became the master of the pratfall, which served him well during his dramatic years onstage. When Jesse died and fell to the ground, the entire audience felt the impact.

Which more or less became his trademark; his ability to turn his *destrudo* into something constructive.

Instead of blowing things up at random—how I remember objects like Legos and blocks flying every which way—he developed an interest in rockets after taking a course at our local science museum. These crafts weren't just balsa wood cutout items being tossed willy-nilly. They could *fly!*

It was a real treat to see him methodically *building* something. The rockets came in an array of colors and had names like Big Bertha and the Monster. Some of them were so sophisticated that they took airborne pictures with built-in cameras. Launching them required lighting a fuse that must have ignited some kind of explosive, because the jets soared upward of hundreds of feet with an enthralling *whoosh!* Jesse's hobby quickly became a pastime that the entire family enjoyed. And, lo and behold, no one got hurt.

I had always felt that Jesse's childhood energy level would serve him well as an adult. And wouldn't you know it, for *once*, I was right. His perpetual motion that drove me crazy is now harnessed into activities like academics, creative and expository writing, acting, photography, and directing.

Recently, my husband and I saw his production of David Mamet's *American Buffalo.* In my humble parental opinion, it was a play worthy of Broadway. The acting was superb, but it was Jesse who cast and directed it. And I do feel that my perception isn't *that* far off. After applying to the university art board for a venue for his next effort, Jesse was given a theater that seats *five hundred and fifty people.* To me, this showed confidence in my son's ability to direct.

Jesse's current academic interest is psychology, where his papers often include no less than forty reference sources. His specific field of interest is aberrant personality disorder.

So we felt this story fit right in. We chose to explore the relationship between Jack the Ripper and his mother, because let's face it, everyone has a mother, even sociopathic, serial killers. And if Freud is to be believed at all, mothers can be influential people in the lives of their children, the prime motivators for deeds and misdeeds, things "nise" or otherwise.

About a year ago, I had a particularly exhausting day, and I asked Jess, who was home at the time, to entertain my then six-year-old daughter with a few stories. After a half hour, he came out of the room, and I asked him how it went. He said she was captivated by his stories just as long as the endings included something or someone blowing up.

Genetics works in strange ways.

When I was small, Mummy would say, *if ye're a good boy, then I will tell you a bedtime story*. But now she cannot because she is too sick. The time has come now that I must take care of her and not the other way round. I must do things for Mummy. I must get Mummy her medicine and buy her spirits. I must bring Mummy her supper every night. Yet, she is not yet so sick and old that she cannot tell me what to do. She has her opinions.

Lately, this has become more of a problem because I want (and she wants me to also, I think) to court a lass or two, and I must bring the lass home to have a proper introduction. Sometimes Mummy makes this very difficult. Her opinions. They are very strong opinions. I am, however, a proper raised gentleman, and I have been educated in the way that makes me respect Mummy even if her opinions are extremely particular and particularly strong. I always do my best to make her happy.

Sometimes, I do wish for a bedtime story, though.

A couple of weeks ago, I decided to go out for a stroll at night. I groomed my mustache. Mummy likes my mustache, and she tells me that I look very right and handsome. I like it when I please her. I straightened my freshly starched waistcoat; then I took my cane, my cloak, and some other things. I did not think it was late in the evening, but Mummy heard me opening the door.

Jack! she called to me.

Yes, Mummy? I said like a good boy says.

Jack, where are y' goin'?

I am goin' for a walk, I said.

It's too late in the night, Jack, she said.

It's not so late, Mummy. I thought of mebbe gettin' a bit of air . . .

Don't go, Jack! she said. She was almost screaming at me from the other room, and her voice was like a very sharp knife. *Don't leave me here, Jackie!*

Her voice made me hurt quite bad. I thought that maybe she was going to die if I left her alone. All of a sudden, I got frightened. So I went to her room to make sure that she was well. When I peeked my head through the door, I could see that she was surrounded by a big pile of pillows (pillows I bought with money that I had earned for her), looking like a fat white man hugging her tight. She was sitting up in bed, and maybe even crying a little. It hurts me when she cries with her voice so little and full of pain. Especially because she looks so weak with her thin bones and white hair.

Please don't go, Jack! she begged.

I will come back soon, Mummy, I said. *I am goin' to bring some spirits. I'll bring y' back a pint.* (I knew that Mummy likes an occasional pint and she would be happy if I offered to bring her one.)

0, would ye, Jack? That would be so nise . . . so nise.

I will come back soon and bring ye a pint, Mummy, I promised.

0, but not a pint. Bring us some red wine, Jack, she said. *Port, if you will, Jackie. That makes me bones very warm.*

Right, then, Mummy, I answered. *Some old red port.*

Thankee, Jackie, said she, gratefully.

I left the house and walked around for a bit. After some time, I was very far from where we lived. I was not certain where I was, although I thought I might be in Whitechapel. I wanted to hear my Mummy's voice telling me a bedtime story, and feel her giving me wet kisses on my forehead. There was a big clock striking the late hour, and I thought that I would get Mummy her wine, and maybe a pint for myself. (Because it was a very soggy night and I wanted to warm my bones.) Afterward, I would go home and go to bed.

Instead, I came upon a lass out walking. She was very short and stout, and she had an ugly smile, but she looked like she wanted to be my friend. I thought that because she walked up to me and said, *Allo, sir, how are ye?*

I said, *I'm fine, thankee. Why are you here so late at night?*

She began to laugh, like a horse throwing its head back and sniffing the air. I could see tiny blue lines in her fat neck where her blood was. It was not a pretty neck, although I have seen pretty necks: long, stretchy, white necks, like swans gliding in the lake in the park. I touched the stiff edge of my collar and waited for her to talk again. Her face was dirty, and the sleeve of her dress was ragged, like it had been chewed.

I know ye want to buy me a nip o' gin, sir, she said. *Will ye buy me a nip?*

Since I had to go get some wine for Mummy, and the lass seemed nise enough, I told her I could buy her a nip.

0, you're a good boy! said the lass.

(Of course, I know I am a good boy because Mummy tells me that all the time. I try very hard to be a good boy for her.)

What's your name, sir? she asked.

Jack, I said.

You're a good boy, Jack, said the lass. *My name is Annie.*

It is an honor to meet you, Annie, I said. Lasses like that, when I talk courtly. Annie liked it, and she laughed again.

Come on, then, she said. *Let's get us a drop!*

I went with Annie to a pub and bought Mummy's port. Annie wanted a gin, and so I bought her a nip. She was thirsty, and she took the whole glass at once. I thought her gulping a bit common and lower class, but when she asked me for another, I bought it for her. Then she asked for a third.

I've not got any more money, Annie, I said.

0, my! she said. *Well, then, I shall have to find another man to buy me a nip. Because it is a cold, damp night.*

No, Annie, I said. *Don't go.* (Because I was starting to fancy her.)

Well, sir, I don't want to go because ye have been so 'nise' to me. But I am very thirsty. Then she laughed again.

I thought that Mummy would be very thirsty by

this time, so I decided that I should go home. But I still fancied Annie.

I said, *Annie, can I ask ye to supper? I can give you a bit of gin that I've got back at home?*

Annie smiled at me with a big brown rotted smile. *It's too late for supper, but I can give ye a bite if you want, sir.*

No thankee, I said for I was not hungry. *Why don't ye come for supper on Friday, then?*

0, sir, said Annie, *that would be quite nise.*

I shall come to get ye, Annie.

Thankee, luv, she said. *Come to get me here.*

Cheers, I said, then left and headed toward home. The whole walk home, I tripped over rats running beneath me in the fog. The misty air was like a big fish swallowing the street. I wanted to be home and to hear a bedtime story before I went to sleep. But when I did get home, Mummy was asleep. I put the wine in the cupboard and went to bed with no bedtime story (which made me feel quite lonely).

The next morning, I told Mummy that I had invited a guest for supper for next week.

Who's that? she asked.

A lass, said I.

Jack! Why are ye bringing lassies home? she scolded me.

She wanted to meet ye, Mummy.

It's not proper to bring lassies home! she yelled. *Not proper at all!*

Then I remembered the port and brought it from the cupboard. While I poured her drink, I said, *She is nise, Mummy.*

Mummy drank a bit. Then she drank a wee bit

more, and smiled. She said to me, *Well, I must meet her if ye think she is nise, my Jackie.*

She is nise, Mummy, I said.

She had another nip and said, *Mummy can tell ye if she is a proper lass or not.*

I said that was why I wanted Mummy to meet her.

Good boy, that y'think of your mummy. You were raised a proper gentleman, my Jack.

I was very happy when she said this. There are times that Mummy makes me very happy. Even if she has her sharp opinions.

The following week, I walked out again and found the pub where Annie was supposed to be. She was not there, and I waited for her. The barman tried to give me drinks, but I did not want to drink anything.

Get out if you're not goin' to be buying somethin'! he yelled. *You're in a pub, you fool.*

I am waiting for a lass, I answered.

Who, then, are ye waitin' for? he asked me.

Annie, said I.

What Annie? said the man.

Jest Annie is her name.

Ye can wait outside, then, said the man.

I waited outside near the door. Annie came, but she was late. She almost did not see me. She almost walked through the door without saying hello. But I took her on the elbow, and that got her to turn around.

Allo, Annie, I said.

Allo, mate, she said. *Buy me a slug, will ye?*

I looked at her, and she stared back as if she did not know my face.

Ye are coming for supper, then? I asked.

Supper? Why would I come with ye to supper? she asked.

I thought she was playing a game. *Annie, ye said ye'd come the night to supper with me,* I explained.

Buy me a nip o' gin, and I'll come to supper with ye, she said.

All right, then, Annie. I'll buy you a nip.

We went inside. I bought her a gin and then a few more. She was soon very happy to come to supper, although I was no longer so certain she should come. She was tipsy, and Mummy does not think it proper for a lass to be tipsy.

I tried to tell her that, but she laughed in my face. Still, she followed me all the way to home. I opened the door, and Annie walked in behind me. *Annie,* said I, *do ye know any bedtime stories?*

Aye, she answered. *I know every story every man wants to hear. But first, I want a nip o' gin.*

I told her soon, after supper. Mummy could not lay the table, being so sick. So I put the cutlery out. Then I took dishes and gave them to Annie.

Lay the dishes, please, Annie, for I must go to see how Mummy is getting on. Then I went to see Mummy.

She was waiting for me. *Is that lass here?* she asked.

Yes, Mummy, she's here, I replied. *Do ye want to eat with us, or shall I bring ye something in bed?*

I think I'll eat with ye, Mummy said. *Bring me to the table, my Jackie.*

I lifted her up and brought her to the table, and Annie was sitting there. She had not yet laid any dishes.

Did ye not lay the table, girl? asked Mummy.

Annie looked at Mummy with bleary eyes and did not say anything, which I thought was very rude.

I brought to the table a piece of cold beef, bread, and water.

Ye said you'd give me a nip, Annie said.

Annie was not behaving the way I thought she would with Mummy present, but I gave her a bit of gin anyway. Then she was quiet for a minute. Mummy ate a few bites of the beef and bread. Then she said to Annie, *What're y'called lassie?*

Annie Chapman, ma'am.

Annie Chapman, said Mummy. *Where did ye meet my Jack?*

Annie drank and did not say a word. But my Mummy continued, *Jack is a good boy, Miss Annie Chapman. Do y'know that?*

Aye, ma'am, answered Annie, *he's a good boy.*

He was not always such a good boy, said Mummy.

Annie looked up from her nip. *How's that?*

Once, when he was a wee lad, he tore up all my linen, Mummy said, coughing and cackling. *Do ye remember that, Jack?*

Yes, I said. I was a bit embarrassed.

Said Mummy, *I was quite cross with him when he was young because he ruined everything. He was a little terror, my Jackie. A terror and a tearer. Jackie the Tearer. But now look how handsome he has grown up to be.*

Aye, Annie answered.

Do ye like his mustache? asked Mummy.

I do, said Annie.

Then Mummy et a bit more. Annie did not have any bread or beef, but she took another glass of gin.

After a while Mummy turned to me, and said, *Jackie, take us to bed will ye?*

I carried her to her bedroom once again. Before I left, she whispered loudly to me, *Jack, I donna like the lass. She is not for a proper raised gentleman like you.*

0, Mummy . . . I said. I was disappointed, but Mummy was sick, so I tried to hide it.

She does not smile like a young lady. Tonight, she did not smile at all, Jack.

I have seen her smile, Mummy. Sometimes, she smiles at me.

Mummy shook her head. *She does not smile big enough, Jackie. Not big like a bright young lassie is meant to smile!*

I listened to her words. They were not nise words, but they were proper. *Do ye think so, Mummy?*

I do, she replied.

Then, what shall I do with her?

I donna care. Just get her away and come back to me, Jack.

I knew she was right. She is right always. *Ye are clever, Mummy.*

I jest want to save me boy from bad lassies, Jackie.

Ye love me, Mummy?

I do, Jackie, said Mummy. *You are my babe.*

I was so happy to hear her say that. I knew what could make her happier. I gave her a kiss on her head full of white hair, and told her I'd be back soon.

I took the cutlery and the dishes to the cupboard and stowed almost everything away. *Come on, then, Annie,* said I. *It's time to take ye back home.*

Give another nip o'gin, luv! she cried.

We've got nothing to give ye, Annie, and so let's get a go.

O, but for a bit of gin!

Back in the pub, then Annie, I said. *Let us go back to where I found ye.*

Aye, luv! she cheered.

We walked a bit. Then I said, *There's a nise pub over here, Annie.*

Where? Annie asked. *I donna see nothin.'*

It was true because the street was dark, and the place was very still.

Annie, said I, *Mummy said ye don't smile big enough.*

I cannot smile when I've got no drink in me, she answered.

I think ye should smile bigger, I said.

She pouted. *Then, why don't y'make me smile bigger, luv.*

I can, Annie, I can, said I.

And then I made her smile the biggest smile she ever had.

When I got home, Mummy was asleep, so I could not tell her about Annie's big smile. I took off my clothes, which were quite wrinkled from walking home in the mist and fog that swallows up everything like a big fish.

The next morning, I did not tell Mummy because I wanted to keep it all a surprise for her birthday, which is very soon. She will know when I tell her. She will see what a good boy I am. And then maybe she will tell me a bedtime story. Perhaps even a bedtime story every night.

But tonight, I shall go for a walk again, and get my

Mummy a wee bit of port for her spirits. I do it because it makes her so happy to have her spirits. It is often hard to make Mummy happy because she has so many sharp opinions. But I try and try. I do it all because I love her.

Marcus Major

~⊶⊷~

On the Move

*Carmen Major and her favorite
son, Marcus.*

The Major family had just completed yet another long journey to yet another new place that for all intended purposes was to be our new home. This time from Fort Campbell, Kentucky, to Starkville, Wisconsin. It was our first excursion into the Midwest, the great American "heartland" my father had reminded us throughout the trip as he scolded his sons in the backseat for not appreciating the scenes of pastoral beauty that we were passing. As far as me and my older brother Ronald were concerned, his appeal had fallen on deaf ears. We had no desire to leave Kentucky and were not looking forward to once again starting over. I was twelve, and he was fourteen, and this was going to be the seventh time we were going to be the new kids in an alien school. This time it was particularly painful because Fort Campbell had been our favorite place to live thus far.

In many ways, a military base like Fort Campbell might be as close to idyllic a place as possible for a child to be raised. There are rows and rows of manicured lawns and cookie-cutter houses, a sameness that was in many ways comforting because you

and your friends were pretty much at the same economic level and everybody's dad (or mom in rare instances) worked for the same boss. The base was
immaculate, kept litter free by the soldiers. The PX,
the teen club, the arcade, school—everything seemed
to be within walking distance or at the very least in
reach by bike. Every day at exactly five p.m. the
bugle-played song "To the Colors" would blare
through the base's many loudspeakers, which would
be followed by a cannon blast and "Retreat." Depending on your proximity to a speaker, the cannon
blast could be so loud that it would reverberate
through your chest and cause your heart to skip a
beat. The newer kids always did the same thing at
the cannon shot. They would dramatically fall over
screaming "Aaargh!" "Medic!" or "I've been hit!"
My brother and our friends would sneer at them. We
had heard over a thousand cannon blasts and had
long ago ceased to find amusement in the ceremony.
If anything, it would put us in a foul mood because
it would usually interrupt our football game (being
soldiers' sons, we all had the good sense to stop
playing during the ceremony) and was the signal
that it would soon be time to head home for dinner,
baths, and homework. So when one of the new kids
(and there are always new kids on a military base)
would fall over trying to wring a cheap laugh out of
us, he would be told in no uncertain terms to get the
hell up and show some goddamned respect.

But once again, it was us who were going to be the
new kids: me, Ronald, and my little brother Ryan,
who didn't seem to be deriving the same angst out of
the situation that we were. We would be the ones un-

familiar with the social graces and customs of the kids who lived in Starkville, the neophytes. What if there was some ceremonial ringing of a cowbell or something, and my behavior during it brought ignominy and scorn on my family's good name? Would we ever live down the shame?

When we passed the sign that said "Welcome to Wisconsin—the Dairy State," I was filled with dread. We passed farm after farm, each one looking the same as groups of cows languidly grazed. When I wondered aloud what the cow to human ratio was in the Dairy State, my parents ignored me. I also kept seeing signs touting cheese curds for sale. My anxiety heightened. I had yet to step onto the soil of Wisconsin and already my naïveté was in issue, for I had no idea what in God's name a cheese curd was. What would I do if I was offered one? It sounded too much like "turd" to eat, that's for damn sure. My father had not warned us that they spoke a different language in the great American Disheartening Land.

We pulled into Starkville. Starkville had a small campus of the University of Wisconsin, where my father would be teaching ROTC. It was summer, and the campus was nearly deserted. We would be staying at the college apartments until my father found us a permanent place to live, during which time the movers would be bringing the rest of our belongings.

After taking our suitcases upstairs, we got back in the car to go find something to eat. My mother would never allow us to eat at a place with a name that she didn't recognize. It had to be at least a national chain,

and then she was often still suspect. She felt that as
Black people, we didn't have the luxury of eating any-
where that was convenient, that we weren't born into
the skin color of universal acceptance, and therefore
couldn't trust just anyone to prepare our food. At the
time, with my youthful lack of worldliness, I just
thought my mom was being paranoid, that her childhood of living in Alabama during the fifties and sixties had left her hopelessly archaic and permanently
scarred.

So as we drove around passing diner after diner,
waiting for my mother to choose a suitable one, me
and my brothers muttered with impatience. It wasn't
enough that she uprooted us from Ft. Campbell, now
she was trying to starve us to death, too? Yes, my
brothers and I blamed my mother for the move. We
blamed her for all the ills of our life while always letting my father off scot-free. Mainly because she was
the sole dispenser of beatings.

My father had endured a childhood of physical
abuse at the hands of his father and had sworn never
to hit his children. He kept his vow, though I didn't
make it easy for him to. I was the requisite asshole of
my family. The mouthy smart-ass kid that waited for
adults, particularly my mother, to stumble so I could
point out their shortcomings. A practice that got me
hit with anything that was within grasp and could
easily be handled by my mother's 115-pound frame.
If she couldn't find anything, she used her hand, or
as I got older, her fist would suffice. I have no data to
back it up, but I believe that my brothers combined
may have gotten smacked one third as many times
as I did. They would get mad at me for putting her

in a bad mood and thus making them more susceptible to her chastisement. Whenever I said something particularly worthy of incurring her wrath, she would often look at me like I was some demon spawn and exasperatedly say, "Boy, you must like when I beat you." She swore that I must of, or I would've learned to "stay in a child's place" some hundred or so beatings previous to the one she was administering at the time. But she was wrong. What she didn't know was that she had an aspiring scientist in her midst. You see, in school I had been learning about astronomy. I was simply trying to discern whether there was any correlation between the gravitational force at work in our universe and the one that seemingly impelled the back of my mother's hand to my mouth. Either that, or I was determined to get her to appreciate my gift of biting wit, and oh-so subtle sense of irony.

Just as I was about to comment that maybe we could wait for one of these cows to die and eat it, which would have probably earned me a date with my mother's fury, my father saved me the trouble.

My father, who was hungry as hell, too, finally gave up. He pulled the car to the side of the road and looked at my mother.

"Carmen, where do you want to eat?"

She looked out the window and then back at him.

"Let's go to Dubuque." Dubuque, I found out later, was a big town or small city, twenty minutes away in Iowa. I had no idea how my mother had even heard of it. My father was evidently as shocked as I was.

"Dubuque? Why Dubuque?" He looked at her with his eyes bugged out incredulously and gave my mom a perfectly executed double take. I always thought my father had missed his true calling, that his career in the military had prevented him from being the next Sidney Poitier. My mother, who was often on the receiving end of his stagecraft, didn't share my appreciation for it.

"Because I want to go somewhere where I can see some Black people. That's why," she replied, irritated.

"Carmen, there are only seventy-five to eighty Black people living in Dubuque!"

Wow, I thought from the backseat. Will wonders never cease? I knew that last week my father had flown from Kentucky to Wisconsin to make arrangements for us. Evidently, he had done his homework as well. For not only was he familiar with this mystical place called "Dubuque," he had evidently done some empirical fact-finding. I pictured my father combing the streets of Dubuque, culling data and making a head count of every Black person within the city limits, just in case my mother made some statement about wanting to see some Black people. What a guy! And he wasn't done yet. For he now had a look of such utter pain on his face, that if he was with anyone besides people who were used to his dramatics, they would have sought medical assistance for him. He balled his left hand into a fist and pounded it on the car door.

"Carmen, you made me leave the best job I ever had in the army to come here . . ."

My brothers and I looked at one another. Aha! So she was responsible for our uprooting.

". . . and now you want to complain because there ain't no Black people? When I think about it . . ."

With the timing of a master thespian, he took his free right hand and started rubbing his stomach, and scrunched his face up even more.

". . . it . . . it just makes my stomach turn sour."

My father's case of severe acid reflux notwithstanding, I now had two major mysteries in my life to unravel. First, I would find out what a cheese curd was. Secondly, I would find out what precipitated my mother making us move.

Me, my brother Ron, and my little brother Ryan were always our mother's sons. The task of raising us fell squarely on her shoulders. Our father was often away from us, either fighting in Vietnam, serving two stints in Germany, or because he and my mother would often separate because they found living with each other intolerable. In which case she would have the three of us in tow. Even when he was with us, like the year we spent in Wisconsin, he was mysterious and distant. It also allowed him to escape culpability and blame, which we heaped on our mother, since she was readily available to us. I know he cared for us but was uncomfortable showing it, while our mother was the centerpiece of our lives and showered us with affection and attention—when she wasn't terrorizing us, usually due to some transgression I had committed.

It was one week before school started, and me and my mother were driving back from Indianapolis, where we had spent the weekend visiting her godmother. She had left my brothers behind in Starkville with our father and just taken me alone with her. The pain-in-the-ass child. Though I was neither her first child or her "baby," for the first ten or eleven years of my life, you couldn't tell me that I wasn't my mother's favorite. By this point and time, we were into the period when we were more removed from each other. Many years later, my mother would tell me that she felt responsible for the breach. I had always been such a sickly child, in and out of the hospital with severe asthma attacks and multiple heart surgeries, that she had feared losing me. She feels that she may have subtly pushed me away to almost prepare herself for a time when I might not be there. This was news to me. I had always chalked it up to the onset of adolescence and the need for privacy that it entails. Though, in retrospect, maybe I did sense something between us had changed. It might explain my incessant craving for attention, and the snotty attitude I utilized to get it.

During the ride, I decided to broach the subject of our recent move.

"Mom, why did you want to leave Fort Campbell?"

She didn't answer right away and kept her eyes focused on the road ahead. "We needed a change," she finally said.

We? I thought. Either my mother was having trouble with her pronoun usage or she had developed multiple personalities, because as far as the males of the family were concerned, we didn't need anything that wasn't to be found in abundance in Kentucky. The weather, my friends, my school—they certainly hadn't needed changing. And in Kentucky, there were no signs of this mysterious cheese-curd phenomenon.

However, I had to be careful how to continue the

conversation. The last place I wanted to get on my mom's bad side was in the car during a long trip like this one. Especially sitting in the front seat. For whenever I was in the backseat and got mouthy, she would turn around while driving and yell, "Come here!" That was my cue to dutifully lean forward so she could smack me upside the head. She would then turn back around and resume driving while yelling at me about what she would not tolerate coming from no child of hers. Ronald, who was usually in the front seat next to her, would be giving me a look of death for getting her in a foul mood again, thereby putting him and Ryan in harm's way of Hurricane Carmen. But, he would be the least of my worries. I was always relieved when she focused her attention back on the road. I hate to think what kind of beating I would have gotten if she had rear-ended someone while dealing with me (Boy! See what you made me do).

For once, I had the good sense to drop the subject. I could tell she didn't want to talk about it, and it was done anyway, so what was the point. Besides, in the front seat I was in too precarious a position. She could expend her entire fusillade of backhands to the mouth, and open-palm shots to the head, with great accuracy and little effort.

The following week, my mother and I were sitting in the guidance office at Starkville Middle School, where I would be attending eighth grade. We had already enrolled my brothers in their respective schools and were waiting to talk to the guidance counselor.

A slightly built man with thick brown hair and a

bushy mustache walked in. He introduced himself as Mr. Perotti, and sat down to talk to us.

At first, he and my mother made small talk about how harsh the Wisconsin winter would be compared to Kentucky, and other innocuous things. Then he started inquiring as to whether there were any other differences that might have concerned her during our time in Starkville thus far.

"Well," she said, "one of the first things I said to my husband was 'Where are all the Black people?'"

I cringed. Up to that point, I had led such a sheltered, naive existence, that I almost hated race to be brought up in any context. It wasn't that I was ever ashamed of my Blackness, but I guess in my youthful folly, I somehow thought that if I (or Black folks like my mother) didn't make an issue of it, for the most part, others wouldn't, either. My favorite movies at the time were anything with Sidney Poitier in it. I fancied myself a younger version of Sidney Poitier's character, Dr. Prentice, in *Guess Who's Coming to Dinner?*, where he belittles his father's antiquated way of thinking by saying, "You think of yourself as a colored man. I think of myself as a ma-hn."

Mr. Perotti nodded his head knowingly and approvingly. He had been fishing for a good way to bring up the issue of race, and now that my mother had bit, he was "allowed" to talk freely.

"Yes, you're going to find that many of the people in this town had never come into any type of direct contact with a Black family."

He said it in such a fashion like he was so much more sophisticated than the yokels that comprised the citizenry of Starkville. He wasn't telling us anything we didn't already know. It had only taken a food-shopping trip at the town's Piggly Wiggly and hearing a little boy proclaim excitedly, "Look, Mom, Black people!" for us to realize that we had entered a strange new world. Everywhere we went, we elicited looks of wonderment.

My family spent one year in Starkville, a year of whose memories the rest of the Majors have long ago sublimated to the deepest, darkest recesses of their psyches. I, on the other hand, had one of the most enjoyable years of my childhood. Excepting for little inconveniences (like having to go seventy miles to get a decent haircut), I kind of enjoyed being the Lone Negro of my school. I was bombarded with attention, as the "liberal" parents welcomed and sometimes pushed their children to make friends with the Black kid. I liked being the one the girls wanted to dance with in gym class because I had more rhythmic coordination than my corn-fed buddies. I liked that everyone knew my name, when nine times out of ten I didn't know theirs. Having already lived in Alabama, Maryland, New Jersey, North Carolina, and Kentucky, to many of my classmates my life seemed so much more exciting than the ones they had led. I learned from them as well. I found out how much land is in an acre. I became a fan of Big Ten football and basketball. And by sheer forced absorption, I learned the lyrics to every John Cougar (Mellencamp) song ever made.

The little bumps in the road, like the occasional "nigger!" that would come spewing from a passing car, I just shrugged off. I figured that kind of stuff happened everywhere.

Meanwhile, on the home front, things were stormy to say the least.

"Ronald, why the hell did you bring us here?"

"Carmen, you're the one that said you wanted to move."

"And you bring us here? Out in the middle of nowhere?"

"I'm in the army, Carmen. I can't tell them where to send me."

"You must think I'm crazy. All those years you have in, you could have requested somewhere else."

Looking back, at least my dad had work to keep him occupied. My brothers and I had school and our extracurricular activities. My mother had nothing to escape the utter boredom of Starkville. She was only in her mid-thirties at the time, and she must have been pulling her hair out. Though, oftentimes it would have been an improvement because she, too, had a long trek to find the sanctuary of a Black hairdresser.

Many times their arguing would get so heated that my brothers (who were always more sensitive than my self-absorbed ass) would leave the house. Then my mother would really let my father have it.

"See? Now, look what you've done! You got my children walking around this lily-ass White town where anything can happen to them. . . ."

I once asked my mother how come the arguments were always my father's fault, when it seemed to me that she started ninety percent of them and she would be the one doing ninety percent of the yelling. Most of the time he would be trying to tune her out. She said it only seemed that way because he would "get her worked up" and then try to play dumb. She then assured me that my father was entirely, solely culpable for instigating every argument in the history of mankind.

With most of my mom's frustration directed at my father, I sailed through my eighth-grade year. I was confirmed in the local Methodist church, got eyeglasses for the first time, played on the basketball team, and maintained good grades in school, despite being a cutup. This did provide me with my one close call. My science/homeroom teacher, Mrs. Olafson, was tiring of my silliness. One time, when she was driving home and I was playing catch with a friend in the street, she stopped her car and motioned for me to get in front of it so she could run me over. To this day, a part of me still thinks that woman's intentions were serious.

However, when she talked about informing my parents about my behavior at the next parent/teacher conference, I straightened up real quick. The thought of what my mother would have done to me if she got a bad report from a teacher makes my spine turn cold to this day.

We only lived in Starkville for one school year, for which I am grateful. I enjoyed my time there, but the novelty of the town on me and me on the town was beginning to wear off.

My mother and I made it all the way to May before locking horns.

As I was nearing completion of the school year, my classmates started to talk about some big end of the school-year dance that was apparently a tradition for eighth graders in Starkville. I was only marginally interested in it.

One day I was shooting baskets after school with a couple of friends, Tommy and Tim, when two of our classmates, Katie and Ellen, approached us.

They were two of the most popular girls in the school. They belonged to the clique of girls that all the nerdy boys dreamed of dating. Tommy and Tim were stud athletes and part of the "cool" group that those same nerdy boys longed to be accepted by. I knew that Tommy was going to the dance with Ellen.

Katie was a dark-haired girl with freckles. She was by far the most pursued girl in the eighth grade, and on a daily basis, boys used to stumble over themselves trying to impress her.

"Tim, are you going to the dance?" Ellen asked.

"Yeah," he answered. "I'm taking Patty."

That makes sense, I thought. She was part of the same clique that Katie and Ellen belonged to. Ellen focused her attention on me.

"What about you, Marcus? You going?"

"I don't think so," I said.

"Why not?"

I shrugged my shoulders. I decided to make a joke out of it.

"I can't find anyone who'll go with me."

"I'll go with you, Marcus," Katie said.

Tim's eyes got as big as the basketball he was holding. Tommy looked at me for a reaction, but there was no look of surprise on his face. I could tell that he already knew.

"Umm, okay, Katie, sure."

Both of the girls smiled.

We made small talk for a little while, and then the girls said good-bye, leaving me with Tommy and Tim, who still had a look of disbelief on his face.

"Wow," he said, looking at me with a combination of awe and newfound respect.

I knew why. In his eyes Katie was the girl. I had been privy to many of the conversations where the fellas discussed where she ranked in the pecking order of eighth-grade females, and their bravado about what they would do to her with their thirteen-year-old schlongs if given the chance. To me, the thing I liked best about Katie is that she laughed at every silly thing I said. I was one of the few guys who never made a fuss over her, which is probably why she wanted to go with me.

When I got home that night, I told my mother about it. Bad move.

"You're going to what?!" She turned down the flame on the stove to let the pot she was cooking simmer, so she could focus her attention on me.

"A dance," I said. "Tommy and I are double dating." I could tell my mom was upset, though I had no idea why. I knew she liked Tommy, his father was in the military and worked with my father, so I threw his name in in an attempt to lessen her anxiety.

"Who is 'Katie'?" she asked.

"A girl from school."

"A White girl?"

Did she know of any other kind of girls in Starkville? I wanted to say but didn't. "Yeah," I said as nonchalantly as possible, hoping that if I acted like it was no big deal, she would too. I went to the refrigerator to get something to drink. I felt her eyes on me, but she was quiet. I took a carton of milk out and went to the cabinet and got a plastic cup.

"I want her phone number," she finally said.

"Why?" I asked, forgetting my thirst for the moment. Surely she wasn't thinking of . . .

"So I can call her family and see if her parents know their daughter is going with a Black child."

"What?! You don't have to do that. They know."

"Then, you shouldn't have a problem with me calling." She walked back over to the stove and started stirring the pot.

I glared at her. In my mind, she had to be the most ignorant person in the world. I took her wanting to inform Katie's parents as her believing that I wasn't worthy of going with their precious daughter because of my Blackness. She was the one with the hangups, and was now forcing me to deal with them. The thought of her talking to Katie's parents, and no doubt saying something embarrassing, was too much for me to bear. I regretted telling her anything.

"Why do you have to make an issue of it?" I snapped at her.

"Because it is," she answered, keeping her back to me.

"It's just a stupid dance. It's no big deal."

"I know. Write down the phone number."

"I don't know it." I was telling the truth. I didn't know it. I rarely spoke to the girl outside of school.

She turned around to look at me. She could tell I wasn't lying.

"Well, if you wanna go, I suggest you get it," she

said calmly, and turned back around. She reached into the cabinet over the stove and pulled out a box of rice.

Her smugness was too much for me to take. Especially considering she was the one so unsophisticated. I mean, really, it was 1984, not 1964. I slammed the cup on the counter.

"Why do you always have to mess things up?"

She had reached her limit with me. "Boy, you'd better go somewhere and sit down."

I sucked my teeth and stormed out of the kitchen, muttering as to how "she was the reason we were in this town in the first place" just loud enough for her to hear. I stomped up the stairs and slammed my bedroom door. For while I may have been too much of a sophisticate for my mother's backwater thinking, I could still throw a good tantrum when the need arose.

I laid across my bed, alternately crying and sucking the snot back up my nose. It was just like Dr. Prentice told his father, it wasn't going to be until my mother's entire backward generation was dead and buried that we would be able to advance as a race. Seeing how my mother was only thirty-five at the time, I supposed I was in for a long wait.

Over the next week, I came up with inventive ways to dodge giving my mother the phone number (which I had since procured), while at the same time making plans to go to the dance. I did an end-around my mother and asked my father to take me and Tommy to the restaurant where we would be meeting Ellen and Katie. Tommy's older brother would then take us to the hall where the dance was being held and also bring the four of us back home afterward. My father had no clue that he was being a party to my attempt to pull a fast one on my mother, because the communication between the two of them was sparse at best by this point.

I came into the house in a good mood after school on a Tuesday afternoon. My mother still hadn't stopped asking me for the phone number like I had hoped. But on the bright side, there were only three days to go until the night of the dance, and I had yet to use my "she was absent today" or "I left it in my locker" excuses yet.

"Marc," she called from the living room. "Do you have that phone number?"

"Nah. She wasn't in school today, so I couldn't get it." I quickly headed for the stairs.

"Boy, you must think I'm stupid. Do I have to go up to the school tomorrow and get it myself?"

That statement made my knees buckle so bad, that I grabbed the rail for support. She wouldn't embarrass me like that. Who was I kidding? Of course, she would. I walked into the living room, unzipped my bookbag, and took out the crumpled piece of paper with the phone number on it.

She didn't scold me for lying to her. She took the paper and inspected it.

"What's her last name?"

"Nelson," I said in as mournful a voice as possible, trying to elicit sympathy from her in a last-ditch effort to get her to reconsider. She was already on her way into the kitchen to make the call. I thought about sitting in the kitchen and listening to her conversation with the Nelsons, but decided it would be too painful to endure. I went upstairs to my room to wait for her to get done.

About half an hour later, I came back downstairs. My mother was watching television with my little brother. I stood there waiting for her to say something.

"You can go," she finally said, without looking away from the TV.

I turned around and went back upstairs.

I waved good-bye to Tommy and his brother and walked into my nearly dark house. My mother had left the foyer light on for me. I thought she would be waiting up. I turned it off and went upstairs to my room. Even though I wasn't the oldest, I had my own room. I think it was primarily due to the fact that I terrorized my little brother Ryan so much that my parents put him in a room with Ron.

I turned on my lamp with the Green Bay Packer lampshade. As I undressed, I reflected on the evening.

I found out why Katie and Ellen had met me and Tommy at the restaurant instead of having us pick them up from home. Mr. and Mrs. Nelson dined at a table about five tables from ours. I didn't begrudge them. Instead, I blamed my mother. I figured that my mom had scared them so much about what could transpire if certain people saw their White daughter out with her Black son that they probably wanted to keep an eye on us.

As for Katie, she wasn't her usual relaxed self in my presence, and I was certain, regretted asking me to go in the first place. In the last few days of school before the date, we hadn't spoken much; neither of us had brought up the phone call my mother had placed to her parents. The reason she had wanted to go with me was, I'm sure, because she thought she would have fun. Again, I blamed my mother. I didn't want to imagine what kind of grief she had gotten from her parents after my far too overly worried mother's call. ("Of all the boys in that school, you had to choose . . .")

There was a soft tap at my bedroom door.

I finished putting on my T-shirt. "Come in."

My mother walked into the room.

"Hi, baby. Did you have a good time, tonight?"

My first impulse was to tell her, "Hell, no," but that would have earned me a pop in the chops. So I was about to follow my second impulse, which was to tell her how her meddling and issue creating had ruined everything, when something strange happened.

I saw a look on her face that surprised me. My mother's normally youthful face was covered with an anxiety that I knew would only be erased if she heard me say that I had enjoyed myself. Even more surprising to me, was my reaction. For all I wanted was for that look to go away.

"Yeah, Mom, I did." I sat down on my bed.

She looked relieved and smiled. She walked over to the bed and sat down next to me.

"That's good. I prayed on it."

"Yeah?" I said looking down at the floor.

"Marc, you might not understand everything I do, but I love you. It's my job to protect you, Ryan, and Ronald the best way I know how. The thing I fear most is losing one of you to some nonsense."

"I know," I said, yawning.

"Well, I know you're tired, you'd better get some rest."

"Yeah."

She stood up. "Do you want me to turn off this lamp?"

"Yeah."

In the darkness my mother navigated her way to the door. Right before she left, I spoke.

"Mom."

"What?" she said softly, not wanting to wake my brothers.

"I love you, too." I hadn't said that to her in aeons. I heard her let out a deep breath.

"Thank you, baby." She walked out closing the door behind her.

AFTERWORD

When I recently asked my mother if she remembered what was said in the conversation with her and Katie's parents, she told me she did not. In fact, she doesn't remember the episode at all—the dance, her dogged pursuit of the phone number, any of it. But then again, I shouldn't have been too surprised. It occurred during our lost year in Starkville, the existence of which she had spent years erasing from her consciousness.

I did find out what precipitated her asking my father to leave Fort Campbell. It was an attempt to save her marriage. She felt that for a number of varying reasons they needed to have a fresh start. However, the desolation of Starkville only emphasized their incompatibility, and they separated the next year. He left for another stint in Germany, and my mother moved us to an all-Black town in New Jersey in an attempt to eradicate any lingering effects Starkville might have had on us.

I never did find out what a cheese curd is.

Maxine O'Callaghan
with John O'Callaghan

Finding Rose

John and Maxine O'Callaghan shooting a short film on location in Southern California.

Rose Dwyer disappeared on a day in late August, just before Sean's fifth birthday. For a long time he was sure if he just struck the right bargain with God, his mother would come back. He promised he'd be the best boy ever, just let her be at the bus stop when he got home from kindergarten. He'd give up his new bike if she would be there when he opened the door, saying, "Hey, baby, did you have a good day at school?" Let her come home for Christmas, and he'd never ask Santa for another thing again.

Eventually, he had to learn life's cruelest lesson: bad things happen; you just have to learn to live with them. Now, almost fifteen years after his mother vanished, Sean was having to deal with that truth all over again because he was losing his father.

At two o'clock that afternoon he had completed his last final at Pasadena City College. Poly Sci, he was fairly sure he'd aced it. Three more classes in summer school, and then in the fall he'd transfer to UCLA as a junior. Until then he had to work as much as possible.

He was scheduled for five o'clock at the video store, which gave him time to go home and have a late lunch. If he grabbed a burger and went on over to the store, maybe he could start early, get a couple of extra hours. And he could avoid dealing with his dad . . .

The twinge of guilt he felt at the thought sent him home to the quiet street in South Pasadena, where he lived with his father and stepmother in an old white bungalow with gray trim and gray shutters.

The town had fought successfully for years to keep a freeway from carving it in half. As a result, time seemed to stand still here in the middle of the sprawling Los Angeles metropolis, whose name was synonymous with constant change. Quite often film crews used the neighborhood for someplace in the Midwest. It stood in for Indianapolis, Cleveland, or even Philadelphia, as long as the cinematographer shot around the occasional giant palm and the jacaranda trees that arched above the street and bloomed in great clouds this time of year.

In the early afternoon sunlight, the masses of flowers on the jacaranda trees were a vibrant blue, shaded toward purple. But when the spent blossoms fell, they overflowed rain gutters and stained sidewalks and cars—the beauty not nearly worth the mess, in Sean's dad's opinion. He'd taken a chain saw to the one in front of their house ten years ago, a sacrilege neither the neighbors nor the city boosters was quick to forgive.

As Sean turned onto the street where he grew up, he felt another stab of guilt at the sight of his stepmother, running down the sidewalk, a good distance from the house. She was so frantic and distracted, it took a moment for her to respond when he braked, rolled down the window, and called to her.

"Gwen? What is it? What's wrong?"

"Sean, oh, thank God it's you," she said, rushing over to the car, stumbling in her haste over cement broken by tree roots and slick with fallen blooms.

Gwen had always been a solid, active woman whose one extravagance was a weekly visit to the beauty salon to maintain her short, curly chestnut hair. It struck Sean now just how much weight she'd lost and how her hair was an ugly iron-gray that straggled around her face and fell almost to her shoulders.

"He's gone," she said. "I swear I just closed my eyes for a minute."

"We'll find him," Sean said. "Get in."

She did, but had barely closed the door when she said, "Better we split up. Take me to get my car. I'm so sorry, I should've known better. But he barely slept last night, he kept waking me up, and I was so tired."

"Don't worry about it," Sean said. "It's not your fault. How long ago?"

"I don't know. Maybe ten minutes."

"Then, he couldn't have gone far."

After dropping her off, Sean drove slowly down the street under the arch of blooming trees. All he could see were the places his father might wander into: backyards, a few open garages that might have unlocked access to the attached houses. And he wasn't sure which was worse, the way his mother had left so abruptly so many years ago, or the way his dad was slowly vanishing a day at a time.

Alan Dwyer had been diagnosed with Alzheimer's disease three years earlier when he was fifty-nine. "So young," people would say when they heard. Victims' families quickly learn, however, that the condition is not necessarily an illness of old age and that it has crept in like a cat burglar long before the memory loss will be thought of as something other than absent-mindedness, or the restlessness and irritability has turned into ceaseless activity and insomnia. By then they also understand that the burglar has not only brought picklocks and keys, but has a hacksaw, blow-torch, and wrecking ball as well.

Sean spotted his dad finally, trotting at a pace that had already put him a good half mile from home. A pair of old gym shoes flapped on his feet, laces un-tied. He wore dirty khaki pants and a green plaid flannel shirt, buttoned crookedly, much too heavy for the warm afternoon sun.

Sean had his mother's coloring, her dark hair and blue eyes, but he looked enough like Alan with his lanky frame and narrow shoulders so that he got a cold chill thinking that he was seeing himself forty-two years from now. Doctors couldn't say for sure that Alzheimer's was genetic, but they couldn't say it wasn't, either.

Calling to his father got no response. Sean had to park, get out, and go up and touch him before his dad stopped and turned with a spark of recognition in his eyes.

"I can't find it, Carl," he said plaintively.

Alan's memories skipped grooves like an old record player working a warped LP. He often thought Sean was his older brother Carl, who had died in the fifties on some cold, forgotten hill in Korea.

"Mama sent me for milk," Alan said, "but I can't find the store."

Sweat plastered the thinning sandy hair to his scalp and ran down just in front of his ears. His skin was pink with sunburn and hung loosely on his cheek and jaw bones.

"That's okay, Dad," Sean said, filled with a combination of grief, repulsion, and love as he took his father's matchstick arm and steered him to the car. "Come on, I'll take you home."

From where Sean sat, trying to eat a sandwich at the kitchen table, he could see his dad asleep on the living room sofa. Exhausted, Gwen had gone to take a nap in their bedroom. Sean's appetite had vanished. He picked at the turkey on sourdough, sipped some Coke, and wondered how much more Gwen could take. At some point they would have to find a nursing home for his dad, maybe soon unless Sean was willing to take over some of the burden of caring for Alan.

He supposed he could work less, take fewer classes, go to Cal State L.A. instead of the university, so he'd have a shorter commute. But he wanted to major in film and had been lucky enough to get into UCLA, so how could he not go? Bad enough that the money his dad had set aside for Sean's education was likely now to be spent on a nursing home and Sean would be saddled with a ton of student loans.

Resentment sat like a big knot in his throat. He took

the remains of his sandwich over to the counter and put it down the garbage disposal.

"Sean?"

Sean turned from the sink to find his father standing there next to the table, looking a little bewildered but otherwise normal.

"I thought you just left for school," Alan said.

"Dad, it's three-thirty," Sean said, and braced himself for an argument.

Usually, Alan never remembered the episodes of dementia and quickly got hostile and angry if you tried to tell him what had happened. Now he sagged into a chair and looked at Sean with a terrible comprehension in his eyes.

"Is Gwen okay?"

"She's fine," Sean said. "She's taking a nap."

"I know what's going to happen," Alan said. "That's the worst part. I know I'm going to forget her. And you. Everything."

Sean wanted to deny this, to reassure his father, but they both knew it was true.

"So while I can," Alan went on, "I just want to say I'm sorry."

"For what, Dad?"

"For driving your mother away. For making her so unhappy she left like that. For not trying to find her. You needed me to do that, Sean, and I never did. Too stubborn, I guess."

It was the first time Alan had willingly brought up Sean's mother. Over the years, he had deflected questions about his missing first wife like BB's ricocheting off stone. If Rose's name was mentioned, he got a set, closed look on his face, and he would say something like, "What's done's done. Best to forget it."

And it was surprising how easy it had been, if not to forget Rose, to avoid the subject. A taciturn neighbor looked after Sean the year he was in kindergarten. There were no relatives or close friends of Rose's nearby to offer explanations. When Sean was in first grade, Alan moved them from the town east of Sacramento to the suburbs of L.A., where he met and married Gwen and had even more reason to bury the past.

Now a hundred questions tumbled through Sean's mind. Before he could frame the first one, Alan said, "That day—she was really upset, she yelled at me on the phone, but I thought it would blow over like it always did. I told her I was coming right home. Maybe if I had—but I got stuck at work, and when I got there she was gone and you were all by yourself. I wish I could see her again, to ask her why, before I . . . while I can still understand. But even if it's too late for me, it's not for you, Sean. I think you ought to do it."

"Dad, my God, you mean look for her? I wouldn't know where to start."

"Well, use your head for once." Alan glared at him and jumped up to begin pacing between the table and the sink. "Do I have to do everything for you?"

"Dad, please, sit down," Sean said, his desperation mixed with dread as he saw his father slipping away. "Tell me about my mother. If you want me to find her, you have to talk to me."

"She drives that old car too damn fast," Alan said,

head down, circling the table. "Mama said we could have cookies later, Carl. But we're out of milk."

Sean felt as though he'd been on a roller-coaster and now the bottom had fallen out. Unable to deal with the emotions his father had sent boiling to the surface, Sean was happy to wake up Gwen and go to work.

Escape was more like running away, however, and short-lived to boot. And all the time he dealt with customers and shelved stock, a part of his mind kept going over and over his father's words and coming back to the same questions. Was it possible to find his mother? Should he even try? What would he say to her after all these years?

When he arrived home shortly after midnight, Gwen had left a light on for him, but the rest of the house was dark and silent. A good sign, he hoped it meant his dad had gone to sleep at a reasonable hour. He tiptoed into his room and closed the door.

Sean usually kept the room picked up, but the small space was messier than usual because of his hectic schedule. He moved a pile of clothes from his bed to the floor, sat down on the edge of the bed, and opened the lower drawer of the bedside table. There at the very bottom, under some old summer camp T-shirts and pajamas he never wore, was a five-by-seven picture in a silver frame and a lace-trimmed, satiny nightgown that had belonged to his mother.

He remembered creeping into his parents' bedroom the evening after she left and taking the gown. For months he'd slept with it, stroking the smooth fabric, wrapped in the lingering scent of his mother's perfume.

The fragrance had to be long gone, but he thought he could catch the faintest smell as he pressed the gown to his face and looked down at the picture. Rose and Alan on their wedding day. A simple affair at a justice of the peace in Sacramento. Alan's arm was around her, and they looked happy and in love.

His mother was beautiful with a cloud of dark hair, a perfect oval face, and so young, his age. His father had been twenty years older than she was. Maybe the difference had been an unbridgeable gap. Sean remembered them fighting, just flashes of raised voices and how scared he'd been.

He had only the haziest of memories of the day his mother left: The pressure of her arms as she hugged him; the thinnest echo of her voice, saying, "Daddy'll be here soon. You be good, Baby;" and a taste of salt lingering in his mouth as he heard a car driving away. What he'd never forget was the feeling of being alone and terrified as the house turned dark and the blaze of light when his father arrived.

Alzheimer's was a terminal illness. Worse, long before the body finally gave up the fight, the mind would be gone. Looked at this way, his dad's poignant wish to know what had happened to Rose might be the last thing he asked of his son.

Sitting there, overwhelmed suddenly by the sense of abandonment he thought he'd put aside, Sean knew something else. His father was right. He needed to find his mother for himself, too, and ask her the questions that had haunted him since he was five.

"Why did you go away? If you loved me, how could you leave me all alone like that?"

He closed his eyes and thought about those last moments with her, recalling the warmth of his mother's body and that strange, lingering taste of salt in his mouth.

A taste, Sean suddenly realized, that had to be his mother's tears, transferred to his lips as she pressed her face against his and held him close that one last time.

By the time he got up the next morning, Gwen said his father had been awake for hours. He had settled into pacing between the living room and kitchen, and Gwen was eating toast and drinking coffee while keeping a distracted eye on him. Sean poured some orange juice, leaned against the counter to drink it, and told her about the conversation the day before and what he had planned to do.

"Oh, Sean," she said, "that's an awfully big decision. Your dad's not thinking straight, you know that."

"He was at that point," Sean said. "I've made up my mind, Gwen. Will you help me?"

"Of course," Gwen said. "But I don't know what I can tell you. I met your dad here in L.A. after the two of you moved down from Rockland. I never knew your mother, and Alan's said very little."

"He must have told you something."

"He was trying to forget what happened, Sean. I know they didn't get along. I'm not excusing what she did, but she was awfully young when they got married and had you."

"That can't be all of it," Sean said. "There had to be a reason why she left. Did Dad ever say what it was?"

Gwen shook her head.

"What was so awful that she'd go off and leave me like that? Did she have a boyfriend? What was going on?"

"Sean, I'm sorry, but I don't know," Gwen said, clearly uncomfortable with his questions and preoccupied with watching his father.

"Well, did Dad look for her?" Sean persisted. "Did he report her missing to the police?"

"The police? No, of course not—"

She broke off at the sound from the living room of the patio door opening, jumped up, and ran out to follow his dad. Sean could see them out in the backyard, Alan with that head-down, one-track determination as he circled the yard, going nowhere, Gwen trying to calm him down.

Sean did a quick cleanup in the kitchen and went back to his room to boot up his computer. Within half an hour he had listings for every Rose Leigh Dwyer the World Wide Web could snare, just three names, and the low number both surprised and depressed him. Phone calls quickly eliminated all of them. One told him in a feeble, old-lady voice that she had never been out of Vermont. Another, who lived in Sedona, Arizona, said she was pretty sure she'd been in his hometown once, lost on the way from Berkeley to Tahoe, and how about buying a crystal guaranteed to help him in his search?

The third call yielded an answering machine. It had been a long time since Sean last heard his mother's voice, but he knew the honeyed accent down in Decatur, Georgia, did not belong to her.

Well, it was a long shot. Chances were that Rose had changed her name as soon as she left, or she may have remarried. Still, he had to try the obvious first.

A bit more Web surfing turned up several sites of people who claimed they could find anybody, but it was obvious from one of the site's questionnaires that there had to be some information to point the way. Besides a name, the questionnaire asked for a birth date, Social Security number, driver's license number, and all kinds of details that reminded him of how little he knew about the woman who had given him life.

He couldn't afford professional help, but without it, where did he go from here? For all Sean knew about his mother's family, she might as well have been raised by wolves. Somebody had told him she was an only child, that her parents died in a car wreck, he didn't remember who, just that it hadn't been his father.

Sean's grandparents on his dad's side were long gone. Besides Alan and Carl, there had been an older sister, his Aunt Paula, who lived in a small town in Michigan, and was now in a nursing home. Two cousins were still in that area. Sean supposed he could get in touch with them, for all the good it would do. The closemouthed Dwyers must have had the smallest telephone bills in the country. Their sole communication consisted of a few words on a card every Christmas.

There had to be plenty of other people who knew his mother and father, even though chances were good they would be scattered to the four winds by now. Only one way to find out, and one place to begin.

He crammed a change of clothes in his duffel bag, called the video store to say he wouldn't be in for a couple of days, then went to say good-bye to Gwen.

The weather might still be mild in the L.A. basin, but the San Joaquin valley was already getting a taste of summer. Wild oats had turned brown on the coastal hills along Interstate 5. On the valley side, rows of cotton simmered in the heat, a deep, dusty green, looking as though the plants had been lopped off knee-high and tailored for a scene in a movie. Or genetically altered to grow that way, that was his second guess.

At the Buttonwillow exit, he stopped for a burrito. Sometime after midnight he pulled off in a rest area and slept for a few hours. Up at dawn, he decided against trying to change his clothes in the public bathroom, found he'd forgotten his razor so had to settle for splashing his face and brushing his teeth. The scruffy guy who looked back from the mirror didn't look improved much.

He arrived at Rockland just before noon. At least that's what the sign said, but he felt an immediate sense of dislocation as he drove into the small town north of Sacramento. He had some memories of the place where he spent the first six years of his life, a few images of the big chocolate-colored house on Pinewood Street, towering trees in a park where he'd sat and eaten a drippy ice cream cone and watched people go in and out of stores, sunlight sparkling on a lake. The lake was there, actually a reservoir, but the rest of the place felt shrunken and skewed somehow, nothing at all like what he remembered.

He drove slowly past the only park in the small downtown area. It was about the size of a tennis court with some scrubby acacias, a couple of picnic benches. A few brown birds pecked in the patchy, drying grass and watched him with black, fierce eyes. The stores he could see offered the basic necessities of life: hardware, appliance repair, dry cleaning, video rental, haircuts. But no luxuries like ice cream.

Streets were laid out in a grid, so it didn't take long to find Pinewood. None of the houses looked the least bit familiar, and, of course, he didn't remember the address. Hungry, tired, and discouraged, he went to find someplace for lunch, not a fast-food joint but a café that looked like it had been around for a while.

The middle-aged waitress who brought him a grilled cheese sandwich and some iced tea looked politely interested when he said he'd once lived in Rockland. Dwyer? No, sorry, she didn't recognize the name or the picture of his mom and dad. He got the same response from the burly guy who doubled as cook and cashier.

Short of going up and down the streets and knocking on every door, he hadn't a clue how to find anybody who might have known his parents. He went in search of a telephone to check in with Gwen.

No phone booth in the café and none outside on the street. Although it looked just like the rest of the nondescript buildings on the block, one directly across from the café announced in black letters across big glass doors: CITY OF ROCKLAND, PUBLIC SER-VICES. Inside, Sean found a big barnlike entrance room with cinder-block walls painted white and a low ceiling covered with acoustical tile. The place looked like it had been converted from some kind of store with minimum expense, deserted except for an older man in a suit who sat on a wooden bench, peeling an orange and dropping the rinds in a paper sack. A directory promised offices for the mayor, the city police, and welfare with an arrow pointing somewhere toward the back.

A display of photographs covered one wall, some kind of historical accounting, beginning with old black-and-white prints and ending with what must have been more recent events done in color. Many of these seemed to be about the reservoir. On the other wall were two big wire trash cans, one marked Recyclables, and a pay phone.

Sean realized the man was close enough to overhear his conversation, although he looked like he didn't care much about anything but finishing his lunch. The smell of oranges overlaid older, undefined odors in the building as Sean made a collect call from the pay phone.

Sounding exhausted and frazzled, Gwen said his father had had a bad night, then added, "Any luck yet?"

"No, I've just started. Gwen, the woman who used to baby-sit me in Rockland when I was little—would you happen to know her name?"

"Let me think. There was a lady we got Christmas cards from for several years. She lived next door to you up there. Molly Something—Hennigan—no Harrigan."

Sean could hear his father in the background, haranguing Gwen with querulous, nonstop questions. He quickly said goodbye, thanking her and promising to call her later.

There was a book, a combined white and yellow pages, secured by a heavy five-inch chain to the shelf beneath the phone. He knew he should wrestle with the thing and look up Molly Harrigan, knew it was another long shot that probably wouldn't pan out.

So he sat down on the bench just as the man tossed his sack in the trash can and walked out the front door. While he worked up his courage, he stared at the photographs, registering little except that much of the black-and-white display told about the original damming of the river that flowed down from the Sierras and the construction of the reservoir, and that the color photos showed some kind of damage and reconstruction.

He couldn't put off the inevitable forever. Dreading another failure, he let his fingers do the walking and, finally, had a change of luck.

Once again, he drove slowly down Pinewood, this time looking for an address. He found it and parked, sat there to stare at the front yard of what had to be Molly Harrigan's home with a FOR SALE sign in the unkempt lawn and a forlorn look of abandonment.

Phone was probably disconnected, too, but of course he hadn't called. And now he supposed he should at least go up and knock, make sure it was really empty. Instead he sat, looking at the houses that bracketed the Harrigan place. He remembered that he had lived next door. He also recalled going upstairs to bed, which meant the two-story cracker box on the right had to be the one.

It was smaller than the house in South Pasadena, no longer brown but painted a Smurf blue. He remembered only grass and no shade at all outside on hot summer days. Over the years there had been time for a sycamore to grow in the front yard and tower over the house and an oleander hedge to become thick and woody.

He might not have gotten out of the car after all, but just then a white Ford Escort pulled into the driveway of the house on the other side of Molly's, and a woman got out bringing a gym bag and tennis racket with her. She looked to be in her sixties, but tanned and fit enough to use the tennis racket either on the court or on him if she had to. Even so she eyed him warily as he left his car and walked over, standing with her Escort's door open and looking like she might jump back in and speed away. So he stopped down at the sidewalk and told her his name and that he was looking for Ms. Harrigan.

"She passed away," the woman said without offering an introduction of her own. "You a relative?"

"No, I used to live next door. She baby-sat me when I was small."

"Your mother is the one who ran off," the woman said, blunt but not unsympathetic. "Molly talked about it a lot."

Sean said hopefully, "Did you live here then? I'm looking for somebody who knew my mother."

"I'm sorry, no. I've been here about ten years."

"Could you tell me what Ms. Harrigan said about her?"

"Not much, just that she could understand her leaving your dad, that they were always fighting, but couldn't believe she'd go off without you."

"Did she have family in town?"

"I don't think so. She had some relatives—I think in San Francisco. You could probably check the records, see who got the house."

"I will, thank you."

She finally gave him the briefest of smiles. "Well, good luck, then. Sorry, but I need to get in out of this heat."

Sean thanked her again and left, feeling like he was going in circles as he headed back downtown.

Inside the Rockland Public Service Building, he walked past the photographic display again and stopped to read some of the captions, mostly to stall off what was sure to be another failure.

Weakened by the big quake in San Francisco in 1989, it seemed the earthen dam had partially collapsed nine years ago. Luckily for the town, this happened at the end of a dry, hot summer when the reservoir was low, and the Army Corps of Engineers arrived immediately to shore up the break, so the flooding was minimal.

The road coming into town had been wiped out, however, and had to be rebuilt. Sean realized that this explained some of his sense of dislocation when he arrived in Rockland. A wider curve had replaced the sharp bend as the road angled into town.

Another series of pictures showed how, in spite of posted warnings about keeping the water supply clean, the sudden lowering of the lake had revealed all kinds of debris on the bottom, including the grisly find of an old car with a body inside.

Sean stood, rooted to the spot, his heart thudding in his chest, his vision restricted solely to the eight-by-ten photograph that showed just the top of some kind of car sticking out of the muddy water. According to the caption, the car was a 1978 Ford Mustang and had been there long enough so that it had been mostly rusted away. The skeletonized remains inside the car had not been identified.

But the body had been that of a woman.

Sean had to wait thirty long agonizing minutes for a detective in the small city police department to speak to him. Oscar Cruz was about forty, lean and dark with the kind of eyes that took in everything and revealed nothing. He led the way into a small, neatly organized office, listened carefully to Sean's stumbling explanation and questions, then pulled a file from a big steel gray cabinet behind his desk.

"Still an open case," he explained. "I inherited it about five years ago and work on it when things are slow." He gave Sean a wry smile. "Which happens a lot around here."

He glanced through the folder. "The license plate was gone, rusted away. The guy before me tracked down the dealer who sold the car by the VIN number, but the place had gone out of business, some fly-by-night used car lot, and he couldn't find any of the sales records. Do you know what kind of car your mother drove?"

Sean shook his head.

"Can you find out? Any records around?"

"I don't know. I can look."

Cruz nodded and went back to the folder. "Checked out missing-person reports, and nothing matched up. I don't remember a report on your mother, Sean. Guess your dad never filed one. There was nothing we could trace like rings or other jewelry on the body or in the car.

"I can look for a dentist who might have had your mother for a patient. We might get lucky. Otherwise, we can do a DNA test, know for sure."

"Where is she?" Sean asked.

"Rockland Memorial Park," Cruz said. "City buries remains after a year. This could take a while. You might as well go on home, Sean. I'll call when I have something. Meanwhile, let me know if you find out about the car."

Cruz arranged for a blood sample to be taken and after that Sean drove out to the cemetery. He found the grave marked with a plain cement square set in the grass and stood there for a long time before he headed back to L.A., thinking of the fragile bones that lay in the ground.

Back in South Pasadena, his dad was pacing the small house, talking nonstop in disconnected sentences, and poor Gwen looked like the last thing she needed was to hear about what Sean had found out in Rockland. So Sean went directly to the storage space in the attic.

The Dwyers were about as big on photographs as they were on phone calls. No albums, no boxes of old pictures, just a few cartons of slides, mostly taken during their rare vacations. These were postcard stuff, as he recalled, mountains and trees and lakes with very few humans involved. He took the slides and the projector down to his room, then came back for two boxes that held old records.

The records first—none went back further than ten years. There was nothing about the house in Rockland or any cars the Dwyers owned back then. Sean had forgotten to look for the screen for the slides, so he used the wall instead.

The slides were bowed in the paper frames, and the projector had to be constantly refocused, but the images on the wall were vivid and bright. He recognized Yosemite, Sequoia, the Golden Gate Bridge. Then, in the last box, he found an envelope marked simply ROCKLAND, containing three slides.

The house on Pinewood, chocolate-brown, as he remembered, a spindly sapling in the yard, a bed of bright petunias by the front stoop. Him on a tricycle on the sidewalk.

The third slide was one of him in his mother's arms. So young and so beautiful, dark hair down to her shoulders—he was overwhelmed by a sudden memory of the way she smelled, like soap and sunshine and flowers, and how he felt so safe in her arms. They stood on the driveway, and down in a corner of the picture he could see the back bumper of a car, not enough to tell make or model but it was blue.

He heard somebody come into the darkened room and glanced toward the door. His father stood there, staring at the projected image.

"That's Rose," he said. "Did you ever meet her?"

"Yes," Sean said. "A long time ago."

"Got a real temper. But it usually doesn't last long. I just wish she wouldn't go running off the way she does."

"You said she drives too fast."

"That's for sure. Promises she won't do it with Sean in the car, but I worry about it."

"What kind of car does she drive?" Sean asked, and felt his breath catch in his throat as he waited for the answer.

"Why, you know, Carl," Alan said. "That blue Mustang. She loves that thing."

Sean heard Gwen call his father, and from the frantic note in her voice, it wasn't the first time. "In here with me," he called back.

"Who is that woman?" Alan asked. "She's been following me around all morning."

"That's Gwen. She's your wife."

"No, she's not. *That's* my wife." He pointed to the image projected on the wall. "Rose—we have a little boy—she's . . ." He trailed off, then asked, "She went away, didn't she?"

"Yes, she did."

"Is she coming back?"

"No, Dad," Sean said. "She's not coming back."

Then something cracked loose in his chest, a dam breaking just like the one that had broken at the reservoir in Rockland. He didn't need to wait for dental charts to be found or DNA test results.

There was no way to know for sure exactly what had happened, but he could certainly come up with a plausible explanation.

Upset and angry, Rose just wanted to be out of the house when his father got home. He had told her he was leaving right away, which meant Sean would only be alone for a few minutes. So she had sped off, driving out of town toward the reservoir. Sean remembered the pictures and the map displayed in the Rockland Public Service Building, how the road made a sharp bend. She had been driving too fast, and the car must have left the road and gone straight into the deep, dark water.

There was an alternate scenario, with his mother leaving for good just like his father had assumed. And another, darker possibility—that she had intended to drive her car into the lake.

But with no way to ever know the truth, Sean looked at the image of his mother holding him, and his heart told him the first one was true, that his young volatile mother had only wanted to be out of the house when his father got home, that she had intended to come back.

As for what followed, Sean could see that, too. Rose had threatened to leave before, and now his father believed she had. He would be too proud to look for her, too stubborn to change his mind, and he would never imagine that she was already dead beneath the dark waters of the reservoir.

"Sean?" his father said uncertainly. "What are you doing looking at these old slides?"

"Come and sit down, Dad," Sean said gently, "and I'll tell you all about it."

AFTERWORD

My son, John, and I share an incredible closeness that always amazes people. This bond formed early. I was a stay-at-home mom who put off my writing career until John, my youngest, was in school full-time, and then I worked only until he and his sister came home.

Growing up he not only loved movies as much as I did, he wanted to make his own. And I not only encouraged him, I helped him out. I'd brainstorm scenes with him, let him use the house to stage them—even ones that called for gallons of blood made with corn syrup and red food coloring.

Later, when his productions grew more sophisticated, I helped him write scripts, scout locations, make costumes, just about everything necessary to put a production together. Once the shooting began, I would cater the food, run back and forth to Hollywood on various errands, fill in as a grip or even act in a crowd scene if needed. We've done three short films together. The last, *Sentinels of the Twilight*, was twenty-four minutes long, had a theatrical run in Beverly Hills, was a selection of the Canyonland Film Festival, and won an award from the Rochester Film Festival.

I think the most special thing about our relationship is not only that we love each other deeply, we also like each other and enjoy being together as friends. We hike, watch baseball games, dissect books and movies, and talk, talk, talk. When we began thinking about what to write for this collection, we decided to explore a very different kind of mother/son relationship. And we came up with a boy who not only grew up without his mother, but one who believed she had abandoned him.

We plotted the story together, playing off each other's ideas, which is a technique we've developed that works well for us. Once the scenes were sketched in, I wrote a draft, which John went over, making corrections and suggestions. Then I did a final draft and polish.

There are shared experiences woven in, like driving together one night past the lake near where I live, and remarking to John how somebody could go right off the road and into the water and who knows when they'd be found. A photo display we saw last summer in Hilo, Hawaii, about a tsunami that devastated the town suggested the one in our story about the reservoir dam breaking.

In the end, we hope our story reflects the love of a son for his mother, and her love for him. We believe we understand those emotions very well.

Lawrence Block

A Rare and Radiant Mother

Lawrence Block, with an uncharacteristic smile, ca. 1941.

The author's parents, Arthur and Lenore, ca. 1932.

It was in 1959, and it seems to me it would have been in early June, a couple of weeks before my twenty-first birthday. I was back in Buffalo after what would turn out to have been my last year at college, and in a week or two I would go to New York, where I intended to support myself writing fiction until it was time to go back to school.

It was dinnertime, and we were at the table in our house on Starin Avenue. My mother and father and sister and I were joined this evening by my Aunt Mim and Uncle Hi, and my cousins Peter and Jeffrey. I don't remember anything about the dinner, but I'm sure it was a good one, because that was the only kind my mother ever put on the table. And I don't remember anything about the conversation, until at some point Leo Norton came into it.

One of the men, my father or my uncle, mentioned Leo Norton, and the other allowed as to how he believed the man was dead. A reasonably intense discussion ensued, and it became evident that, while there was a certain division of opinion on the subject, no one at the table could say with anything approaching certainty whether Leo Norton was in fact alive or dead.

For my own part, I'd never heard of the man before. I don't know who he was or how his name came up, but I think it's safe to say he didn't play a central role in the life of any of the eight of us, or somebody would have known whether or not the man had a pulse.

The discussion proceeded apace, until my cousin Jeffrey stood up and left the table. He consulted the phone book, picked up the hall phone, and dialed a number. The table went silent as we waited to see what the hell Jeffrey was up to. "Hello," he said. "Is Leo there?" There was a pause, and he beamed. "Just checking," he said, and hung up.

Leo, Jeffrey assured us, was alive and well. We acknowledged Jeffrey for his resourcefulness in solving the puzzle, and we speculated on the reaction the phone call must have produced in the Norton household, and then the conversation turned to another topic, and that was that.

A year and a half later, in December of 1960, my father died suddenly and unexpectedly the day before his fifty-second birthday. An aortic aneurysm ruptured during the night, and an hour or two later he was dead.

I was in New York when this happened. I had indeed moved there shortly after the Leo Norton dinner, and had moved back to Buffalo six weeks later. I wrote paperback novels and pulp short stories, bought a half interest in a downtown jazz club, and began dating a woman. In March of 1960 we got married and moved to New York. I sold my half of the business back to my partner and went on writing fiction, and in the middle of the night the phone rang and Moe Cheplove, doctor and family friend, told me my father was dead.

It was a shocking death. My father was one of the first in his social set to die, and there'd been no warning; he was apparently fine one day and gone the next. My mother was devastated, and so was my sister, and so was I.

I could dredge up memories of the several days in Buffalo following his death, and indeed I've been unable to avoid them, but I'll spare you. There's just the one incident that's relevant here, and it happened at the funeral parlor, as I sat next to my mother while one person after another came over to express regrets. There were a great many people there whom I knew, and many I did not, and I wasn't expecting anything when a man I'd never seen before walked up to my mother.

"Lenore," he said, "I'm very sorry. I'm Leo Norton. . . ."

Well, I lost it.

Perhaps you saw that classic episode of the *Mary Tyler Moore Show*, the one centered on the funeral of Chuckles the Clown. (He was dressed up as a peanut, and an elephant tried to shell him.) Nobody could resist making jokes about his death, and Mary thought they were in very bad taste. Then, at the funeral itself, with everybody appropriately solemn, Mary can't keep from laughing.

Jesus, I know just how she felt. I'd been bawling like a baby for a couple of days, and shell-shocked to numbness the rest of the time, and here was this doofus I'd never seen before, and the only other time I'd heard his goddamn name was when eight of us sat around the dining room table arguing about whether he was alive or dead. "Is Leo there? . . . just checking!"

I could not stop laughing. I knew I shouldn't be laughing—I was at my father's funeral, for God's sake, and you don't laugh at your father's funeral—but there was nothing I could do about it, and the inappropriateness of my laughter just made the whole thing that much funnier.

And here's what my mother did: She put an arm around me, and she *soothed* me! "It's all right, Larry," she said. "Go ahead and cry. It's all right."

She knew I wasn't crying. She knew I was laughing, and she knew *why* I was laughing, but she was the only person in the room who did. Because she played her part so superbly, everybody else believed just what she wanted them to believe—that her son, overcome with grief, was sobbing uncontrollably.

I got it together, as one does, and the day went on. And that night we were talking, and we laughed about our Leo Norton moment. "God, that was funny," she said. "Your father would have loved it." Her face clouded. "And I can never tell him," she said, and we wept.

It must have been fifteen years later when I got an envelope in the mail addressed in my mother's handwriting. I opened it up and took out a newspaper clipping, with a two- or three-paragraph obituary for Leo Norton.

The name didn't register at first, and I turned the piece of paper over to see if there was something relevant on the reverse. There wasn't. Then I read it again and the penny dropped.

I called Buffalo. "I got that clipping," I told her,

"and it took me a minute, but then all I could do was laugh."

"I had the same reaction when I read it in the paper," she said. "It's a fine thing. The poor man drops dead and we laugh."

That story may be familiar. I've told it before, fictionalized, in a short story I called "Leo Youngdahl, R.I.P." I changed Leo's last name, and some other names as well—Jeffrey to Jeremy. I moved the family from Buffalo and changed our background from Jewish to Pennsylvania Dutch. I made the narrator a woman, and had her recount the story to the man she was living with. I chose some of these changes, I suspect, in order to distance myself from the story, to make it less about me, less about us.

Because, you see, it is not my nature to write about my own self, my own life, my own family. All honest fiction, to be sure, is autobiographical, in the sense that every character is a projection of oneself, every incident a projection of one's own experience. In that sense, who I am and what I've done and where I come from informs everything I've written.

But my characters rarely bear much resemblance to me, and the stories I tell hardly ever derive from experience. I almost never base a character on someone I know. There is, I believe, an unconscious process of synthesis that operates, so that characters are comprised of bits and pieces of people I've known or glimpsed or heard about, but that's about as far as I go. I've observed elsewhere that fiction writers fall into two basic categories, those who report what they've seen and those who recount what they've imagined. I'm not a reporter, I'm an imaginer.

I'm thus not terribly eager to sit down and tell you about my mother, and my natural reluctance is greatly augmented by my sense that my mother is probably equally reluctant to be written about. I have reason to believe this. On two occasions, Buffalo expatriates of my generation have written revealingly about their parents, and in both instances my mother found the whole business upsetting. David Milch, the television writer, included in a memoir one chapter about his late father, a prominent and respected heart surgeon. My mother thought it was deplorable that David portrayed his father as a pill-popping compulsive gambler. What David wrote seemed to me to be enormously affectionate and loving, but all my mother could see was that he had told truths about the man that should have been kept private.

Similarly, Elizabeth Swados, the writer and composer, wrote at length about her Buffalo family, about her schizophrenic brother, about her problematic relationship with her father. My mother found the whole business unfortunate and questioned why she'd had to go public with that sort of thing.

I have no family secrets to reveal in these pages. I'm not here to show you my mother's dark side; if she has one, I haven't seen it myself. I have, and have always had, a warm and loving relationship with the woman. I visit her in Buffalo once or twice a year, talk to her on the phone several times a week. And, when I finally sat down to write this piece after months of stalling, I wrote three sentences and had to go lie down.

I'd just as soon go lie down now. But I'll keep at it, and I'll tell you a thing or two about my mother. Some facts, some memories, some impressions. Make of them what you will.

She was born September 21, 1912, in Buffalo, New York, to native-born parents who were themselves the children of immigrants. She grew up in a two-family house on Hertel Avenue. Her father had bought the house, occupying the lower flat with his wife and children, installing his mother and his two unmarried sisters upstairs.

We lived less than a mile from that big white house, and I spent much of my childhood there. My father's parents died young, and what family he had was geographically and emotionally remote, so our extended family was in fact my mother's family. My grandmother was a legendary cook—everybody says this, but for a change it's true—and I think we must have gathered around her dining room table every couple of weeks. I know all holidays and family occasions were celebrated there.

My grandmother was widowed in 1952 and died in 1963. After her death, my great-aunts, Sal and Nettie, moved downstairs and rented out the upper flat. Nettie died in 1983, Sal in 1990. We put the house on the market, and somebody bought it.

My mother's name was Lenore Harriet Nathan. She had two younger brothers, Hi and Jerry. She went to PS 22, just a block from her house, and Bennett High School, just a few blocks away on Main Street. She was salutatorian of her high school class, and should have been valedictorian on the basis of her grade-point average. There was, I gather, some question as to just why she was screwed out of her higher office. One school of thought held that it was because she was Jewish, the other that it was because she was female. (A little of both would be my guess, but who cares?)

On a recent promotional tour to Florida, I met a woman who told me she'd known my mother as a girl. She and her older sister would come over to my mother's house, and the three of them would cut through the backyard as a shortcut to PS 22. "Your mother was always so nice to me," the woman remembered. "She was my sister's age, and I was eight years younger, but she didn't treat me like a baby."

"I remember her," my mother said. "She was a pest."

My mother won a scholarship and went to Cornell University. In due course, both of her brothers followed her to Cornell. I suspect they were there on scholarships as well. The Nathans were a bright family.

These were competitive scholarships, awarded through examination and sponsored by Cornell University and the New York State Board of Regents. I don't know if she would have qualified for a scholarship based on need. My grandfather, who dropped out of high school to support his widowed mother, had a company called Buffalo Batt & Felt, with a factory in Depew, New York. I don't know what they did there, but gather it had something to do with by-products of the cotton industry. (One summer my grandfather delivered a load of cottonseed waste to our house, where my mother spread it on the gardens for fertilizer. It lay there stinking for months.)

In high school, my mother had shown more than a little talent at the piano and as a visual artist. Her piano teacher encouraged her to think about a concert career, while her art instructor hoped she would draw and paint professionally.

Did she ever seriously entertain such hopes? I don't know, but my sense is that she did not. She was, I gather, vastly popular at Cornell. Family lore has it that she once had three dates on a Saturday night, and somehow contrived to keep them all. (If I wrote sitcoms, I probably would have found a use for that one.) She was nearsighted, and evidently vain enough to go without her glasses on all social occasions; while she attended all Cornell's home games, she never actually saw a football game until, married, she put her glasses on. According to my father, who exaggerated wildly for the sake of a story, she was surprised to discover that there were men down there on the field.

She was an English major. I don't know how seriously she approached her studies, but her grades were always good. She signed up for second-year Spanish because it fit her schedule, without having taken first-year Spanish. She got a B. The rest of her grades were generally A's, and she made Phi Beta Kappa.

In 1974 I fell in with a small crowd of people who went to jazz clubs six nights a week. (They stayed home on Saturdays; Saturdays were for amateurs.) They were older than I, and one had been at Cornell at the same time as my mother. When I told him her maiden name, his eyes widened. He knew right away what sorority she was in (Sigma Delta Tau) and had the wistful look in his eyes of someone who'd gone to school with Grace Kelly. "Please remember me to your mother," he said later that evening.

When I did, she allowed that his name was familiar, but she didn't remember who he was.

Arthur Jerome Block, a New Yorker, won the same scholarship and attended the same college. He was four years older than my mother, and got to Cornell a couple of years earlier than she did. After three years as an undergraduate in the arts college, he transferred to the law school.

His mother had died while he was an infant, and he'd been raised by his father and by a couple of aunts. His father was a plumber who made some money in real estate, and my father was forever moving and changing schools. During his first year in law school, his father, forty-two, died suddenly of pneumonia.

I think being abruptly orphaned must have predisposed my father to early marriage. He felt entirely alone, and he wanted a wife and a family. And he met my mother and they fell in love, and they did something that was both dramatic and unusual.

They ran off and got married in secret.

This was in 1932, when college students did not get married. Indeed, most colleges had a rule against it. If two students did get married, it was generally for an obvious reason. She was pregnant, and he was Doing the Right Thing.

That wasn't the case with my parents. Their plan,

you must understand, was to keep the marriage a secret from virtually everyone. (My father's roommate,
Jimmy Gitlitz, was in on it, and served as best man. I
suppose my mother must have had an attendant as
well.) They went off to Cortland and got married by a
Baptist minister. (Their first choice, a justice of the
peace in Trumansburg, turned them down.) Then they
drove to Albany for a weekend honeymoon, intend-
ing to return to Ithaca, where my mother would continue to live in the dormitory. They'd be married, but
nobody would know.

Why, for God's sake? Not to thwart parental oppo-
sition; my father had met my mother's parents, and
they liked him, even as he was drawn to the warmth
and solidity of their family circle. Not to legitimize an
impending birth; she wasn't pregnant, and wouldn't
become pregnant for four more years. (She had a miscarriage two years or so before I was born in 1938.)
Did they marry so they could sleep together lawfully?
Or was it simply that my father wanted to be married,
wanted the security of it?

I know it was his idea, and he must have been per-
suasive. His was not the first marriage proposal my
mother received. There were, I gather, several young
men who wanted to marry her. She found it easy to
turn them down, so you'd think she wouldn't have
found it difficult to put my father off for a couple of
years.

I guess they were crazy in love. I think that must
have been it.

Anyway, the plan went kerblooey. Student marriage was a genuinely rare occurrence at the time, and
the local paper in Cortland ran an item about two

Cornell students having gotten married there. Jimmy Gitlitz drove all over Ithaca in his Model T Ford, heroically buying up all the copies of the Cortland paper before anyone could read it. But the item was somehow deemed newsworthy beyond Trumansburg, and another paper—Albany? maybe—picked up the story, and that was more papers than Jimmy could buy.

Word got out. The bridal couple went directly from Albany to Buffalo and had a religious ceremony with the bride's family present. "And you'll celebrate this as your wedding anniversary," my grandmother said.

No, said my father. They'd celebrate the first date, February 26. "Would you want your daughter to have lived in sin for four whole days?" he demanded. "And believe me, did she sin!"

They lived briefly in New York, where my mother spent a semester at Barnard. My father had finished law school and was admitted to the bar, and had a promising future in New York, through a connection with the successful law firm that had represented his late father. But they wound up in Buffalo instead. I think my mother missed her family, and I think my *father* missed her family. He had a stepmother whom he detested, and . . . well, this is her story, not his, but I think he may have been more eager than she to relocate to Buffalo.

So they found an apartment in Buffalo, and he found a job, and she spent the next twenty-eight years as a wife and mother.

It was a very different world. There were, to be sure, women who entered the professions, women who made careers for themselves in the arts. But I don't think my mother even saw this as an option. It was not what women in her circle did, and she was very much a member of her own social circle.

Nowadays, as my wife would say, the worm is on the other foot. Nowadays a woman who does not work, who allows her husband to support her while she devotes her time to *küche und kinder,* feels guilty about it, or thinks she ought to feel guilty about it. She's presumably wasting her talents, her education, her whole life.

It was different then. When the wife of a man of the business or professional classes took employment, she was not only reflecting unfavorably upon her husband's ability to provide for her. In addition, she was depriving her children of a full-time mother while taking a job away from a woman who genuinely needed one.

My father always supported us, and we never missed any meals, but we were a far cry from well-off and could certainly have used a second household income. It was never a consideration. Did any of my friends' mothers work? I can't think of a single one that did.

This is not to say that my mother's life was one of idleness. She did have some household help while my sister and I were growing up, but she kept an immaculate, well-ordered home and prepared an excellent dinner every night. She did volunteer work and belonged to high-minded organizations, frequently serving as secretary. ("Sometimes," she told me, "I'd like to write the minutes the way they ought to be written. 'Mrs. Fingerhut suggested that the window be closed. Mrs. Wisbaum responded that it was warm in the room, and that if Mrs. Fingerhut didn't dress like a tramp she wouldn't feel the draft.'")

She played cards regularly—bridge in the evening with my father and other couples, bridge and canasta and mah jongg on regularly scheduled afternoons with her friends. Often enough there would be a game at our house, and I'd be playing on the floor in the next room while a table of nicely dressed ladies moved cards or tiles around and dished their absent friends. Looking back, I'm struck by what an opportunity it provided for a future writer, and how I let its knock go unanswered. They prattled on, destroying reputations on a regular basis, and I never paid any attention.

And she played the piano. There was a Gulbrandsen upright in our front room for years, and I took lessons and practiced on it, to no purpose and with no discernible effect. Sometimes she played, by herself and for herself. Chopin, more often than not, but sometimes Czerny, and sometimes show tunes. She could play anything by ear, and could transpose from one key to another with relative ease.

When I was in high school, she took up painting again. There was a class given once a week at the Jewish Center, and once a week she attended it, and while she was there she painted. Her work was representational at first, and became increasingly abstract; for several years, until she gave it up a decade or so ago, she painted hard-edge acrylics reminiscent of the work of Al Held.

Once, when I was eighteen or so and home from college for a few days, my parents and sister and I

were going out for dinner. Betsy was in the car, and
my folks thought that I was there as well, and that
they were alone in the house. But I'd forgotten something, and had come back to get it from my room.

Betsy had a parakeet at the time, and you were supposed to cover its cage when you left, and I overheard
the following conversation between my parents:

My Mother: Are you ready? We're running late.

My Father: Okay, let's go. Oh, wait a minute. We
have to cover the parakeet's cage.

My Mother: Oh, the hell with the little bastard.

I couldn't believe it. While I wouldn't have phrased
it so inelegantly, I had until that moment regarded my
mother as a woman who wouldn't have said shit if
she had a mouthful. And here she was, talking like
you or me.

"Oh, the hell with the little bastard." With those as-
tonishing and unforgettable words, my mother unwit-
tingly allowed me to realize that she was a real
person.

I think their marriage was a good one. If they
fought or argued, I never knew it. It seemed to me
that their interests diverged over the years, but not in
such a way as to imperil the marital bond. I've no idea
if either or both of them sought fulfillment elsewhere,
and I have to say I'm perfectly content not knowing.
It is manifestly none of my business . . . and, if I did
know, it would be none of yours.

My father was an unhappy man. I suspect today
he'd be diagnosed as having a bi-polar personality.
He was certainly a depressive, with occasional peri-

ods of elation. His moods were never uncontrolled, never required hospitalization, never led him to seek treatment.

In the last half-dozen years of his life he would wake up very early—four or five in the morning—and would get up and have breakfast and start the day. After dinner he would get in bed with the television set on and be unable to stay awake past eight or nine o'clock. On the weekends, when he and my mother had a social engagement, I think he stayed awake without difficulty, but during the week he drifted into this pattern of early to bed, early to rise.

She would be up until midnight or one in the morning. I lived at home from August of 1959 until I got married the following March. I was writing paperback novels at this point, and worked out a curious schedule; I would have a cup of coffee with my mother around midnight. She would go to bed, and I'd go to my room and work all night, finishing in time to have another cup of coffee with my father around five or six. Then I'd go to bed.

I think my father probably regarded himself as a failure. He wanted to be rich, and became impatient with work that didn't reward him quickly enough. Consequently he changed careers prematurely. If he'd stayed with any of several things he tried, he probably would have been rewarded in the long run. But it was not in his nature.

On the way to the hospital, he said this to my mother: "I hope you get a better guy next time." Then he was admitted, and joked with his nurses. And died.

*   *   *

I was a good student, and, while I was never a candidate for valedictorian, I was always on the honor roll. The only academic difficulty I got into was in the first semester of my third year in high school. I was taking intermediate algebra, and during the first two of three marking periods, I did the homework and took the tests and got grades in the 90's.

Then, abruptly and for no particular reason, I stopped doing the daily homework assignments. Don't ask me why. I guess they struck me as boring and stupid. I stopped doing them, and nobody said anything, and life went on.

At the end of the semester, we all took the regents exam. The following week, Miss Kelly announced that only one person in the class had earned a perfect score on the final. "And that same person didn't hand in any of his homework assignments during the past six weeks," she said. "So on his report card I've given him 100 for the final examination, and 65 for the last marking period."

Everybody thought it was pretty funny. Then I went home, and my mother asked me what grades I'd received.

"Well," I said, "I got the seven in English."

"The seven? What does that mean?"

"Ninety-seven," I said. "And, let's see, I got the two in Spanish."

"The two?"

"Ninety-two. And I got the five in algebra."

"What does that mean, ninety-five?"

"No, sixty-five," I said, sarcasm dropping like acid.

"And how about Latin? What did you get in Latin?"

It was a good stratagem, but only for a day or so, until I brought the card home and showed it to her. Her sense of irony and poetic justice was at least as good as Miss Kelly's. I got the dollar for acing the final, and grounded for a month for the 65.

It was in my junior year at high school that I decided to become a writer. In English class, I wrote a composition on career plans, discussing the various career choices I'd entertained since early childhood. (At four I'd announced that I wanted to be a garbageman, abandoning that dream when my mother told me they all got chapped hands.) I concluded with the observation that, uncertain as my future was, one thing was clear: I could never be a writer.

My teacher, Miss Jepson, wrote in the margin: "I'm not so sure about that!" And I decided on the spot that I would be a writer, and never had a moment of second thoughts on the subject. I'd never previously considered being a writer, and from that day on I never considered anything else.

I'd already had some success. In eighth grade, I had to write an essay on the subject of Americanism, for a contest jointly sponsored by the American Legion and the *Buffalo Evening News*. A year before then we had to write essays on the plight of the Buffalo waterfront, and for some reason I couldn't understand what the hell the teacher was getting at, and never turned in the assignment. I suppose my mother wanted to make sure this didn't happen again, and this time around she gave me a little coaching. I wrote the essay, but in retrospect I can see that she put ideas and phrases in my path.

Well, I won a trip to Washington. Not a bad payoff for 250 words.

When I announced that I wanted to be a writer, I got nothing but encouragement from both my parents. They read the poems and sketches I turned out and found something to praise in them. In my senior year I applied to two colleges—to Cornell, of course, which was essentially the family school, and to Antioch, which my parents suggested. They'd heard about it through a friend, and thought it might be a nurturing environment for me.

Both colleges expressed a willingness to admit me. I took the same exam my parents had taken years earlier, and won the same scholarship. It would have substantially reduced the cost of sending me to Cornell, and was of no use at an out-of-state school.

We were not in great shape financially—I'm sure I would have been eligible for financial aid at Antioch, had my father not been unwilling to fill out the requisite forms. As it was, I could have saved a good deal of money by going to Cornell, and I'd have received in Ithaca an education every bit as good and rather more prestigious than what was on offer in Yellow Springs, Ohio. I wanted to go to Antioch, but I can't say I had my heart set on it, and at any rate I wouldn't have dreamed of making a fuss. But there was never a suggestion that I take the money and go to Cornell. They completely supported my going to Antioch.

They were just as supportive when I dropped out two years later. I had sold a story and found a summer job at a literary agency, and I decided the job was too good to give up to return to school.

*   *   *

In February of 1958, I had my first story published. It was called "You Can't Lose" and it appeared in *Manhunt*, a crime fiction magazine. I'd written it in 1956, in the fall, and had sold it the following summer. By the time it appeared in print, I had dropped out of college and was living in New York, working for a literary agent. I was nineteen years old, and thought of myself as mature beyond my years. I was misinformed.

My parents in Buffalo had been awaiting the story's appearance in print, and were quick to buy copies and tell their friends, some of whom dutifully bought copies of their own. (It may have been *Manhunt*'s peak month in western New York.) The story, such as it was (and it wasn't much), is narrated by a thoroughly unscrupulous young man, living by his wits, and getting started in a life of crime. For at least one of my mother's friends, it embodied nothing so much as a loss of innocence—specifically, that of the young fellow who'd written it.

"Oh, Lenore," she said with a sigh. "How do they grow up so quickly? Where do they learn it all? You tell them to dress warm, you hope they'll wear their rubbers . . ."

"Now more than ever," my mother said.

My sister, Betsy, was five years younger than I. Just as I took after my mother's side of the family, so did she take after our father's. "She has my features," he said, "but on her they look good." (He was being unnecessarily modest, and was in fact a handsome man.)

As a child I could never detect this sort of resemblance, and now I wonder how I could have missed it.

Betsy definitely looked like my dad, and there is a picture of his mother that could be a picture of Betsy in a period costume. The resemblance is uncanny.

She also inherited his emotional makeup, and on her it didn't look good at all.

What amounted to moodiness in my father manifested far more severely in his daughter. She began acting out around the onset of puberty, and was hospitalized after a psychotic break a couple of years later. The eventual diagnosis was manic-depressive psychosis, and it had her in and out of state mental hospitals for the rest of her life.

She was tall and beautiful, bright and funny, and she had a terrible life. She was married twice, had a child with each husband, and wound up in Roswell, New Mexico, where lithium finally seemed to be keeping her emotionally stable. She died there in 1978, a few months after her thirty-fifth birthday, a few days after my fortieth. Her lithium levels created problems, and a doctor prescribed something to help, and instead it killed her.

My mother never knew what the hell to do about Betsy. There are, I am sure, worse things than being the parent of a mentally ill child, but I'd be hard put to tell you what they are. Nowadays I suppose there are support groups for this, as there are for everything, and I suspect they help. God knows my folks could have used one.

Instead, they blamed themselves. Forty years ago, few people were apt to suggest that madness might be cellular or biochemical in origin. If a kid didn't turn out right, the logical assumption seemed to be that it was the parents' fault. For years my mother was haunted by the thought that there was something she might have done wrong, or something she might have failed to do, that had led to Betsy's difficulties.

I think she got over this. What lasted longer, I suspect, was the nagging sense that there ought to be something she could do to help.

What she didn't like to do was talk about it. She talked with my father, and later with her second husband, and she talked a great deal with me, but she avoided discussing the subject with her friends. Part of this stemmed from a natural inclination to keep family matters private. She was concerned, too, at least early on, that Betsy might recover and resume her rightful place in society, only to be handicapped by widespread knowledge of her past.

There was something else, though, and it took me a while to understand it. What she wanted to avoid was having the same futile and tedious conversation over and over with well-meaning friends. I'm sure they thought she was avoiding the subject, and consequently politeness and consideration led them to avoid bringing it up. And that was fine with her.

I used to think she was being hypocritical, or playing ostrich with her head in the sand. I've long since ceased to see it that way, perhaps because I've found out how annoying it is to wind up having the same conversation over and over, even on a subject that is not painful but merely tedious.

Well, I take after her. But on her it looks good.

My sister's first marriage ended abruptly. Her husband was a Hawaiian, a lifer in the Marine Corps. He was also an alcoholic, and she told me he abused her physically, but I never knew whether to believe her. When Betsy reported something, you couldn't be sure if it was true. She never lied, but she sometimes remembered things that hadn't happened.

His name was Everett Collins Poohina, and he was called Po. At the end he was based at Camp Pendleton, in southern California. My sister bore his son, David, and was hospitalized again at Patten State, near San Bernardino. While she was there, Po went AWOL, wandered around drinking for a couple of days, then picked up a hand grenade and took it out onto the range. He pulled the pin and didn't stop counting at ten.

My mother and I flew out there and saw the baby, who was being cared for by friends of Betsy and Po. Po's father was planning to come over from Hawaii, and had expressed the intention of taking his grandson back to the islands with him.

After we left the couple's house in Oceanside, my mother kept stressing the baby's physical appearance. He looked Hawaiian, she said. He looked like his father. He didn't look like us at all.

I was confused. That sort of racial observation was uncharacteristic of her. But then I realized what she was doing. She knew that the baby was going to wind up in Hawaii, that he would be separated from his mother and indeed from all of us, and that it was probably better for him that way. And so she was preparing herself for lifelong separation from her grandson by stressing his otherness as a way of distancing herself from him. He was one of them, not one of us.

*   *   *

My mother was forty-eight when she was widowed, and left with nothing aside from the cash on
hand, the house on Starin Avenue, and the proceeds
of a small insurance policy. My father had bought the
house in 1943 for $8500, and she sold it in 1961 for just
about twice that. (I suppose it would bring $200,000
now, something like that.)

She moved to an apartment a few blocks away and
got a job at a library, where she quickly made herself
indispensable, taking evening courses in library science toward a masters or some sort of certification.
After an appropriate interval she began accepting
dates, and began keeping company with a man
named Bill Bregger. They dated for a year or two, and
had come to an understanding. Then he went into the
hospital for a routine prostate operation. A successful
pharmacist, he knew all the doctors and hospital per-
sonnel, and was assured of the best care.

And one thing after another went wrong post-op,
and he stayed in the hospital for weeks until finally
his kidneys failed and he died.

She was in a curious position, a sort of unofficial
widow. His daughters knew and liked her—she's still
close to them—and she was in some respects the chief
mourner.

I was living in Buffalo at the time. My wife and
daughter and I had moved back from New York several months after my father's death, probably out of
guilt from not having been there at the time. We were
there for two years, and then I accepted a job editing a
numismatic magazine in Racine, Wisconsin. I took it,
it seems to me, as a graceful way of getting out of Buffalo.

Shortly after we settled in Racine, my mother mentioned that Frankie Rosenberg, who'd been in poor health for some time, had died. The Rosenbergs lived directly across the street from us, and Joe and Frankie had painted in the same weekly class as my mother. He was an otorhinolaryngologist, and had taken out my tonsils when I was five years old.

I never held it against him. And, when I got off the phone with my mother, a curious thought flashed through my mind. Now she and Joe can get married, I thought. It was, really, a ridiculous thought, and I let it go and forgot about it.

And, a year or so later, they did.

Her second marriage was just about perfect. With Joe she found a true companion, and the delight they took in each other's company was remarkable to see. They traveled widely, collected art together, painted together, and obsessed together over the decor of their home. (She was back on Starin again, directly across the street from the house I grew up in.)

Joe had lost a kidney early on to diphtheria, and had survived bladder cancer, but he was the furthest thing from an invalid. He was wonderfully energetic and enthusiastic. They had eleven great years together, and then, driving to work one morning, he had a heart attack and died.

She sold the house, bought a condo in a good building downtown. She had quit work at the library to marry Joe, and wished in hindsight that she'd stayed on another six months to qualify for Social Security. She didn't go back to the library, or look for anything elsewhere. She was sixty-four, and young for her age, but I was not surprised when the years passed without any more men coming into her life. That chapter had ended on a high note, but it had ended.

Some months after Joe's death, before she sold the house, I came to visit for a few days. I overheard her talking to a friend on the phone, and she was saying that it was good to have a man in the house. "I'll tell you," I heard her say, "it's a pleasure to find the toilet seat up!"

Nice line, but here's what I really like about it: Years before their marriage, Joe had had a bladderectomy. He wore a prosthesis, a bag that he emptied at appropriate intervals, and he didn't have to raise the toilet seat to do it. So he never left the seat up.

She'd been widowed about a year and a half when Betsy died. Coincidentally, she was visiting New York when the call came, so we were able to fly out to New Mexico together for the funeral. Betsy, who'd had a Reformed Jewish upbringing, had become Christian somewhere along the way—attending her total-immersion baptism into one denomination or other had been a peak experience for Joe and Lenore—and belonged to the Salvation Army toward the end. I wondered how my mother would handle the service, with the hymns and the eulogy, but she was fine with it.

Afterward, back at our motel, she said, "Well, now at least I don't have to worry about where she is and what she's doing."

Huh? Where she was was in the ground, and what she was doing was lying there. We no longer had to worry that something bad might happen, because the worst possible thing *had* happened. Where was the relief in that?

I didn't get it. Now, just over twenty years later, I'm beginning to. It's easier to endure the worst, I guess, than to sit around waiting for it.

After the funeral, she had a drink. I kept her company, but I didn't have one with her. I'd stopped doing that about fifteen months earlier.

When I was three or four months sober, I'd flown to Buffalo for the weekend. I'd decided to tell my mother that I'd stopped drinking, and I knew what her response would be. "Don't you think you're overreacting?" she would say. "Why do you have to take everything to extremes? Why can't you just drink sensibly?"

It was not a conversation I was eager to have. But I blurted it out, told her I'd realized I had a drinking problem and that, a day at a time, I was staying away from the stuff.

"I think that's wonderful," she said. "I think you've made a very wise decision, and I'm happy for you."

Go know.

In July, 1988, my wife Lynne and I attended an international conference of crime writers in Gijón, an industrial port in northern Spain. I got a phone call from my cousin David, who had tracked me down, God knows how. My mother had been in an auto accident. She was in critical condition, and it was impossible to say whether she would survive.

Early the following morning we flew to Madrid

and continued on to New York and Buffalo, not knowing whether we were rushing to a bedside or a funeral. When we arrived she was alive but her outlook was uncertain, and it stayed that way for a long time. She was in intensive care for a full month, and comatose throughout. She had sustained broken ankles and a cracked pelvis and had gone into respiratory failure.

When she finally recovered consciousness and got out of the ICU, there was a period of a couple of weeks during which she was not herself. That's an overused expression, but in this instance it was literally true. The personality inhabiting her was not her own. She was nasty to her nurses, mean-spirited, and, well, not herself. Lynne and I were put in mind of Stephen King's *Pet Sematary*, in which the dead return to life, but incompletely, their souls misshapen, their psyches with pieces missing. She was alive, but who the hell *was* she?

Maybe this sort of thing happens frequently after such massive insults to the body and soul. I wouldn't know. It was clear, though, that the internal decision she had made to return to life was not one she endorsed wholeheartedly. She was back, but she wasn't entirely sure it was where she wanted to be.

I remember that I brought her a book of Gary Larson's *Far Side* cartoons while she was in the hospital, and it turned out to be an unfortunate choice. She kept finding cartoons she didn't get, and it bothered her profoundly that their humor eluded her. "Why is this funny?" she kept demanding. "What's funny about it?"

I knew what was bothering her. She was afraid that

some mental impairment might have resulted from the accident, and that was something she had always dreaded far more than death. "If I ever get like that," she'd said, of someone suffering from Alzheimer's, "I hope I can count on you to kill me."

I don't think she really relaxed until I brought her a book of Double-Crostics, and she knocked one off in half an hour. If she could still do that, the brain damage couldn't be too severe.

Lynne and I stayed in her apartment while she was in the ICU, and for the first few weeks after she came to. Then we went on with our lives, and, a few weeks later, she was discharged from the hospital and went on with her own.

I made one executive decision before we left. I found the packs of cigarettes she had on hand and tossed them.

She'd been a heavy smoker ever since college, and had never attempted to quit, or even considered it. Smoking may have been a contributing factor to her post-traumatic respiratory failure; it certainly slowed her recovery.

I figured she would probably start smoking again after she got out of the hospital, and I felt she had the right, but I also figured if it meant that much to her, she could damn well go out and buy a pack. So I rounded up the cigarettes and got rid of them.

She never did resume smoking. I eventually mentioned what I'd done, and she said she'd almost certainly have started again if there had been cigarettes around the house. But there weren't, so she didn't.

*   *   *

The September before her accident, she'd thrown herself a seventy-fifth birthday party at the country club. Dozens of her friends attended, and all the family. She was the belle of the ball, young for her years, and very much on top of her game.

The auto accident constituted an abrupt transition from middle to old age. She'd become a traveler after my father's death, traveled extensively with her second husband, traveled again in her second widowhood. She went to India, to China. When my daughters Amy and Jill each graduated from college, she took them in turn to Europe.

She'd have taken my youngest daughter, Alison, too, but the accident intervened. There have been no more trips to Europe, or even to New York. But she has remained very active, going to plays and concerts, playing cards with her friends, dining out at restaurants several nights a week. She watches a good deal of television, and is especially fond of *East Enders*, the British soap, and HBO's *Oz* and *The Sopranos*. ("I was watching *Oz* the other night," my daughter Jill told me, "and trying to come to terms with the fact that Nana never misses an episode. I mean, is that a show for your grandmother to watch?")

Three years ago I bought her a computer for Christmas. Arthritic fingers don't exactly dance on a keyboard, and the requisite memorization is easier for the young than the old, but she got the hang of it and surfed the Net like a kid.

She still reads, though less than she used to. I send her my books in manuscript now, so she won't have to wait for the printed book, and because the typeface is larger and easier to cope with. She still knocks off Thomas Middleton's Double-Crostics in twenty minutes. Mentally, she really hasn't lost a step.

But her feet never entirely recovered from the accident, and arthritis complicated by late-onset diabetes has her in pain pretty much all the time.

Well, she's eighty-six years old.

I had this piece mostly written when Lynne and I flew up to Buffalo to spend Passover with her. Our visits, once or twice a year, are like time-lapse photography. Every time we see her it's a little harder for her to get around, and she has more hours where the pain and discomfort immobilizes her. It's always a joy to see her, and I always come home deeply saddened.

We ate in several different restaurants, and each time she brought half her entrée home in a doggie bag. Her sense of smell had faded in recent months, she told me, and perhaps as a consequence her appetite was considerably diminished. She still enjoyed her food, but she didn't eat as much of it.

In our family, that's not a good sign. Hearty appetites are a birthright, and emotional blows don't interfere. My mother certainly endured some crippling losses in the course of her life, but nothing ever stopped her from eating a good dinner.

In Gijón, after I'd made arrangements for our flight the following morning, Lynne and I went out with another couple as planned, and fell to like loggers. My mother, I assured Lynne, would understand.

I don't know what it means, this ebbing of the appetite.

One afternoon I had her windshield wipers replaced. The car's the one she bought to replace the one in which she had the accident, and it must be ten years old by now. The mileage is low, though, and the car seems to be in good shape.

"This will be my last car," she said. "It'll outlast me."

I had printed out what I'd thus far written, and brought it along, thinking I might let her have a look at it. Once, when she asked what I was working on, I was on the verge of telling her about this piece. But I didn't.

Maybe, now that it's done, I'll print out a copy for her. Maybe I'll wait until the book comes out.

We'll see.

I spent weeks trying to figure out how to approach this essay, or article, or whatever the hell it is. I'm by no means thrilled with the result. What does it say, really, about her, or about me, or about anything?

What do I know about writing this sort of thing?

She is, to my mind, a remarkable woman, but I don't know that you could prove it from what I've written. She's hidden somewhere under all these damned words, but where?

I haven't even known what to call her. "My mother." "She."

When I talk about her—to Lynne, to my daughters, to anyone who knows her—I call her Lenore. (My father used to quote Poe: "A rare and radiant maiden whom the angels call Lenore.") When she's in the room, I call her Mom.

There is a metaphysical school of thought that holds that you choose your own parents. The soul, buzzing around in hyperspace, picks out the vessel in which to be reincarnated.

I'd say I chose well.

Eileen Dreyer

Variations on a Theme

FREDRICK B. DREYER

*Kevin and Eileen Dreyer at a family function
(he's the cute one with the beard).*

"I love you, Mom."

There she stood in her best new dress, a rose corsage tickling her neck and tears tickling her eyes, as she stared up at the six-foot-tall young man she'd known all his life. She heard him say it, saw his smile, and knew that what he was saying wasn't really *I love you*. She'd learned that lesson so young. She couldn't have been more than twenty-five. Years ago now. He'd been the one to teach her, this handsome young man. He'd taught her the magic fact that children communicated in a language of their own, and boys in a language that was even more arcane.

She'd thought she was a pretty well-educated woman when she'd had this son of hers. She had a bachelor's degree in science, held a challenging job, knew witty and erudite people who looked to her for conversation and advice. She'd already voted in two presidential elections, managed her own retirement account, and spoke four languages.

Unfortunately, the only language she didn't speak was the one she suddenly needed the most.

Child.

She'd first realized this oversight when her son

began to babble. Face screwed up in concentration, hands waving in the air, eyes bright and delighted, he talked to her for hours. No, he waited just for her before he began his dissertations. Insistent, impatient, as rapid-fire as a college professor trying to impart age-old wisdom to the stupid undergraduate. She'd talked back to him with her own nonsense as if the two of them bandied conversation at a cocktail party.

"Gna, gna, da da spppph da da gna gna."

"You're right. I didn't like the color either, but Rauol is supposed to be the best hairdresser in seven states. What do I know?"

"Gna gna DA DA DA!"

"That bad, huh?"

She'd laughed, and he'd laughed as if he'd saved it all up for her, the sound as enchanting as fairy bells in a summer wood. It was the first time she heard *I love you* from her son.

She didn't realize it, of course. Not until the day she walked down to find him trying to hold just such a conversation with her neighbor Marge. Same insistent tone, same imperious waving of his arms to give greater emphasis to his very important baby thoughts. Same creased, furrowed forehead, as if the universal translator had just broken down.

And then, just when it looked as if he would curse in frustration, he caught sight of her. And he laughed. Out loud. Delighted, relieved, certain, his entire body participating.

And she heard it, there in her head, instead of all the diphthongs he'd delighted in practicing the last few days. *I love you. I've been waiting for you. I don't find anyone else as interesting or pretty or wonderful.*

Okay, he was probably also thinking that she was the one who always provided lunch, but nothing said loving like something in the stomach.

He had been three when she'd learned the next important lesson, that the words *I love you* didn't necessarily translate the way she imagined. It was summer, she was in the home office she'd set up so she didn't miss a day of his high impact childhood, and he'd been out in the backyard allegedly playing with the dog.

She could see him out the window. She could hear his high-pitched giggles and the brisk orders he dictated to the confused golden retriever who seemed to be acting as his one-dog army. Chasing around the yard in smaller and smaller circles until the two of them fell in a big tangle of arms, legs, laughter, and barking. Even with her attention on the client she was trying to haggle prices with, she smiled. Where the heck did the kid get his energy?

She only took her eyes off of him for a minute. She was trying to make a very important point with the client, and her attention was on her computer screen and the voice over her earphones. She didn't notice quickly enough how quiet the backyard had gotten. She did notice, however, when she got off the phone just in time to feel sturdy little arms wrap around her legs as she stood at her desk.

"I *love* you, Mom."

Smiling like a game-show contestant, his hair moussed with sweat, his jean shorts and Sesame Street T-shirt looking as if they'd just been scooped out of the dustbin. Scraped and bruised from headlong flight, and redolent with a suspiciously familiar smell that wafted too intensely from his hot little body.

"What did you do?"

His smile grew, and she knew that this *I love you* was a preemptive strike. He'd done something that was going to really tick her off, and he was already hedging his bets. A real pro, this kid. After all, who could resist such an impish smile and those magic four words?

I love you, Mom.

It was the day she learned to laugh off whatever he brought her with that particular recitation of the magic words. The day she spent cleaning all that dog pooh off her good carpets after her son had finished his spurt of decorating.

The Picasso of Poop, her husband called him. Houdini, she said instead. After all, he'd made her fury disappear in a puff of smoke and replaced it with grudging respect.

Not that he escaped being punished, of course. Not then, and not any of the other times he tried that trick.

But the trick still worked.

Every time.

At six years he had gifted her with a particularly boy version of *I love you.* She'd had such a bad day. Her mother was sick, and she'd spent the day in the hospital with her. And she so hated hospitals. There was something about that smell, that purposeful hush that bespoke death and decay. The hidden term limit in the heart of every human. In hospitals a person dealt not simply with the fragility of the life she visited, but the fragility of the life that did the visiting.

All of existence seemed so transient as she drove home from that place, wanting nothing more than a shower. Than the reassuring bulk of her son's growing body in her arms.

If she could hold him still long enough.

Six meant sports teams and war games and the invasion of girls into his securely male little life. Moms didn't count of course, because moms were so very asexual to a six-year-old boy. But girls were yuckie.

Just that was enough to make her smile, knowing that when she got home from that place of death she could resurrect her good spirits on the promised whimsy of her son.

And then he met her at the front door. Nervous, balanced on one foot at a time, hands behind his back, forehead again furrowed. He knew Nana was in the hospital. He'd visited her the other night, snagged briefly in her paper-thin arms like a comet catching the edge of a planet's gravity. Too impatient for that place of endings, this child of discovery.

He'd asked her a few times about his nana, and he'd hugged her once, patting her back just as she did his when he hurt his knees. Today, though, he waited in terrible uncertainty, his eyes down, his face pursed.

"Hey, handsome, what do you have for me?" she asked, crouching down to his level. Desperate for a hug. For the bolstering of his life against hers.

But he didn't give her a hug. He darted toward her, a hummingbird skimming the edge of a flower, and dropped something in her hands.

"For you," he said, and ran.

She looked down at what he'd given her, and knew she'd smile later. Now she felt tears.

He'd made her a gift.

He'd taken his three favorite Hot Wheels, an ambulance, a blue Mustang, and a yellow convertible of some kind, and he'd smashed them to a pulp. Not only that, he'd nailed them to a hunk of old cedar her husband had left lying around in the garage after a shelf-building binge a few years ago.

He'd given her the most precious things he had to make her feel better. And after living with a mother who loved pretty things, he'd arranged them into what, for a boy, was a pretty thing.

An easy jump from there to *I love you*. One of her most precious. One she could sit on her desk and reach out to touch for reassurance like her own mezuzah, even when he wasn't there. Even years later, when he'd given her much more beautiful gifts, more eloquent statements. His little Hot Wheels sculpture still drew her eye the most, because he'd still been young enough to be mortally embarrassed when she'd chased him down in his room to wrap him in the biggest hug of his life.

The next lesson she called the FAO Schwarz variation. A simple adaptation, a universal scene any mother with a credit card and working knowledge of a toy store would be familiar with. The most memorable was the year he was eight and Christmas was coming. A dangerous time of year to venture near toy stores, but he was invited to a birthday party, and they needed a present quick. The problem was, of course, the toy store, a terrible temptation at any time, was now a veritable cornucopia of excess, games and dolls and balls and bikes stacked to the ceiling, disembodied voices urging parents toward recklessness over the loudspeaker, squeaking, tumbling toys placed with near-demonic precision to waylay even the most stalwart of children.

And her son was no more immune than any other red-blooded child on the planet.

What was worse, the toy of the year was a soldier action figure. Bets were already being taken that it would rival the talking furball that had decimated parental pocketbooks the year before. Not only were betting people laying odds that the toy would be gone from the toy-store universe within a fortnight, but the store had just gotten in a rare stock.

She didn't buy her son frivolous toys. She didn't bribe him with water pistols or McDonald's. Well, not often. She should have been able to withstand the pleading, puppy-dog eyes, the near-window-shattering pitch of his whine. She should have gotten out of that store with the one single, damn whiffle ball set she was planning on getting the birthday boy.

And then her son had gone and done it.

"I love you, Mom."

Not *I love you*, mind. *Ple-e-e-e-e-a-s-e. I'm so cute you can't say no. I'm your only son. You love me too much to deny me.*

Tears in his big green eyes and a tremble in the lower lip, his melodramatic sighs more dead-on than Demi Moore in *Ghost*. He was telling her that his heart was breaking, but that was okay. He still loved her. Even if she didn't (sob) get him this one, perfect, life-sustaining gift.

She came perilously close to applauding. By now, of course, she was wise to the ways of little boys. She wasn't immune, necessarily, but she'd certainly survived her share of guilt trips. Enough, in fact, that she knew for a fact that parents only visited the evil things on their children for payback.

But in that Christmas season when he was eight, she succumbed to his blandishments. She got him the damn toy. And then she went home and poured herself a drink.

Little boys especially are fond of telling their mothers they love them by decorating the floor in mud. This was one of the most persistently learned lessons of her motherhood, especially after he had a sister to play with and teach in the ways of aiding and abetting.

The chances of this form of communication being visited on a mother increased diametrically with the effort she'd just gone through to get the floor clean. Usually after a long day yanking sense out of a diabolical computer, when her husband was out of town and the cat was sick on the carpet. Inevitably when the only accomplishment she'd actually managed with any success that day was the scrubbing of every scuff mark and dog track on the white kitchen floor she'd thought was so pretty when she was still childless.

By the time he was ten, she should have anticipated it, like knowing just which puppy-faced soldier was going to get creamed in a war movie. Cute and cuddly, one point. Family back home, one point. The desire to raise rabbits in Montana, ten points. Bang, he was dead.

In her own personal war movie, the sniper had just gotten her in his sights.

She'd just eased herself down into a chair after spending more time than usual scraping the detritus of the last week off her floor. The business partners were coming over that night to celebrate the sealing of a deal. Her house, dammit, sparkled.

And then, like shark music in *Jaws*, she heard the door slam. Footsteps. Raised, breathless voices. And without even hauling her aching butt out of the chair, she knew just what her sparkling white floor was going to look like when she walked in there.

"Mom! Mom! Look what I found for you!"

Just as inevitably, the surprise would be of a type found most often in stagnant ponds. Boys particularly liked stagnant ponds. Her son reveled in them. There were days she saw him growing up to be an ecologist, just for the excuse to play in primordial ooze.

The footsteps skidded. Silence took hold for a second.

"Uh-oh."

She smiled. Another type of *I love you*. He'd obviously seen the wake he'd stirred up across her floor. But, knowing his pattern, he was already halfway across.

"Come on," she said without getting up. "You can help me clean it later."

"It's just so cool!" he rhapsodized. "I knew you'd want to see it."

Now, she hated stereotyping. She didn't think of herself as a "girly" girl. She was appalled at the Donna Reed type of housewife who trilled and tittered and grew faint at the sight of scales. But she did not like snakes. Neither did Indiana Jones, if it came right down to it, so it wasn't necessarily a gender thing. But no matter the personal disgust for her son's latest predilection, she kept smiling.

"He wrapped right around my arm, Mom! Can I keep him?"

He'd brought his discovery straight to her. Just as he had all his discoveries. The pretty rocks and the snails in the yard and the license plate from Alaska that had washed up down the block when the water main broke. He didn't declare it an official discovery until Mom had oohed and aahed over it. Which was why she knew that *I love you* could be spelled in mud on the kitchen floor.

One of the hardest lessons a mother needed to learn was when *I love you* meant *I'm sorry.* Sometimes the lesson was small, sometimes costly, sometimes painful. He was fifteen and learning to drive. He'd found an affinity with her computer she'd never quite been able to enjoy. He delighted in installing his war games on it so that when she sat down to type up a prospectus, she'd find tanks and stinger missiles infesting the screen.

They needed another computer, but with two growing children in the house, somehow the money was never there for it. So he used hers. And one night after he finished his homework, he came to tell her that her hard drive was about full. She turned to her husband, but he was an English teacher, so what did he know?

"It's okay, Mom," her son said with a big brash smile. "I'll take care of it."

By the time he finished, the missiles still resided in

her computer. The records of her last year's transac-
tions didn't. Her son sat ashen-faced before the
screen, terrified to tell her what he'd done. Not sure,
to put it to the point, what it was he had done.

"What happened?" she asked, just as ashen-faced.

"Did you back up your records?"

"What . . . happened?"

His eyes closed. His hands went limp on the desk-
top. "I love you, Mom."

This time had been an easier lesson. She had backed
up her files. She even ended up learning how to work
the program that reclaimed erased files the next time
her son decided to help her. And she learned that the
I'm sorry I love you was the most special, because it
took courage to admit it.

Thank you. Another variation that was sometimes
wonderful, like the day after he passed his test to
drive and she actually, without more than a small
groan of dismay, handed him the keys so he could
show off for his newest girlfriend.

First his eyes widened. Eyes that had gone from
impish to deadly, long lashed and light green, handsome, winsome eyes that were catching girls' attention. Too-intelligent eyes on her suddenly tall,
suddenly good-looking son.

"You mean it?" he asked, actually picking at the
collar on his precious Tommy Hilfiger shirt.

"Yes." She tried to sound enthusiastic when she
smiled. She really did. She did manage a smile, however tight. "I mean it."

He forgot for a moment he was quite the grown-up
young man. He forgot he was taller than his mother

and raging in hormones that made him question her intelligence, taste, sense, wisdom, and relationship. He grabbed her up in a bear hug and swung her around, her feet several inches off the floor.

"I love you, Mom!"

Her ribs hurt for two weeks, and she was sure at least one of her hips dislocated. But she made it back to the floor with a real smile on her face that lasted well past the time he walked out the door, and she began to fear for his life and the life of everyone on the street.

The *thank you* I love yous were also sometimes painful, like when that little girl he'd grown so fond of found someone else to be fond of.

It wasn't exactly that he told his mother. She simply saw part of that special light that was his personality go out. It was as if he dimmed, grew smaller. Quieter.

She finally braved even his room to make sure he was okay.

The Hilfiger shirt was on a pile on the floor along with his wrestling gear and all the filled notebooks from last semester. He was stretched out on the bed she'd bought when he was three and a big boy, and suddenly she realized it was too small. Not that his feet hung over the end or anything. She just couldn't imagine him having space to roll over.

He didn't look as if he'd get the energy to do even that for at least another year.

"Can I help?"

There wasn't a chair with seat space available, so she perched on the edge of his bed, as she'd done all the times he'd needed her, through fevers and night-mares and disappointments. Joy filled the house. Sadness constricted to the smallest space possible.

He kept an arm over his eyes. "No."

"I'm sorry, baby."

"It's not your fault."

"Doesn't matter. You hurt. I hurt. And you hurt."

She didn't say, *that little tart hurt you,* like she wanted to. She didn't even tell him that she'd never liked the little tramp, and that she wanted to push her little dimpled face in. She just stroked his hair, just as she'd done when he'd had the croup and the day he'd dropped the pop fly that would have gotten his team out of a close play-off game two runs ahead.

She sat there for a while in silence, just being Mom for a gangly, handsome young man who only needed her quite so much now when he was sick or sad.

And when she finally left him to his disappointment, he raised the arm off his face. "I love you, Mom."

Standing at the open door, she told him he was welcome. "I love you, too, baby."

And now, standing here in her best dress, wanting to sneeze from the roses, she faced the worst *I love you.* The sweetest, the saddest, the most inevitable.

There were tears in his eyes. There were tears in hers, because her baby, whom she'd rocked and chattered with and cleaned up and wept over, had found another woman. He'd met a sweet young lady who stroked his hair when he was sad and laughed with him when he found something new to delight him. Which brought him here to stand at the back of the church as the organ music began the intro into the Mother of the Groom piece and smile at his mother as he said those momentous words.

"I love you, Mom."

She knew she had never heard any words more terrible, yet more promising. She knew she could only answer in kind, because he had to know that it had all been worth it, that she would do it again in a heartbeat. That she would always be there for him no matter what, but that she gave him gladly to the arms of his new wife who would be the one he'd run to first now, just as it should be.

"I love you, too, baby," she said, and for the first time in her life, turned away from him to let him walk on alone. Because with this *I love you*, her son had told her good-bye.

AFTERWORD

My son Kevin is now twenty-one and living in the dorm. There is no question he inspired this story. My mother once nicknamed him "World War II." Nobody could keep up with him. And, as a matter of fact, I do have a very special Hot Wheels sculpture in my office, along with the other sculptures and paintings Kevin has done, since. All I can say is that it's a good thing I was a trauma nurse, because it came in handy. When we came up with the concept for the story, we had a great time going back over some of the highlights of life in a household with a child who my father called "all boy," and putting them to paper. Even though I still have yet to visit the chapter that closes our story, I can't wait to stand in the back of that church, and, indeed, to see his sons grow as tall and handsome and fine as he is.

Eric Jerome Dickey

—∞—

Fish Sammich with Cheese

COURTESY OF VIRGINIA JERRY

*Eric Jerome Dickey,
ca. 1963.*

COURTESY OF VIRGINIA JERRY

Carolyn "Doll" Dickey.

TRI TRAN PHOTOGRAPHY

*Eric Jerome Dickey,
today.*

I never lived with my birth mother.

When I was about ten months old, she "dropped me off" at the baby-sitter and never returned. Guess she forgot. Maybe something more important came up. This was how the story was related to me. So, I suppose, that was how we became unrelated. I didn't have much early memory of her, but I already knew at five that I strongly feared, dreaded my mother. I didn't know why. I didn't know if it was because of everyone's attitude toward her, or if it was due to her actions and attitude toward me.

I was living with an elderly couple from rural country, Grenada, Mississippi, who had taken me in as family. Vardaman and Lila Gause. Lila was in her fifties; Vardaman a little older. The Gauses bought my clothes, sheltered me, made sure I went to school, fed me. No one asked them to take care of me, they just did. Neither had much of an education. Lila couldn't read; don't think I ever saw her write anything but her name. Functionally illiterate. Still she was a good God-fearing woman who cherished her Bible and gave up much love. She had an older son, Junior, who I don't remember being around the house until I was at least thirteen. She had experienced one miscarriage after Junior was born. I think her second son was named James. I remember reading a certificate of death or some type of document that said he was stillborn or something. She never spoke of it, but I remember hearing she miscarried while working either the cotton fields or in her own garden. That's what I heard. I often wondered if she saw me as the replacement for that loss. A godsend.

Vardaman could read and "do figures"—as he called it. Back in his day, children only went to school for a short while, maybe to sixth grade, then quit to work the land or do something to support his family. He worked at Sealy Posturepedic in South Memphis, adjacent to Riverside Park (renamed Martin Luther King Park) until he retired, then had a series of strokes and died in the mid-seventies.

I never really saw any white people in my neighborhood, but when they showed up on Kansas Street they were always in nice cars, never on foot or the bus, and they never stayed long. They ran sundries in our neighborhood and often came by to collect insurance money, often with attitudes, on Fridays. Taking.

Vardaman was a deacon at White Stone M.B.C. on South Parkway East and Third Street. Lila, the woman I will always call Momma, was a member of the Mother's Board. Daddy had a reserved seat under the minister facing the front. Momma sat on the left front row, always in the same seat. Rain or shine, we went to church every Sunday. They loved me as if I were their own. Yep, these were the only parents I knew. Momma and Daddy.

Still, I was alone. I don't remember ever having a consistent playmate. No brother. No sister. No best friend. So I felt lonely. As a child I didn't recognize this emotion, nor could I clearly articulate the need for a companion. I relied on my imagination for entertainment.

We lived in a white five-room house at 1858 Kansas Street, the south side of Memphis in one of the colored districts, not the best-looking house in the neighborhood but far from the worst. Landscaped by hedges. Two big trees in the front that I would sneak and climb. A plum and a peach tree in the back by the clothesline. There was a garage that Daddy had built in the back for parking his car and storing his tools. He called it "the shed."

The shed was my refuge, where I played every day. I could pick up pieces of wood, or use one of Daddy's tools and make believe it was a secret weapon and pretend I was a superhero defending the world. And after I disposed of all of the evil forces, everyone in the world wanted to come out and play with me. I was the play-king. I picked the games, and I made the rules.

One day as I dictated the rules of a new game to my imaginary civilization, I heard my name called. All of a sudden I felt fear, dread, anxiety. My name rang from the lungs of Carolyn "Doll" Dickey. My birth mother.

She called me "Roni," as in Rice-A-Roni, that San Francisco treat. Guess she thought it was funny, but I hated that. How could she dare give me a nickname, especially since I didn't know her? My Uncle Darrell called me Fat Head, and since I stuttered, kids on

Blair Hunt Drive called me Porky Pig. But that was different. They knew me. I knew them.

I went around to the front of the house, and she stood there next to Lila; Lila was wringing her hands, what she did when her nerves were acting up, doing that over and over as she rocked side to side, biting her lip and forcing a smile. A worried and unhappy smile. Lila always had a distressed expression on her face, always wrung her hands when Doll showed up, which wasn't very often. Her reputation preceded her.

Doll leaned over to me and said, "Give your momma a hug."

You aren't my momma, but I'll hug you because you're bigger and could beat me up. I remember now. You have beat me up for less. You have hit me, said bad things to me, did whatever you wanted just because you were my "momma" and had the right. I'm five years old, and you have never given me anything but grief and a good backhand, occasionally a pimp slap, to make yourself feel superior. You have never called or remembered me on my birthday.

"Ain't you gonna speak, Roni?"

"'Lo. How you doing?" I responded like that robot on *Lost in Space*.

I crossed my fingers behind my back. *Please don't make me call you Momma, please. God make her drop dead right now so I can go back to my kingdom and finish my game. My subjects need me. How can they play if they don't know the rules? Are you listening, God? What about Jesus? Can He help or is He busy, too?* In church they said He was always listening and everywhere.

"You had anything to eat yet?"

"No, ma'am. I been playing in dah shed."

"Let's go up to the snack bar and get you something to eat," Doll said.

I wasn't hungry. But then I thought, she has never taken me to get anything to eat. This was unusual. It seemed nice. Maybe everyone was overreacting. Maybe she was really a nice person and loved her bastard child.

"Will you loan me five dollars, Miss Gause?" Doll asked.

Loan? You ain't got no job! I had heard them say that about Doll. A flag went up. User alert!

"I only got a couple of dollars," Lila said as she dropped her face and looked at the ground, still shifting side to side.

"Okay," Doll immediately said, snapping and overlapping.

Momma hurried into the house and came back with three wrinkled greenbacks. As she stepped off the porch and came back out underneath the shade tree, she frantically pulled at the dollars as if she was trying to straighten them out and make them more valuable, more appealing to her aggressor.

Momma got close; Doll whisked her hand out, palm opened. Momma looked at me, then slowly raised her hand and paid the ransom. I didn't want her to give her money to Doll. I knew that Momma got her money from Daddy, so she was giving her Daddy's money. I knew Doll wouldn't give it back. She had never meant to give it back, because she never did. She looked people in the eye and lied to them. Good people I cared about and who cared about me. I wanted to be bigger so I could take it back.

I tried to summon my kingdom. Maybe they couldn't hear me. Maybe my telepathic signals couldn't make it to the backyard. Maybe I wasn't concentrating hard enough. Maybe Doll was causing the interference.

Three whole dollars. I was sure three dollars was about fifty cents short of being a million dollars.

"Let's go to the snack bar," Doll said.

Doll hurriedly put the money in her bra, her personal pocketbook. All of Doll's clothes looked beaten and worn and would definitely have been rejected by the Salvation Army.

"Let's stop by your grandmomma's house on the way," she said.

My grandmother? Why? What about the food she promised? Had she forgotten so quickly?

My grandmother lived at 1826 Kansas. Seven houses north of 1858. My grandmother, Virginia Jerry, had three of her six children living with her. Regina. Darrell. Michael. These were the children by her second marriage to Herman Jerry. Doll, Verna Jean, and Mary Alice were products of her first marriage to Herman Dickey.

I didn't really know my maternal relatives at this point in my life. I knew who they were, they lived on the same block. But I didn't know the history of our tree. I would stop by to say "Hi" occasionally on my ventures to the corner sundry to replenish my coconut or chocolate chip cookie supply.

Lila looked at me. "You wanna go visit Sister Jerry?"

My eyes said "no," but fear had seized my tongue.

"I'll bring him right on back," Doll interrupted, signaling that my answer would be insignificant.

Doll grabbed my hand and led the way as we exited the yard. I remember wishing that Daddy was at home. He wouldn't have let her take me away from my comfort zone. Doll wasn't as tough, not as disrespectful, when he was around.

Still, Momma was protecting me from Doll the best she knew. Doll was just nineteen years older than me, much younger than Lila. We were taught to respect older people, to defer to them and their wisdom, but I believe Doll intimidated her. Doll was my real mother, so I guess that meant she had the right. The law or something. If Momma didn't do what Doll wanted, Doll would threaten to take me away.

I kept looking back to the shed.

Helpless. Hopeless. Powerless.

It seemed like it took an eternity to get to my grandmother's house, but on the way I devised a plan that would allow me to regain my freedom, and I immediately put it into effect. I began stepping on all the cracks in the sidewalk, the wider ones twice. "Step on a crack, break your momma's back," I had heard other kids say.

Crack. Step. Wide crack. Double step.

My eyes went up to Doll. "How you feeling?" I asked.

"Fine."

Walking straight. Not missing a beat. Damn. Back intact.

I held my head down and tried to think of another plan as we walked north along Kansas. Doll spoke to people along the way. We lived in the south, among Mississippi transplants, a community of nosy people, where everybody knew everybody, so everybody spoke to everybody.

"'Lo, Miss Odessa. Good Evening, Mr. Wright. Long time no see, Miss Lucille. Mr. Roy. Hiya, Ethel Mae. Kaye. Faye. Y'all, getting big. Mr. Ernest, Miss Betty. Mr. White. Hello, Miss Bennett. Hello, Mr. Steve. Miss Ira."

At a few houses, kids my age were out on their porches, or playing in their yards. Doll's clothing was tattered, maybe out of style, her face always bruised. The kind of things that embarrass a child. And the kids saw me with her, being forced to hold hands while I walked at her side. I didn't want to view the looks of astonishment, hear the giggles, being delivered from my dirty-face and snotty-nose peers. Didn't want to be weak and give any indication of my dread. If I had shown I was wounded, they would attack me with insults upon my return. That was the way of the ghetto children. We rank. We bag. We played the dozen. Did it extremely well. But those slurs would cut deep, because I knew they would all be true.

Why won't any of you grown people intervene and save me? Haven't any of you read Hansel and Gretel? *Can't any of you recognize the witch? Look at her crooked nose? Her missing teeth? Can't you smell the aroma of brew spewing from her pores? You people are of no help. Useless.*

We arrived at my grandmother's front door, and I stepped back as she knocked. The front door was open, but the screen door was fastened. Inside, house shoes dragged across the floor. I trembled. My fate was uncertain. Thought that Madear was in on this scheme. But my grandmother was shocked twice. First to see Doll. Second to see Doll with me. Even she knew that sight wasn't right.

"Hello, Madear," I said.

"Well, good afternoon, Jerome," Madear replied, and smiled sunshine at me.

Not "Roni." Jerome. I loved the way she said my name. It was my middle name, and even though I didn't like it, she was the only one who said it right. My grandmother has a powerful voice that makes it seem as if she is shouting when she isn't. Madear was a nononsense type of woman. Brilliantly logical. Very religious, but not overbearingly so. Madear lived directly across the street from Shady Grove M.B.C., which she attended.

"Hi, Madear," Doll said.

Madear said, "Hello, Doll."

The smile had left Madear's face. No facade here. That's one quality my grandmother had, you knew how she felt about you. Exactly. Doll became a child in my grandmother's presence. She had fear and respect for Madear.

Besides, Doll wanted something.

After a few moments of empty conversation, Doll got to the point. "I was wondering if you could lend me ten dollars," Doll asked as she pulled out another Kool, making her question seem trivial.

"Ten Dollars?" Madear replied with a you-must-be-crazy tone, leaning back in her chair.

See, it was 1960 something. Ten dollars was a mega-fortune. In some third world countries or on some corners in some ghettos, it still is.

"Mrs. Gause made me to come get Roni," Doll said, "so I'm taking him to stay with me, and I need cab fare to get back."

What?

Doll held me close, looked at me and winked, as if she wanted me to collaborate on this falsehood. I dropped my head and busied myself playing with my hands and biting my dirty nails so I could pretend I didn't hear any of this.

"I ain't giving you no ten dollars. How you gonna pay me back? You ain't got no job."

That's what I was thinking.

"I'll give you cab fare to get back home. That's it," Madear said with finality. The emotions were in the air. I felt Madear just wanted to get rid of her. Something about Doll irritated her, bothered her. Maybe because parents want to see their children do better in life than they did, or at least become independent, giving them the ability to be proud of their reproductions, happy knowing they have added another strong branch to the family tree. Maybe.

I wouldn't know how much all of that pained Madear until I was over thirty years old, back in Memphis for a few days, standing by her side at Doll's funeral. Doll would be fifty-two; Madear in her early seventies. Madear would cry, and keep repeating, "I did all I could for you. All I could." She was a small woman, hardly five feet tall. All my life I had thought she was so much bigger, maybe because she was a giant in my mind. When we stood in a cemetery off South Parkway East, giving Carolyn

Dickey back to the ground, the moment the first dirt hit her pink coffin and thumped like a final heartbeat, even though I said I wouldn't, that was when I cried.

Madear grumbled, but she gave Doll three dollars. Maybe now I'd get my fish sammich wit cheese and a lotta hot sauce.

A couple of minutes later, Doll picked up the phone and called a cab. I thought, surely she wasn't going to take me with her. But when the cab pulled up, she placed me inside first. I cringed. Didn't like being this close to her. My asthma didn't like the smell of her Kool cigarettes.

She gave the cabdriver directions.

Kansas Street disappeared as we drove off.

We rode almost as long as I could hold my breath, then the taxi dropped us off right up in front of one of the neighborhood liquor stores.

When the driver told Doll the fare, she handed him a twenty-dollar bill. A twenty-dollar bill. She already had money. Liar. User. Chain smoker.

We got out, walked across the lot, by all the black men who were standing around with brown paper bags in their hands, and went to a car parked on the side street. Inside were two people I had never seen before. I sat in the backseat with the older lady. Doll sat up front. I have no idea who was driving.

"Roni."

Arrgh!!!

"Speak to your grandmother," Doll said.

My grandmother? This wasn't Mrs. Virginia Jerry. Who was this imposter?

"This is your daddy's momma," Doll explained with a smile.

Daddy? Which one? I remember once that Doll told me that I had seven daddies. Seven. A man named Jimmy—he bought me a chocolate Yoohoo soda one time; I liked him—and six other names that escaped me. At the time I didn't know that this was biologically impossible. I believed it. First I thought, Great!

Then I wondered why none ever came to visit me, or bought me birthday presents, or took me to get a fish sammich with cheese.

"Hello," my newfound grandmother said.

"Good morning," I said.

"It's afternoon," Doll interjected.

I didn't question the authenticity of this new relation. Children were taught not to question adults.

We drove over to Florida Street, one street over, turned right, went over the railroad tracks, turned left at the next street, Belz Avenue, turned right into the shopping center off Belz just west of Parkway. Southgate Shopping Center.

I wondered if we were going to buy something. The driver parked in the back behind Skaggs Drugstore. I had never been to this section of the center. This part of shopping was boring. There were no stores back here to buy toys or comic books from, so this area of the center didn't interest me.

Doll and my fraternal grandmother took me upstairs. A small room with chairs. Air-conditioned. White people behind the counters.

After a while a white lady called us to a desk. My

fraternal grandmother showed her some papers. "He is my grandson. My son was his daddy."

Was?

The grown folks continued talking about stuff I didn't understand and was not interested in. Words were going back and forth, voices raised, Doll had a slight attitude.

I was quiet, practicing verbal constipation.

The white lady looked at me.

"Eric, where do you live?" the lady asked politely.

I looked up. My new grandmother, Eula Reed, watched me. She wasn't upset, not like Doll had sounded. My little brown eyes went to Doll, requesting permission to speak. She didn't respond. Her lips were tight, arms folded. Tense. This didn't really bother me at the time, because I hadn't done anything. I had been quiet while they talked, didn't interrupt, was well behaved in front of the white people. Being a good boy. Showing them I had home training.

"Eighteen-fiddy-eight Kansas."

"With whom?" she smiled.

I didn't know what "whom" meant, so I assumed she was slow and had mispronounced "who." Maybe she came to work on a short yellow bus.

"Vardaman and Lila Gause," I stated, as if she should already know. "Eighteen-fiddy-eight Kans-ass Street, Memp-fist, Ten-ahsee."

She smiled. "You're a smart little boy."

I smiled.

She motioned toward Doll. "Do you live with your momma here?"

"No, ma'am," I said, eyebrows crinkled, wondering

why the strange woman with the long yellow hair asked me that, hoping she would take me back home.

Somebody groaned.

The conversation went back to the adults. Desperate voices. My fraternal grandmother stared at Doll in shock, maybe disapproval. The white lady had said something offensive, something that had offended Doll, and Doll let go of the fake smile.

Afraid. I remember being afraid something awful might happen to us because of her actions. You didn't talk like that to white people. Everybody knew that. Colored people were maimed, went to heaven for less.

What had happened?

It would be years before I actually knew what that scenario was all about. It would take time for me to recollect. It would take time for the significance of this event to register.

My father, Vernon, had been killed in an auto accident down in Louisiana. They said he had been drinking. Drove off a bridge. Motor went through his chest. I didn't know him, had never heard of him before that day. Don't know if he knew about me. Doll had contacted my father's mother right after the death. A tragedy she could capitalize on.

My father was married to someone else at the time of the sperm donation. This kind of explains why my birth certificate only shows one parent. Asexual reproduction implied. The section for the information about the father is blank. Null. Yet to be determined. We'll think about it and get back to you later.

So, Doll was attempting to initiate Social Security benefits from this. However, she had tried, but couldn't accomplish this alone. Since somebody had forgot to fill in the blank, confirmation of the father of the illegitimate heir was required. Doll needed my fraternal grandmother to make this possible. She gathered everything and everybody she needed, got whatever was requested by the administration. Me, my recently discovered grandmother, and paperwork to verify I was his son. And mostly my grandmother's word.

Sounds noble. Keep reading.

The Social Security Administration reviewed the literature, interviewed the necessary individuals, and came to a conclusion. I was eligible for a monthly disbursement to ease my economic condition. Yippee! Yes, there is a God, and she's blonde and works for the government! I could receive payments until I was eighteen, or twenty-one if I went to college. Would cost nobody nothing. Zip. No skin off anybody's butt. It was there for me. It was built into the system. Ironically, I could be supported because someone I would never know had met with an untimely demise.

I had an uncle named Sam, and he was looking pretty good to me.

The problem?

The administration would send the check to where the child lived. That location, that house, in the name of the primary care givers. No ifs, ands, or buts. After interviewing me, they wanted to send the check to 1858 Kansas under the name of Lila and Vardaman Gause. The people who had taken care of me every day since I was in diapers. The people who had taught me how to walk, stayed up with me when I

was having asthma attacks, the people who had sacrificed their own finances to take care of me.

Doll had a problem with that. A serious problem.
That was when she stopped being polite. When the
attitude came in. When she started being defensive.
Her scheme had fallen apart unexpectedly. My simple
answer wasn't part of the equation. In other words,
that was when the shit hit the fan.

"Why can't you send the check to me?" Doll demanded to know.

Why was she getting mad at the nice white lady?

"We have to send it where he lives," she replied
firmly.

"Send it to me, then I'll take him the money."

"We have to send it to where he lives," the woman
reiterated for the hundredth time. "The checks have to
be in the name of the people he lives with."

Papers were drawn. Forms filled out. All that was
left, the last thing required was Doll's consent. The
government needed her permission. Once again, she
had a choke hold on my future, on what would become of me. All that was left was for her to sign her
name on a piece of white paper at the bottom of a
bunch of words to set everything off. A monthly check
plus a lump sum back payment was at stake. Nothing. It would cost her nothing.

"Forget it. Keep your money," she snapped.

I was surprised, because, well, I had never heard
her turn down money before. My new grandmother's
eyes were wide, her mouth gaping.

Doll was shifting and rolling her eyes, smoking her
Kool cigarette, blowing out her disgust in long
streams of smoke.

More arguments. Then a white man came over.

Doll grabbed my hand, and we abruptly exited the office.

My brand-new grandmother had been earnest, honest. She was sincere in her effort to right a wrong. To do the right thing. To help with no expectations of reward. She wasn't a part of this plot. She, like me, had been used. We sat in the backseat of the car.

My mother had tried to pimp me. I had been put out on the corner to bring in the money. Although she didn't prevail, I had been violated. I had been raped of my livelihood. My future had been molested.

Yep, it would be years before I realized the significance of this day. I'd think about it when I was in college, a full-time student, working three jobs.

When we were away from the white people, my new grandmother had a few words with Doll. Words that said she was disappointed, that what just happened wasn't right. She hugged me good-bye, left us. Then another taxi was called.

"You taking me to get a fish sammich wit—"

"Hush."

The taxi dropped anchor in downtown Memphis. Beale Street, long before it was rebuilt. There were no neon lights, no shine, no blues clubs. We passed through a park, and I remember seeing a bronze statue of a black man. Didn't know they made those. Later I would find out that was W. C. Handy, father of the blues, holding a trumpet, standing tall, smiling wide. It was the first time I had ever seen a statue of a black man. He was big, strong. Almost as if he could reach down and take me away to safety. Years down the road, when I passed through this park, I would clearly remember this day, giving Mr. Handy a special place in my life.

The streets were littered with homeless people, back then they were bums, all sharing pints of various brands of "medicine." Men. Women. All looked old to me, just some looked a lot older than the others. All looking as if they needed to bathe and shelter. I was afraid of these people. There were so many. They were so big. I had never seen so many grown people walking around in their play clothes.

Doll was at home, more comfortable here than she had been on Kansas Street or around the friendly white lady she had made mad.

She introduced "her baby" to almost everyone she came in contact with. Almost everyone responded the same way. They first said, "I didn't know you had a baby," then looked to me for confirmation. I became a trophy, an animal on display. Pushed from stranger to stranger, passed around like a joint. She made me ask people for change as a gift after each introduction, and if they complied, she took my offerings and pocketed them. She said she wanted to "keep" it for me, and kept it she did.

Then she took me to a bad place. Old. Streets smelled of urine and dirt combined with alcohol. I don't recall if it was a house, or an apartment building. I do know that from the outside, it didn't look like a place where I thought people would live. There was a steep flight of stairs at the entrance. We went up one level. Then downstairs. She knocked on a door, and an elderly lady answered.

"Doll!" the old lady said as she opened the door.

The old lady let us in. It was a complete apartment.

Complete meaning it had its own toilet. A kitchen was to the right. An elderly gentleman watched television. He turned when I entered, and he smiled. A man and a woman, shacking. Or a husband and a wife. Either way, a family. I felt safe in their presence.

Doll began the introductions. Once again, I was her little boy. And again they didn't know she had a child. They went to the kitchen. I couldn't hear their conversation, but if somebody spoke to me, I responded, "Yes, sir," or "No, ma'am."

Something had caught my eye. A telephone. A big black rotary phone.

The elderly couple were very nice. I assume they were the managers or keepers of this establishment. Food. I smelled food. Stomach growled. I still hadn't had my fish sandwich wit cheese and how long ago was that? Five, six hours? I was hungry, but I didn't want to do anything to cause her to lash out at me.

Why-tall-tu-fo'-tree-fo'-nyne . . .

Doll said good night to the elderly couple. It had gotten dark, past my bedtime, and we proceeded to go up the stairs. Under her weight, the stairs creaked. None creaked under mine. Too small. Too light. The hall had a musty, dusty, moldy smell. Walls, stairs needed painting.

At the top she opened a door on the right side of the hallway, took me inside a cave. A small room with a bed against the wall, a short dresser, a small round table. No windows. No bathroom. A box. Was this where she lived? Was I to live here? The bed wasn't made up. Momma always made up the beds in the morning. Maybe nobody told Doll she was supposed to do that. Cigarettes overflowed the ashtrays. Why didn't she clean up? It was only one room.

Why-tall-tu-fo'-tree-fo'-nyne.

I sat down on the bed, nervous. Sheets smelled stinky. Then I heard someone come up the stairs. Creaking loud enough to let me know it was somebody big. Feet dragging. The footsteps stopped in front of the door. Someone was out there. Standing still. Contemplating.

First fear made me back away, then hope made me lean forward.

Could it be someone from my kingdom who had followed and waited for the right moment to put their plan in motion?

The doorknob clicked, creaked as the door eased open.

A man with a stubbly beard. He was huge.

He frowned down on me.

Nope, not from my kingdom.

He slammed the door behind him. He was definitely angry. A cool sort of anger. But still angry. Had I done something? My eyes went to Doll. I wanted to hide behind her. She began fumbling with her clothes, her hair, wringing her hands like Lila did. I'd never seen her like that before. A crooked smile came over her face. I wondered who was this person who just walked into Doll's room, into my life.

Doll looked at him and said, "I want you to meet—"

"Where you been all day?" he injected sharply.

"I went to my momma's house."

"How you get there?"

She hesitated.

"I said, how you get there?"

"I took a cab," she said with a little snap.

He took a step forward. Heavy feet in black work boots.

"Where you get car fare from?"

"Momma paid for it."

Oh, boy, to the tenth power. I knew that was a story (I was forbade to use the word lie). I sensed trouble.

"Somebody done stole twenny dollars out of my pants pocket."

"I didn't take your money," she replied quickly, then she looked at me. *What're you looking at me for? I didn't take it. Hell, I just got here.*

Then she winked at got, like this was a game and I was to play along.

What she was doing, now that I look back on that day, was telling him, *Not now, don't act like a fool in front of my child.* And telling me not to tell him that I'd seen the twenty when we were in the cab.

Like he cared.

"It was there last night," he rumbled.

Her eyes left me, went back to the man.

Again, the sky-high man in the black boots frowned down at me.

My eyes went to the wooden floor.

His voice hovered over my little head, "Step out in the hall for a minute, pard-nah."

"I gotta go number one," I said, holding up one finger like they taught me in church.

"The bathroom's down at the end of the hall," Doll said, voice nervous, finger pointing toward her right, my left. Away from the stairs. Away from freedom. I walked out into the musty hallway of that unknown world, afraid. I wanted to escape this place, these evil people. Fear raced through my veins. Heart beat too fast. Forehead sweated. Could barely breathe. Thought I was about to have an asthma attack, and that made me want to cry. I wanted to fall into a corner and whimper and wish all this away.

"Lying motherfucker!" spilled into the halls.

Crashes and bumps and thuds.

I raced back to Doll's door, stood there shaking. It sounded like the man was attacking her the way I had seen Daniel Boone (Fess Parker) attack bad guys—or was that the way I had seen the bad guys attack Daniel Boone?

"Look at this shit. Why you hiding this money in your bosom?"

"Stop!"

"Answer me, nigger!"

"Momma gave me ten dollars!"

Bravo! I was amazed that even under these circumstances, she still could lie. Guess she'd had a lot of practice. Was this the type of life she led every day? Is that how she got the bruises on her face?

I thought of church and the Bible and people saying "do unto others" and how "we shall forgive" and that nice black man who was always on television walking and marching with a bunch of people saying "turn the other cheek" because we would overcome, someday.

Then a new terror.

Since she had stolen his money and offended him, would he not turn and batter me as well? After all, we were related. I had heard them say in church something about the children carrying the sins of the father. Something else I didn't understand. Talk of angels and devils, but the pictures in the Bible always showed both as white folks.

No one to protect me from the tall mean man in the black boots. No one had protected me from her. I was alone, far away from my kingdom.

Why-tall-tu-fo'-tree-fo'-nyne.

Small steps. I took small steps backward.

Listened.

No response from the other side of that door. The argument, that fight was still going on strong. His yells, louder. Her cries, weaker.

Another step.

No response.

I cautiously went down the stairs. I hoped they didn't creak, or break like they did on the *Lone Ranger*, or give any other warning of my unscheduled departure. I looked down. Being afraid of heights didn't help, not at all. The number of steps seemed infinite. The pathway to freedom, so steep and treacherous. I would descend a couple of steps, then listen for my master or her intruder to realize their property had fled, listened to see if they had sounded the alarm. I made it to the bottom undetected.

The hall was empty. Cars passed by on the dark street.

I stood in front of the elderly couple's apartment trying to regain my composure. Act normal, like everything was hunky dory, peachy keen. I didn't want them to suspect. Didn't want them to return me up the stairs.

I knocked softly, loud enough for the people inside to hear, too low for the sounds to travel.

The elderly lady opened the door, and she smiled down at me.

I calmly and quickly asked, "Miss Ma'am, can I use y'all phone? To call home?"

She smiled but looked confused.

I realized that what I had said came out too fast, blending into one word.

Please don't ask me questions, please, please, please.

"Sho' you can," she chuckled. "You know the number?"

"Yes, ma'am," I slowed. "Why-tall-tu-fo'-tree-fo'-nyne."

She dialed the number, which seemed to take forever, waiting for her eyes to find the correct number, place her fragile finger in the hole, rotate the number, wait for the spinner to come back so she could dial the next digit.

Finally, she handed me the phone.

It rang once. Momma answered. Hearing her voice, I wanted to cry. I missed her and Daddy so much. I was afraid. I hoped she wouldn't be mad at me for calling so late, for being up past my bedtime, for crossing the streets, for being a problem. I didn't want to be trouble.

When I heard her voice, I said only four words. I spoke very softly, trying not to be a crybaby, "Momma, come get me."

"Where you at?"

I didn't know. Dumb. Stupid colored boy. Idiot. How could you plan an escape without that information? My watery eyes went to the elderly lady. My shaky little hands held the phone up to her.

I had been defeated. Someone must get word back to my kingdom that they must choose a new ruler and go on without me. Be good to my shed, new ruler.

"Hello," she said to Momma.

I stood close, as close as I could. Wanted to hear everything she said. My eyes were on the door, my ears with the old lady. I didn't trust her. At that moment, inside that fear, I didn't trust anyone.

They talked forever, maybe only a few seconds. My fear kept me watching the door, expecting Doll to burst in in agony and reclaim her bastard child. I wished they would hurry.

She hung up the phone and slowly looked down at me. The smile gone from her face, her eyes misting. Sorrow radiated from the depths of her soul. She put her hand on my shoulder, patted softly.

"She'll be here dah-recktly," she said softly.

Miss Ma'am pulled out a chair for me to sit in the kitchen next to her. Her eyes were on the door, too. Mr. Old Man was still sitting watching television. I have no idea what was on after dark in 1968. My diet consisted of Popeye, Bugs Bunny, and Porky Pig. Mr. Old Man looked back at me and smiled.

"Where yo' momma at?" he asked.

I didn't know what to say. Miss Ma'am smiled slightly. Maybe she wanted to know, too, but wasn't going to ask.

All I could say was, "She up in her house."

Mr. Old Man turned back to his black-and-white television program, a fat white man with a balled-up fist telling his wife that he was gonna send her to the moon. My little brown eyes, trying not to cry, went back to the old lady. She was still watching me in a way that expressed "everythang will be alright in a minute."

A horn blew. Without saying a word, I ran to the door, for that wasn't the sound of just any tooter, it belonged to a white two-door Buick Wildcat that had whitewall tires, manual windows, and an AM radio. My Wildcat. The one that has blown for me and Momma every Sunday morning at eight-thirty, right after Daddy had backed the car from the shed to the front of the house. Whenever his whistle sounded, it meant you had best be ready because it was time to go.

And now it was time to go.

The car was right outside the front door, curbside, its interior lights on. Momma had the window down, worry in her eyes. Daddy leaned forward, strained to look out, checked to see if he was at the right address. I ran out, exited abruptly without consideration, but in the midst of my flee, I paused. Paused a moment to look back up those stairs.

The hallway was quiet.

Momma pushed the passenger door open as soon as she saw me come out, and I jumped in and shut the door. We waved back at the old lady to signify that we had found each other. The old lady looked relieved.

Momma had a strange smile on her face. That of release. Since I had left walking up Kansas Street, she had been worried, fidgeting, wringing her hands nonstop. That's why she had stayed up late and answered the phone on the first ring. That's why she had Daddy bring her out past his bedtime to rescue me. That's why she had made it clear across town in record time.

And I realized for the first time, I loved her.

I couldn't express myself at that age, but I knew what I felt. I understood that bond. That unbreakable bond. She loved me like I was her own. We belonged together, needed each other.

Daddy asked me no questions. I was glad because I didn't want to tell him what was going on upstairs. I didn't want to return to that troubled cavern. Didn't want anything to prevent or further delay my flee. I felt safe again.

And I wasn't ashamed.

Actually, I was proud.

Like James T. West, or Captain James T. Kirk, even James Bond, I had single-handedly masterminded a daring escape. Now I could return to my kingdom a hero. A hero with a story to tell of witches and beggars and dragons and statues of golden Negroes and angels and devils and chariots of fire.

Downtown was behind me. I was no longer that scared little boy at the mercy of people I didn't know, of people who didn't care about me.

I stretched out and leaned against Momma. Back in my comfort zone. Momma put her hand on top of my head and rubbed my wooly hair. Maybe she would tell Daddy to give me a haircut tomorrow. It was a short drive, but I fell asleep on the way home. In my siesta I fantasized about a fish sammich wit cheese and a lotta hot sauce on it.

Tomorrow Momma would make me a special pineapple cake, all done from scratch, something she did for every one of my birthdays up until she was put on her back by a stroke and called to heaven in 1983, a couple of months before I graduated from college. I marched alone, but I felt her there. Nope, it wasn't my birthday, but she'd make that cake. She'd make sure Daddy left enough money so I could have my fish sammich wit cheese for lunch.

There was one thing that I would always remember. Something that Lila taught me.

Why-tall-tu-fo'-tree-fo'-nyne.

WHITE-HALL-two-four-three-four-nine.

942-4349.

Diana Gabaldon
with Sam Watkins

Mirror Image

Diana Gabaldon and her son Samuel.

The man in the dock looked very like his father. Especially seen in profile, thought Lord Malmsley. Of course, a profile was all that remained of the King, dead these twenty years; the long nose and noble brow stamped on the coinage of the realm, large eyes set wide in a blank stare of gold benevolence.

Not the eyes, though, thought Edward, Lord Malmsley—as he had thought many times before. The young man's eyes were from his mother. The Queen had come from the East, and both her sons had had the dark hair and the almond eyes that had made her exotic beauty the focus of the court's fascination.

The famous almond eyes were fixed on her son now—the one remaining. The Queen sat in her place, alone above the court, behind the spot reserved for the Chief Justice, the tables for the lawyers and clerks, the open benches where the spectators crowded and jostled, murmuring speculation as they stole glances—or gawked openly—at the Prince in the dock.

"Oyez, oyez!" cried the clerk. "All men rise!"

All men did—and after a moment's hesitation, so did the Queen, acknowledging the power of the law.

The Justice walked slowly into the well of the court, resplendent in horsehair wig and ermine-trimmed gown, followed by the barristers, severe in black, their white bands gleaming. His face was set in official grimness; he was an old man; he had been appointed by the King. The last thing he would have wished was to preside over such a trial as this, Lord Malmsley reflected—and yet he would do his duty. As they all would. As they all must.

Now the peers came: the peers of the realm, from mightiest duke to meanest baronet, each in the panoply of his full regalia, gleaming with jewels, glittering with his chains of office and honors of war. It was a sight meant to awe, and it had its effect; the crowd drew in its collective breath with a gasp, followed by murmurs of excitement, nudgings and pointings as this or that lord came pacing slowly in.

Edward regarded the procession with somewhat more cynicism—but then, he was personally acquainted with the men themselves, and was not dazzled by the trimmings. In essence, this was all for show—not only the solemn procession of lords, but the trial itself.

William, Prince of Thilesia, Duke of Shrewsbury, and the duchy of Bonmir, Count of this, that, and the other—was still William the prisoner—was still William of the house of Holborn; a prince of the blood royal. As such, no man could claim to be his peer— save perhaps the brother he had killed—and none of these peers, no matter their grandeur or their power, could sit in judgment on him. No matter what the verdict of the court, the Queen alone would pass judgment.

There was a space in the solemn procession, and the crowd held its breath, watching the empty arch through which the lawyers and the lords had passed. A generous gap was left between the last of the peers and the man who came behind, as though a sanitary cordon was required to prevent the contagion of death from touching the hems of the fur-trimmed robes.

The room was still as the headsman appeared. The silence lasted as he crossed the great hall and took his place, the great ax laid with ceremony upon the table before him; a symbol of ultimate justice.

That was the point of all this pomp and circumstance. Justice must be done—or must be seen to be done. The King had been dead for more than twenty years; he had died a month before the birth of the twin boys who bore his name, and the country had teetered on the edge of civil war for years, hauled back from the brink only by the efforts of the Queen and her counselors—Edward of Malmsley chief among them. His bones still ached from two months spent on horseback, riding the border counties with Prince Kyle—Kyle, who would ride no more.

The Queen was an excellent regent, a skilled ruler— and yet she held the throne only in trust for the heir. For William. There were no other heirs of the blood royal save the brothers, no one with a sound claim to the throne. And yet the lords and the people would never accept a fratricide as ruler; with Kyle dead and William attainted by his murder, the kingdom would be torn by war as this peer or that strove to seize the throne—if the kingdom survived at all; there were enemies on every side, only watching for the opportunity to prey upon it.

There was only one answer, and Edward had seen it at once, urging this course upon the Queen, who had reluctantly agreed. An open trial, in which all evidence could be presented under the noses of peer and peasant alike—and from which, God willing, William might emerge exonerated, able to claim the throne that would be his.

If one came down to it, only the Queen had the power to condemn a noble—let alone a Prince—no matter what the result of this trial. But if William were proved guilty, might she be compelled to do just that? That was the risk that turned her knuckles white under the ornate rings, and that blanched her cheeks beneath the artful cosmetics she wore to hide both grief and terror. Edward shared her emotions; yet he looked out over the courtroom with an air of remote detachment, as though nothing of great import were happening.

The Justice mounted to his high bench and took his place. With a small rustle of dread, everyone sat down. Everyone save Edward, Lord Malmsley. He remained standing, close to the Queen as always. He was her Minister; it was his duty to attend her, to serve her in any way necessary.

The preliminaries were over; Edward took a deep breath, feeling his chest tighten as the charge was read out.

"That you, William Henry Edgar George Holborn, did feloniously, treacherously, and treasonably murder Kyle Gresham Robert Clarence, Prince and Lord of this realm, upon the seventh day of May, in this year of our Lord . . ."

Treason? Edward felt a small shock at the word, but it was correct; to spill royal blood must by definition be treason—even if the murderer's veins throbbed with the same precious fluid.

Prince William stood straight and silent, head held high as the charge was read. His dark eyes burned, fixed on the small gallery above the hall, where members of the royal court were seated. Edward followed the direction of the Prince's gaze, to the empty seat among the courtiers. He had wondered himself if she would come; that had been the prevailing topic of speculation in the street markets and taverns—would she come to see her husband tried for the murder of his brother—for the murder of her lover?

Opinion in the taverns was mixed, of course. *Had* he been her lover? The women said yes. The men— perhaps affected by startling blue eyes and an appealing air of porcelain frailty—or perhaps unaffected by jealousy—said no.

He glanced at the Queen, straight-figured and composed, her face set in stone, a royal enigma. And what did *she* think? Lord Malmsley knew her as well as any and better than most; he had had years of practice in interpreting her slightest move, her lightest wish. The tones of her voice and the play of light upon her features yielded meaning to him as the stink of sulphur and the glow of flame yielded secrets to an alchemist—and yet just now, her face told him nothing.

On the other hand, the Queen was a woman. And the Princess, Lady Eilidh, however innocent, was the cause of the death of one son—and maybe both. Innocent she might be, but Lord Malmsley doubted that the Queen would hold her blameless.

The tiresome preliminaries were complete, and a stir of anticipation fluttered through the great hall as the Prosecutor stepped forward to state the case against the accused. The Prosecutor was a small man, but fierce in aspect, rather like a kestrel, Edward thought.

"Your Majesty, my lords and ladies . . ." the formalities began, the punctilious address that set the ponderous machine of Justice in movement, gears beginning to turn slowly, slowly. The oil of evidence and supposition would lubricate them, the machinery would pick up speed, until finally the juggernaut rolled mercilessly to its end, flattening whomever stood in its path.

At last, the Prosecutor launched himself upon the description of the crime.

". . . that on the morning of May seventh, the prisoner did willfully murder . . ."

Edward felt a shudder run through him. He had no need to hear this; he had seen it.

It had happened near the family mausoleum, that marble monument to the Holborns. Set in the center of a maze of clipped yew, surrounded by flowering trees and benches for meditation, the royal tomb and its chapel were a peaceful retreat, and it was not unheard of for impious couples to use its messuages for less-than-reverential purposes, particularly in the warm weather. There were few men at court who had never stolen at least a kiss—and often more—in the shadows of the royal tomb or the hidden alleys of the yew maze.

Edward surreptitiously removed a handkerchief and blotted sweat from beneath his pointed black beard. It was more than warm in the courtroom, with its press of unwashed bodies.

The weather had been warm on May the seventh, and the Princess had taken the opportunity—she said, the Prosecutor added, with a heavy emphasis—to fetch fresh flowers to the tomb, to honor the old King's spirit on the anniversary of his birth.

She had come to the tomb alone, without the company of her ladies, her pageboy, her dog—with no attendants whatever. *How very suspicious*, said the Prosecutor's tone, though his words did not.

It *was* suspicious. Princesses did not live alone, and very seldom *were* alone. If they were unmarried, they never stirred far without a coterie of ladies, guards, and attendants. They moved constantly but slowly, like giant roses swaying in the wind, surrounded by bees. If married, they were sometimes alone—but only with their husbands.

Prince William, Eilidh's husband, had been heard to say the night before that he proposed to spend the day in solitary hawking. No one supposed, therefore, that the Princess might be found in his company; she did not care for the blood sports that were her husband's joy.

More and more suspicious, the Prosecutor's face said plainly, bright eyes gleaming as he traced the threads of his story, like a kestrel hovering, tracing out the path of his scampering prey.

It had, in fact, been suspicious enough for the Lady Marietta, chief among the ladies in waiting, to have come looking for her mistress. Quietly, discreetly, raising no outcry. The Lady Marietta had grown up in the same household with the Princess; they were as close as sisters. Lady Marietta would have been careful to do nothing that might harm her mistress, or cause talk. Unable to find the Princess, and worried by her absence, therefore, she had gone to find Edward, himself the soul of discretion—and the only person at court who could be trusted to keep secrets, for he kept everyone's.

Oddly enough, he had sensed nothing amiss when Marietta found him. It was a glorious day, with the scent of apple blossom on the breeze and pale green butterflies floating over the lawns. No wonder if the Princess had risen before dawn and had gone out alone, drawn by the silken touch of the air, the song of lark and blackbird. Anyone might wish a few minutes alone, to savor such an untouched morning.

So he told Lady Marietta, reassuring her. But he would go himself to look—just in case. Sending Marietta back to search the stillrooms, in case her mistress had been seized by a domestic impulse (he thought it unlikely, but one could never tell with women), he turned to the gardens, and began to quarter the paths and parterres in methodical fashion, enjoying the task, even as he wondered with half a mind what the Princess might be doing.

He had had his horoscope cast only the day before; *a day of change*, the astrologer had told him blandly. So much for augury!

When they asked, later, what had led him to the mausoleum, Edward said merely that he had thought of paying his respects. There was a chapel next to the mausoleum, and it was not uncommon for him to go there, he was the King's elder half brother, after all—born of a different father, but close to his royal sibling until the latter's unfortunate death.

In fact, what had led him there was a scream. He had finished his search of the orchard and the herbary, and was headed for the rose garden and its ornamental grotto, when he heard the scream from the center of the maze.

He knew the maze well, and it took no more than moments to thread the paths through the eight-foot walls of yew. What he saw when he arrived, breathless and disheveled from running, was what the Prosecutor was even now describing, in a deceptively simple fashion that, if anything, enhanced the grisly power of the image.

"Prince Kyle lay upon the grass at the lady's feet, dead of a dagger wound. Prince William, his brother, was present, his arms locked about his wife."

Almost true, thought Edward. No supposition by the court as to the nature of William's embrace. By avoiding such supposition, of course, it was left open whether it had been a true embrace of husbandly support—or an attempt to keep Eilidh from hurling herself upon the body of her fallen lover. And by not stating it baldly, the Prosecutor left room for people to imagine the worst—something people were always ready, willing, and quite able to do.

The other small detail lacking from the Prosecutor's account was the fact that Kyle had not been quite dead when Edward arrived upon the scene. Edward had, however, thought it entirely unnecessary to tell the crown's investigator that Prince Kyle's last word had been "Whore!" gasped in the direction of his brother's wife. Evidently, neither William nor the Princess had found it desirable to mention this, either. There were no other witnesses; by the time the Captain of the Guard arrived, a few moments later, Kyle was forever silent.

". . . This vicious crime of fratricide, perhaps planned, perhaps with the connivance of other parties . . ."

"No! That is not true!" All heads turned, gaping in surprise. The Prince stood upright in the dock, broad hands gripping the rail as though to tear it out.

"Your Highness . . ." began the Prosecutor, but the Prince's own barrister was already there, a restraining hand upon the Prince's arm, muttering in his ear.

The Prince at length relaxed his grip upon the wood, and with a grudging nod, stood back—but his burning eyes were now fixed upon the Prosecutor, rather than on the empty chair across the room.

At last the Prosecutor ceased speaking, and the Queen's Counsel, the barrister who would speak for the Prince, stood up. QC was a large and florid man of commanding presence. Just to look at him made one feel that things were in good hands; there was a sense of relief among the crowd as he turned slowly round, meeting the eyes of each peer in turn before he began to speak.

"My lords," he said, and his voice was low and pleasant, though it carried clearly to the back of the hall. "We are met upon this sad occasion in order to discover the truth. Not to witness the destruction of a man—to discover the truth, and only that.

"There is no question that a terrible tragedy has occurred; a man lies dead. There is also no question how that death came about; Prince William admits that his brother met his death at his hand."

A collective sound of awe and excitement rumbled through the crowd, instantly stilled as the QC held up a large and immaculate hand.

"The truth that we must discover, my lords, is *why*. What events led to this horrible occurrence, this unspeakable tragedy which has afflicted the royal house? The truth, my lords, is this."

He bowed very low, as though in apology for what he was about to say, in the direction of the Queen. She did not acknowledge the respect, but sat immobile, waiting to hear what he would say. It would come as no surprise; Lord Malmsley had spent hours with the Queen's Counsel the day before, rehearsing versions of this speech.

The QC began, with great eloquence, to paint a picture of the Prince's marriage. True, it was a marriage contracted for reasons of state, but one—he said—that had grown into a relationship of great attachment. The Prince and his wife were known to be a most thoroughly united couple, devoted to each other. And how could this be otherwise, in view of the great virtue and saintly character of the Princess Eilidh? Heads turned to steal a glance at the empty chair— but it was no longer empty.

Princess Eilidh sat in her place, the small oval of her face dead-white, but her head held up and her chin raised proudly. She wore full mourning, and the black silk set off her pale skin and fiery hair like pearls and rubies in a setting of jet.

Excitement flared among the crowd, with small cries and spontaneous cheers, quelled with some difficulty by the bailiffs. All eyes were upon her—even the Queen's—but not Edward's. He looked instead at the prisoner. The young man's eyes were fixed on his wife, but there was no sign of relief upon his countenance, or thankfulness at her appearance. He looked both shocked and fearful.

Luckily, the look of fear left his face in an instant, as he recollected his position. He stood up straight and stern, once more in possession of himself, every inch the King's son. With luck, Edward thought, glancing covertly round the room, no one else had noticed that momentary lapse.

William met his wife's eyes now, nodding encouragement. His hands were clenched tight on the wooden rail, and his body leaned slightly toward her, as though he wished to vault the rail and run to her.

Eilidh did not smile back, though her trembling lips made a small attempt. She did meet William's eye, though, and made no effort to look away—doubtless QC had coached her well.

Pleased with the effect of his showmanship, the Queen's Counsel had paused, to let the audience enjoy the full effect of this dramatic reunion.

"Alas," said the QC, a tone of deep sorrow entering his voice, "the lady's beauty of form and character had attracted the notice of her brother-in-law, Prince Kyle." QC was careful to face the ranks of the peers as he put this delicate part of the case; he would not face the Queen as he painted her dead son in the vilest colors.

Edward couldn't see the Queen's face—he knew she would not change expression, in any case—but he saw her fingers curled tight over the rounded ends of her chair's arms, nails dug into the furling fiddle-heads that formed its ornamentation. He wanted very much to take the one step forward that would bring him close enough for her to feel his presence, and be reminded that he was there.

"It is necessary," he had told her, with emphasis. "Kyle is dead; nothing can harm him further. But no one was present save William and his wife. If we are to save William, we cannot merely insist that he is innocent—plainly it was his hand that struck down Kyle. The only possibility is to provide an explanation for the deed that will exonerate him in the eyes of the populace."

He delicately refrained from pointing out the fact that this explanation was the one that both William and his wife had—however reluctantly—supplied, and that there were no other explanations apparent. No matter how loath the Queen might be to believe her younger son a seducer and a rapist, no matter how painful it might be to hear him so described . . . the only alternative was to brand William a cold-blooded murderer, his wife an accessory—and condemn them both.

QC concluded his own judicial condemnation, and heaved a great sigh. He was sweating visibly, his heavy face damp and red, broad shoulders slumping under the weight of his tale. *Such a pity*, his sorrowful manner suggested.

"A tragedy, a waste," he said, very quietly. "I beg you, my lords, do not compound the tragedy. Let it stop here."

He bowed to the peers, again to the Justice, and finally, deeply, to the Queen. The court stood recessed.

* * *

The Queen vanished through the door at the end of the hall, moving like a small, self-contained storm, followed by a black cloud of attendants. There was nothing Edward could do there; perhaps he might be of use elsewhere. Ignoring the greetings and muted cordialities of the assembled peers, he slipped away and out of the massive building that housed the court.

Once free of the sense of oppression and constraint that filled the place, he felt his breath come freer, in spite of the press of townsfolk around him. Soberly dressed as he always was, and with a dark cloak hiding his silk doublet and gold chain of office, he passed unnoticed—as was his usual practice. In the taproom of the Goat and Grapes, he might have passed for one of the prosperous merchants who mingled with the lower classes in a common thirst for the local cider.

A good many of those at the public house had come from the court, eager to exchange views on the morning's experience. Edward found himself wedged into a dark corner, listening to the conversation of a carter and a couple of cloth merchants.

"A dreadful thing," one cloth seller said, shaking a heavy head. "Dreadful!"

"'Tis," agreed his companion. "I cannot think who I am more sorry for—the Queen or Her Highness. Poor women!"

"Aye. Still, thank the good God it was *him*," the carter said, then crossed himself, no doubt feeling such a wish unworthy, if not quite blasphemous. "Might have been Prince William, I mean."

Unworthy the sentiment might be, but almost universal, judging from the conversation surging to and fro around him. While the twins were as like to look at as peas in a pod, their personalities could not have been more diverse.

Born on either side of midnight, one was day and one was night. Oddly enough, it was William, the night-born, who shone like the sun, full of bonhomie and courage, gaining repute as a warrior by the time of his eighteenth birthday. Bluff and cordial, he was possessed of the common touch, and was a popular figure.

Kyle, the day-born, lived always in his brother's shadow—unavoidable, Edward supposed, given that William was heir. Still, Kyle was shier than his brother, and given to sullenness. Lacking his brother's delight in sport and combat, he had the reputation also of a weakling, if not an outright coward—though Edward, who had had the opportunity to observe the boys closely since their babyhood, was not so sure.

Still, public opinion was already favorably disposed toward William, so far as Edward could tell—and he was skilled at judging such things. With a small sense of optimism, he made his way back through the crowded streets toward the court.

The trial resumed and a string of witnesses was called, to repeat obedient testimony to the great devotion between husband and wife. Some were more convincing than others, Edward thought cynically. He had himself heard rumors of trouble in that marriage, and had not been surprised.

William's public face might be sunny, but in private, he had a tendency to brood, and no compunction over letting his bad moods affect those closest to him. He was sufficiently considerate as a husband, Edward supposed, and there was no open coldness, but he had himself seen no sign of great rapport between Prince William and his wife. It was a marriage of arrangement, and while both Prince and Princess were undoubtedly dutiful, he thought there had never been great passion—not till now.

Still, on the surface, all had seemed well, and no testimony was brought forth that said otherwise.

The next witness was more disturbing. An assistant groom, trembling with nervousness, who was nonetheless brought to admit that he had overheard portions of a quarrel between the brothers, a few days before the crime.

"Where did this quarrel take place?" The Prosecutor leaned forward, hands folded, bright eyes fixed on the squirming witness as though he were a tasty mouse.

"In the stable," the groom muttered. He looked down into his lap, reluctant to meet anyone's eye.

"And you were yourself present?"

"No. Yes—I mean, I were in t'stable, but they couldn't see me. I were cleanin' of t'harness in the tack room, and they were in the main part."

"I see. And will you tell the court, sir, what you heard?"

The groom blew out his cheeks, disconcerted at the prospect of formulating sentences. With skillful prodding by the Prosecutor, though, he reluctantly supplied such bits of conversation as he had overheard. The Princes had been quarreling over a woman, he was sure of that much. No, the woman's name had not been spoken; they only mentioned "she."

One man was reproaching the other for his treatment of the woman, the other retorted that his brother had no business to be concerned. There was the sound of a brief scuffle, of boots scraping stone, and the noise of a solid object striking the wooden door of a stall. One man walked away, fast. The other—presumably him who had been thrown—said something in a low voice that the groom took for a curse, and departed a moment later.

QC, upon arising to question the witness, led him slowly through the sequence of events once more, but halted at one point in the testimony.

"Wait. One moment." The QC raised one finger, considering. "Did he say, 'You have no business to concern yourself in this matter,' or was it perhaps, 'You have *no reason for concern?*' Might not the speaker have been assuring his brother that his suspicions were unfounded?"

The groom stared at him, hopelessly befuddled.

"Dunno . . . sir," he said.

Likewise, he had no notion which of the Princes had said what—but he was confident that it had been Their Highnesses, on that point he was sure. No one doubted it; both young men had distinctive voices, deep, with a slight rasp; neither could be mistaken for anyone else.

A brief recess, and the court reconvened, to hear the testimony of the Lady Marietta, chief lady in waiting to the Princess.

No, she said. She knew of no trouble between the Princess and her husband, though—honesty compelled her to add—naturally no one was privy to the couple's most intimate moments.

The Lady Marietta was either a very poor liar, Edward thought, or a very good one. Had it been a mistake to call her—or a clever ploy? His musings on the possibility were sharply interrupted with the calling of the next witness—the Princess.

She came to the witness box on the arm of the Chancellor, walking like one in a dream. A bad dream, at that. The crowd was riveted; murmurs of deep sympathy ran through the room like ocean currents.

Even the Prosecutor's manner was modified from its usual sharpness; the stooping hawk became a dove, cooing reassurance and leading the Princess by gentle stages into the labyrinth of her narrative.

"How did Your Highness come to be in that particular place?"

"I—I had gone to take fresh flowers to the chapel. It was the old King's anniversary."

"Quite." The Prosecutor gave a polite nod, approving of this filial piety. "Did anyone accompany you on this errand?"

"No." Eilidh was so pale that the slight reddening around her nostrils made the skin look raw. "I was alone. I . . . wished to ask a special blessing."

The Prosecutor lifted a brow, considering whether to inquire about the nature of this blessing, but discarded the notion in favor of his next planned question.

"Ah, yes. Tell me, Your Highness, when did the Princes join you?"

She grew paler still, the final vestiges of color leaching from her lips.

"My—that is—Prince Kyle . . . came out from the maze. He said he had been f-following me."

The story emerged in fits and jerks, hampered by the Princess's obvious reluctance to speak, compelled by the Prosecutor's gentle persistence. Prince Kyle, she said, had been . . . forward in his manner. This forwardness progressed, and the Prince had horrified her by making a declaration, proclaiming his love for her, and desiring her to come away with him—to leave her husband, and flee to some far country.

Edward glanced at the dock; William stood like stone, burning eyes fixed on his wife. She did not look in his direction.

"This proposal was unwelcome to Your Highness?" The Prosecutor put the question with delicacy.

"I—yes." She swallowed, and every eye in the room followed the delicate ripple of her throat. The last traces of bruising showed beneath the edge of her high collar, smears of yellow and green on the whiteness of her skin.

"You refused him?" the Prosecutor asked bluntly.

A low growl from the dock caused several heads to turn in that direction, but they turned immediately back, eager to miss nothing.

"I refused him."

"What was his reaction to your refusal?"

"He—struck me. And he . . ." The Princess lowered her head, but the sudden wave of crimson that swept up from her collar was clearly visible.

"He attacked you?"

She nodded, head still down. Her fingers twisted the fabric at the neck of her gown, as though to tug its modesty still higher.

"And what happened then?"

She shook her head, speechless for a moment. Then she cleared her throat, struggling to speak.

"I—I am not sure. I was dazed, you see . . . he . . . he choked me, and I had lost breath, my eyes had gone dark. I thought I was d-dead." She sniffed and gulped, and there were echoing sniffs from among the audience.

She had come to herself lying upon the grass, with her husband's arms about her, his voice calling to her as he tried to rouse her. It was not for several moments that she came to herself enough to recall what had happened, or to look about her. When she did . . .

She stopped speaking, a look of dull horror on her face.

"Your Highness?" the Prosecutor prompted.

She did not answer, but only stared blindly, as though seeing in the recesses of her mind the dead man upon the grass and the flowing blood. Her eyes rolled up, and she sank senseless to the floor.

Court was recessed for the day, amid pandemonium.

"So far, so good." Edward leaned against the closed door of the chamber, and let his muscles relax momentarily. The effort of anxious hours standing in court, controlling the slightest twitch of face or body, followed by more hours of pushing through the crowded streets and fetid inn yards, had left him feeling as though he had ridden for days.

"You think so, do you?" the Queen answered dryly. She stood in the recessed window, looking out over the south lawn. Far away, at the edge of the ornamental wood, was the dark green smear of the yew maze.

"Why, yes." Edward crossed to stand beside her, and took one of her hands in his. It was well tended, but small and cold. "The Prosecutor made good show of impartiality, QC made better show of outraged innocence—and the talk in the taverns is much in support of William. I should be much surprised if he is not acquitted upon the morrow."

"I should."

He glanced down at her, startled. The strains of the last week had ravaged her face and shadowed her exotic beauty, but she looked in no way distraught by her grief.

"Whatever do you mean?"

"I mean," she said with a small sigh, "that William is dead."

He should, he thought, have been more shocked than he was. He did feel the jolt of her statement—felt it clear to the bones of his feet—but in the center of his being, some small uneasiness slipped over the edge into open acknowledgment. He had not known—but knowing now, was not in truth greatly startled. Something in him, watching the young man in the dock, must have sensed the truth.

If not startled, though, he was certainly appalled.

"It is Kyle? You are sure?" Even as he spoke, he knew that was a foolish question. She took her hand from his, with a small gesture of impatience.

"Certainly. To mimic William's manner is no great trick; half the boys at court have done it. I saw Kyle himself do it once—but only once."

Edward nodded. He remembered. The brothers now and then had exchanged names and places as japery when they were children, just as any twins might do. As they grew, though, and their characters became distinct, they ceased to take each other's identities, each jealous of his own growing talents. Once, though, at a masque, they had done it, William becoming Kyle and Kyle William—and a young and flighty girl who fancied William had made much of the brother she thought *was* William, only to make a scene upon discovering the truth. Kyle had never again adopted even the slightest shadow of his brother's essence. Until now.

Edward's mind, jarred by the concussion of shock, began to work again.

"Does Eilidh know?" he asked, and was rewarded by a small nod of approval from the Queen. A good question.

"I don't know. She hasn't seen him since the crime, and quite possibly she could not tell from his demeanor in the dock. So the question really is—does she know which of them was killed?"

"Almost certainly." He had seen no point at the time in distressing the Queen with the detail of her dying son's final word, but clearly matters had altered now. He acquainted her quickly with the truth, and watched her almond eyes darken as she heard it.

"Whore," she said softly. "Her *husband* called her whore?"

"He may have been mistaken," Edward reminded her.

"Mistaken or not," she said with an edge to her voice, "no man makes such an accusation without grounds."

There was a great terrestrial globe near the center of the room; a pretty thing inlaid with semiprecious stones, its seas dark lapis, with the masses of land in mother-of-pearl, the cities picked out in glowing jewels. The Queen rested her hand upon it, then gave it a sudden strong push, so it spun upon its axis. Edward watched the globe spin and slow in silence. It was an inescapable implication; that Kyle had indeed been Eilidh's lover. If William had killed his brother in defense of his wife's honor, it was both scandal and tragedy, but one that left husband—or supposed husband—and wife with their lives and reputations intact. If Kyle had seduced his brother's wife, then killed William with the intent of taking his place . . . Edward shuddered briefly, feeling as though a cold hand had touched his spine.

"If it is true," he said at last, reluctantly, "William's death might still have been an accident."

He caught a glance from dark and brooding eyes.

"Accident? He was stabbed through the heart." Her lips pressed tight together; he could see grief at the thought constrict her throat. He realized that for her, this revelation was like living through the death of her son once more—having suffered Kyle's death, now she must suffer William's. And whatever joy there might be for her in finding Kyle still alive must be overwhelmed in the enormity of his crime.

"There is a difference, surely," he said gently. "If William came upon them suddenly, perhaps began to threaten Eilidh, or to attack his brother . . . then Kyle might have struck in self-defense. Not the same thing as a cold-blooded plot, to murder William and steal both his wife and his inheritance."

"No," the Queen said bleakly. "Not the same thing—but most likely with the same result."

He knew what she was thinking—that having lost one son, she was now faced with the immediate probability of losing the other as well, if the truth were revealed.

"Regardless," Edward said firmly. "We must know the truth—*you* must know the truth."

"Yes," she whispered, and set a hand on the globe to stop it. Her hand was ivory, her rings glowing like submerged continents—truth rising from the depths. "Go and find out."

Kyle first, or the Princess? Edward hesitated outside the Royal quarters, then turned in the direction of the Princess's suite. Kyle was under close guard, and while Her Majesty's Minister could of course gain access to him, it would cause comment. Also, he knew from experience that Kyle possessed considerable stubbornness; best to learn as much as possible, then, before he spoke to the heir to the throne.

Was that it? he wondered, as he made his way through the labyrinthine hallways. Did he do it to be King? Kyle might have been jealous of his brother's popularity, but he had never shown any sign that he envied the responsibilities of rule. Of course, Edward reminded himself, Kyle was evidently much better at keeping secrets than anyone had suspected.

And as to the keeping of secrets, of course . . .

Was it even vaguely possible that the Princess did not know which brother had killed which? That she was under the illusion that her husband was still alive?

No. Impossible. Kyle might—by keeping quiet as much as possible—fool most people into believing he was William, but he had not fooled his mother, and surely could not fool William's wife; certainly not in the midst of committing murder.

Which meant—Edward paused outside the Princess's quarters to draw breath and straighten his doublet—which meant that Eilidh was an accomplice, at the least, to whatever events had occurred in the maze. But might she have been something more? The instigator of the crime?

In the event, Edward got no further than the outer chamber of the Princess's suite. Her Highness was asleep, he was informed with great firmness, and could not be disturbed, by order of her doctor.

The doctor himself was just taking his departure; Edward caught a glimpse of the distinctive square-topped red hat vanishing around the turn of the staircase below. Seized by impulse, he thundered down the stairs in pursuit, formulating questions as he went. An inquiry as to the Princess's state of health was quite in order; a cautious probing as to anything she might have said upon recovering consciousness could probably be slipped in without exciting too much attention.

He caught up with the doctor outside, just as the latter was ascending the steps of his carriage. The doctor turned, frowning at the hand upon his sleeve, but immediately altered his expression to one of cordial respect upon seeing his interlocutor.

"Oh, your lordship."

"Doctor." Edward bowed, gasping slightly for breath. "If I might—a small word with you?"

"I must go—I'm called to a birthing—but come along, why don't you?" The doctor gestured toward the open door of the carriage. "We can talk on the way, and my driver will bring you back."

Edward stepped into the soft dimness of the coach, congratulating himself on a stroke of luck. Now he had the doctor safely sequestered, away from prying ears, and plenty of time to question him with subtlety.

Subtlety turned out to be unneeded; while the doctor of course had the discretion of his profession, he clearly thought it unnecessary to be discreet with the Queen's Chief Minister. The Princess, he said, was quite healthy—allowing for the strain of circumstances, of course. Still, he had advised complete rest, in case the emotional distress should lead to unfortunate results.

"Unfortunate?" Edward raised his brows, hoping that the light provided by the tiny lantern that hung near his head would be sufficient to convey his expression of encouraging curiosity. "Do you mean . . . ?"

Evidently so; the doctor smiled, with an attitude of proprietorial benevolence.

"Yes, she is with child. A great blessing and consolation—to Her Majesty, as well as to the country, at this sad time. Even if Prince William should . . . er . . . that is to say . . ." The doctor coughed, embarrassed, and muttered, "a great consolation," a few more times.

"Yes," Edward said dryly. "I'm sure it would be." The throne would have an heir, even if William—or rather Kyle—were to be executed for the murder of his brother—but he thought the consolation to the Queen might be somewhat less than the doctor evidently hoped.

"Mind you," the doctor said, leaning close in confidentiality, "care must be taken. The Princess is in good health, and I see no cause for alarm, but it's early days, you know, early days." He shook his head, frowning slightly. "Much can go amiss. I took the precaution, after seeing Her Highness, of inquiring as to the details of her diet and other habits. Teas she might be fond of, medicines she might take—all that sort of thing."

The doctor reached into his bag and drew out a small bundle, wrapped in cloth, and tied with a length of thread, and handed it to Edward. Seen close to, the thread was really three threads twisted together; one of red, one of yellow, and one of black. A tiny ornament of carved stone was tied to the end of the thread, and Edward felt a small internal tremor at the sight of it.

"What do you think of that, hey?" the doctor demanded. "Know what it is?"

Edward raised the bundle to his nose. It smelled of bayberry, hellebore, and something else he could not name, but recognized instantly. In a flash, he was no longer seated in a carriage, bumping down the road. He was in the back room of a filthy inn, staring into the face of an old gypsy crone, counting the stumps of her remaining teeth as she counted out his pieces of silver. He shut his eyes hard, blinked, and found himself once more in the coach, the lantern swaying beside his ear.

He sucked the inside of his cheek, trying to bring a little moisture to a mouth gone suddenly dry.

"A charm of some sort?" he hazarded.

The doctor snorted. "You could say that. Gypsy rubbish. A tea of some kind, the lady said. Probably some foolish love-philter or the like."

"What lady?" Edward handled back the bundle, gingerly, as though it might explode.

"The Lady Marietta. Her Highness was too indisposed to speak, so I put her to bed, then made her chief lady in waiting come with me to look over her medicines and answer questions. This is likely harmless"—he tossed the bundle carelessly in his hand—"but no sense in taking chances. No telling what the gypsies might have put in. Thought I'd best take it away with me, just in case."

"Very wise of you," Edward murmured. "Very wise indeed."

It was late by the time he returned to the palace, and he was both tired and hungry. He didn't pause to eat, though, but went at once to the Princess's quarters, in search of the Lady Marietta.

The lady was asleep, her maid insisted, scandalized—but Lord Malmsley was not one to take no for an answer at the best of times—and at the worst of times, mannerly considerations went up before him like chaff in a fire.

He smiled pleasantly at the maid, who was a small woman. He reached out and took her by the waist, then picked her up and set her on top of the ornamental cabinet by the door. Her mouth was still open in shock as Lord Malmsley pushed through the door. As she opened her mouth to call for help, she heard a grating sound from the other side. Edward had bolted the door behind him.

The Lady Marietta, he saw, was *not* asleep. As he stepped from the sitting room into her boudoir, he saw her standing by the window, fully clothed, a lighted taper in her hand.

"Waiting up for someone?" he inquired pleasantly.

She whirled with a gasp, dropping the taper. It went out before it struck the floor, and Edward gallantly bent to retrieve it.

"Permit me, madam."

She reached hesitantly for the taper, and he grasped her wrist, dragging her away from the window.

Ordinarily, the Lady Marietta looked anything but rodentlike, being tall and lissome, with a sweet round face and a guileless gaze. At the moment, though, she bore a strong resemblance to a trapped rat. Black eyes gleaming in terror, she wrenched at her wrist, trying to pull away. Edward gripped harder.

"I know who is dead and who is not," he said, speaking low. "If you and your mistress do not wish to join Prince William, you will tell me what you know, and tell me now!"

"Join him? In prison?" Marietta looked horrified, but he had felt the tightening, then the relaxing of her arm. She knew, all right.

"In the grave, madam." He let go of her wrist, quite suddenly, and crossed to the window. From this window, there was a view of the royal stables, with the wood beyond. And far in the distance, barely visible beyond the trees, the rounded dome of the King's tomb. Everything outside was peaceful, the garden below bathed in starlight. Nothing moved.

He turned from the window. Marietta backed warily away from him, stealing a glance at the door to the sitting room beyond.

"Pamela!" she called. "Pam, come here, I want you!"

"Want all you like," he said. "The door is bolted, with your maid on the other side." He came forward and took her—more gently—by the arm, bringing her to the big window. He sat down upon the window seat, and compelled her to sit down with him. She sat opposite him, head down, ostentatiously rubbing her bruised wrist.

"I have been talking with the doctor," Edward began, speaking pleasantly. "Fortunately, he had never seen a *tezana* bundle before. I have."

Marietta was regaining her poise.

"I am not surprised," she said coolly. "You have the reputation of a man of the world, Lord Malmsley—and no known bastards to your credit."

He ignored that.

"Was it you who procured it for her? How did you know where to go?"

"I know a lot of things." Her face was calm now, but her eyes made no pretense of guilelessness.

"You know where to get the medicine to rid a woman of an unwanted child. I suppose that also means you know exactly why the child *is* unwanted."

"It is not unwanted." Her lips pressed tightly together. "She would not take the medicine."

"Indeed." Edward pursed his lips, studying the implications. "Hm. Does Kyle know about the child?"

"Kyle is dead." Her forehead was puckered. "Isn't he?"

He had thought in court that she wasn't a good liar. He still thought so. He sighed with exasperation.

"Cease this pretense, madam," he said. "If Her

Highness trusted you with one secret, she has trusted you with this one, as well. I'll ask again—does Prince Kyle know that Eilidh is with child?"

Her lower lip protruded as she glowered at him, like a sulky child.

"I can ask him," he reminded her. "And I will." She sighed, shoulders slumping in surrender.

"No. He doesn't know."

Edward took a deep breath, in some obscure way relieved. It didn't *prove* that Kyle hadn't been Eilidh's lover, he reminded himself—but it did seem to lessen the probabilities. He tugged at his beard, considering—and then stopped suddenly, feeling as though he had been hit in the stomach. He glanced sharply at Lady Marietta.

"It cannot be Kyle's child. She would have no difficulty in passing it off as William's, were that the case."

She smiled ironically, waiting for him to make the next deduction.

"Unless William had reason to believe that any child of his wife's was not sired by him."

She inclined her head, acknowledging the conclusion.

"My lord hasn't shared his wife's bed in six months." She studied her nails. "I didn't ask why."

Edward drew a hand down over his face, dragging the skin over his features. It was very late, and he felt as though he had been awake for years. He sighed.

"If Kyle doesn't know about the child, why should he have killed William?"

"To be King?" Marietta suggested. "Or—perhaps for love of my mistress?"

"I have never seen any evidence that Kyle desires the throne," Edward said slowly, "and I know him well. The other . . . perhaps. Though that, too, seems unlikely. It is difficult to hide the signs of such passion as might result in a child—in a place like this?" He waved a hand, indicating the palace around them, with its thousand eyes and its thousand tongues. "I cannot believe that Kyle might have pursued such an affair, to the point that he could commit murder—and have Eilidh accept it—without some indication. And I should know, he has been with me—" He stopped, the next word dead on his tongue.

"I am a fool," he said softly. "Kyle has been with me for two months, on the borders. The child cannot possibly be his."

The Lady Marietta bowed again.

"Perhaps you are tired," she suggested sympathetically. "I am sure you would have recalled that sooner, if your mind was working with its accustomed brilliance."

Edward stood up, too agitated to notice her sarcasm.

"Who?" he barked.

"Do you think I know?" she asked innocently.

He seized her wrist again, in a grip that made her cry out.

"You do, and you will tell me," he growled. "You owe no loyalty to a woman who would deceive her husband and then lead his brother to risk death for her sake!"

"She wouldn't!"

"She did!"

"Not—not Kyle. If the verdict goes against him, she will speak. She told me so."

"And what good would her speaking do? Speak and tell everyone who he is? It would only serve to condemn him more certainly!"

"Not if she speaks the truth." Lady Marietta pulled away from him, her round face pale in the shadows. He made a motion toward her, and she put out a hand, gesturing to the window seat. "Sit. I will tell you all you want to know. Will you have wine?" She waved a hand at the jug that sat on the table nearby.

"No. I—yes, I will have some. Thank you." So he sat, sipping wine, and watched the lady pace slowly to and fro on the Oriental carpet, as she told him the story.

William had married as had Eilidh, for duty, but finding himself mismatched with his quiet, shy wife, had sought refuge in the company of his companions, hunting, drinking, and wenching in the towns. When his wife ventured to criticize his behavior, he turned sullen, avoiding her company or speaking only in cruelty when with her.

Lonely and frightened of her husband, the Princess had been vulnerable to . . . sympathy.

"Sympathy," Edward said dryly. "I see."

Marietta turned sharply on him.

"I do not say it was right. I understand it, that is all. It was only once. Easy enough for you or me to say she should have been stronger. It was sympathy she wanted. What she got—" She shrugged and turned away to resume her pacing.

There had been a quarrel that morning. William had come in late from an evening of drinking and been roused early by the Princess's dog, yapping near his bed. He had rolled out of bed and kicked the dog across the room, then abused its mistress, shouting curses and threats at her.

The Princess, much distressed, had left their chamber as quickly as she could, and seeking to hide herself, had gone to the maze. William pursued her, though, full of threats and vile names. Kyle had been in the garden, talking with Marietta. Seeing his brother stomping through the herbary, down the path Eilidh had just taken, he took a hasty leave of Marietta and followed William.

"So he came upon them at the King's tomb, and—what? Killed William because he was threatening Eilidh?"

Marietta sighed.

"He did not kill William."

"What? You do not mean to tell me that the Princess—?"

"Certainly not," she said crossly. "Though I should myself have thought her justified." She frowned at him. "You are very stupid tonight, Lord Malmsley. Kyle was not the only one who heard William uttering threats against his wife."

"Ah, the unknown lover," Edward said, sarcastic. "You mean that he—this man, whoever he was—is the murderer?"

"I do."

"Very convenient," Edward said in a tone of utter disbelief. "How gallant."

She stamped her foot in exasperation.

"Believe me or not, as you like! He heard the things William was calling Eilidh, and sprang to the conclusion that William knew about the child. It was not gallantry, it was cowardice! If William learned that he had seduced the Princess, he would be arrested and executed—so he dashed from the maze, snatched William's dagger from his belt, and stabbed him."

Edward drained the rest of his glass in one gulp and lowered it, glaring at her.

"And Kyle then came upon this scene, and—"

"And thought that the Princess had killed William," she interrupted. "He—the man—heard Kyle coming and ran away, back into the maze. There are a dozen blind alleys where one can hide; you know that."

He nodded, somewhat dazed.

"So Kyle is pretending to be William, and to have killed himself, because they might conceivably get away with the notion of a husband killing to defend his wife's honor—and he is doing this for her, even though he thinks she killed his brother?"

"He knew William," she said simply. "And he does love her, I think."

Edward heaved a sigh that came from the roots of his soul.

"And if he is condemned, she will confess everything?"

"Yes. She would never see an innocent man die for her—or even a guilty one." An odd note in her voice made him look up, to see her staring through the window. The moon was setting, just visible above the trees, its silvery radiance setting the dome of the King's tomb aglow.

"The Captain of the Guard," she said, almost gently. "He will have escaped the city by now; I saw him ride out from the stables just as you came in."

* * *

A glow of red stained the eastern sky, as Edward spoke to the guard outside the place where the Prince was held prisoner. It was all most irregular, but Lord Malmsley *was* the Queen's Minister—and when the uncertain guard sent to seek advice from his superior, it appeared that the superior in question could not be found. As a ripple of inquiry began to spread through the barracks, the heavy door swung open, and Edward stepped in.

"Your Highness," he said.

As the air lightened to the pale fresh gray of dawn, a small procession made its way through the palace, toward the great double doors that guarded the Queen's private quarters. The Queen's Minister, Lord Malmsley, with two guards, their halberds stiffly held across their chests—and the hollow-eyed figure of a young man, who stumbled slightly from the fatigue of a week of sleepless nights.

The Queen turned from the long windows at the far side of the room as they entered. She had plainly not slept, either; the fine-boned face was like cracked ivory, the almond eyes dark holes. But a small glow seemed to rise in her face at the sight of them.

"Kyle," she said softly. "Oh, Kyle!"

Until that moment, Edward would have said that she had loved both twins with complete impartiality. Perhaps she had—but now the son she had thought dead was restored to her, and she grasped his hand as though she would never let it go.

She held it still, as Edward began his story, her face changing from anxiety to shock, settling at last into an expression he knew well—the small frown of duty. She released her son's hand, and stood thinking for a moment, then turned to him with great formality.

"It is yours to say," she said. "What will you have us do?"

What, indeed? If the truth were revealed, Kyle would be free, his reputation restored—but as for the Princess and her unborn child ... And yet if the truth were not told, and the fiction allowed to stand, Kyle—as William—would live with the weight of his brother's death. Kyle—as Kyle—would not only be dead, but forever dishonored.

Kyle's face was shadowed, but not by indecision.

"I am William," he said softly. "Let it be."

"Can you truly do this?" asked his mother, the frown growing deeper. "Bear the burden of your brother? Let your honor stand in dishonor, your own name forever tarnished, your brother's bright, though he was unworthy of it? Take a woman who does not love you, and a child not your own? Forswear yourself and live another's life?"

He knelt suddenly, took his mother's hand in answer, kissed it, and pressed his forehead to it.

"I am William," he said again, definitely.

She laid her free hand softly on his head.

"Then, rise, and be the man that neither you nor your brother was—but perhaps the man you were meant to be. Be the King."

He lifted his head and looked up at her, searching her face. The dawn light lit his profile—the long nose and high brow that would one day grace coins of his own.

"And you, madam," he said. The old Kyle flickered

in his eyes momentarily, suspicious. "Are you content, then, that a child with no trace of royal blood shall one day inherit this throne that you give me?"

The Queen hesitated at that; the stern curve of her mouth softened as she looked at her son. And then the dark eyes flickered to her Minister.

Edward held his breath, heart thundering in his chest as her gaze touched his face; he felt it, burning like fire, as it traced his features—the distinctive lines of the long, straight nose, the noble brow he had shared with his half brother, the King. The King, dead these many years. The beard disguised the strong resemblance—but not enough to hide it from anyone who had reason to look closely.

His eyes met hers, with the understanding between them of those who had known each other's heart for many years. He nodded slightly. It was her choice, to speak or not. She was the Queen; he was her Minister, and lived to serve her, in whatever way he might. As he always had.

The corners of the tender mouth lifted slightly, secretly, in a way that turned his heart to water. Then she turned again to her son—their son—the smile once more hidden behind the mask of duty.

"I am content," she said.

AFTERWORD

Why did my son and I write a story on this theme? Well, because the anthology is titled *Mothers & Sons*, so we thought that's what the story had better be about.

I read everything—though possibly more mysteries than anything else—while Sam's tastes run to fantasy, tales of heroism and gore. So we sat down together to figure out a story line involving mothers and sons. A Royal Kingdom, that we could agree on, and a throne at stake. Sam suggested the Queen and the rival sons, and the story began to take shape. Then we got into the complexities of motive.

"Mom!" he said. "That's not a story, that's a *soap opera!* We need an assassin."

And so the brainstorming went on, to result in a fantasy of murder—and love.

All of my children are avid readers and capable writers, but Sam is the only one of the kids who writes for fun. He reads mostly fantasy, and writes it, too, spinning complex tales of adventure and magic. A night owl like his mother, he often comes up to my office at night to discuss his latest plot or tell me the details of a story.

One night, very late, he was sitting on the floor of my office by my feet, telling me the latest installment of the story he was engaged in writing. He sighed and said, "You know, I wish I could really *do* magic—you know, cast spells and make things happen."

And I sat there, with my hands on the keys and the words on the screen glowing in front of me, and said, "Oh, you can, Sam; it's just much harder work than people think."

Stuart M. Kaminsky

In Search of My Mother

Stuart M. Kaminsky and his mother,
Dorothy, two decades ago in
Evanston, Illinois.

I hid my first short story in the loose wooden leg of our living room sofa. My mother found it.

I was twelve years old with no thought of becoming a writer. I just wrote the three pages with a Number Two pencil on small sheets of white paper, folded them, and not wishing anyone to read what I had written, hid the creation in a place that I thought only I knew.

I was wrong.

My mother found it while she was cleaning. A lot of cleaning was required in our two-bedroom apartment on Chicago's West Side. In addition to my sister, my mother, my father, and me, my cousin and aunt lived with us. We also took in a boarder, who slept in the dining room.

The boarder, a young woman about twenty, worked in an office somewhere. She was pretty. I was twelve. I never looked at her directly. I did think about writing a story about her.

When I stood before my parents the night of the discovery of my hidden tale, I was thankful that I had not written about our boarder. Instead, I had written about an imaginary argument between a man named

Manny, who lived across the street, and his daughter Mitzi, who was two years older than I.

"How do you know this happened?" my mother asked, looking at the unfolded story on the kitchen table.

"I made it up," I said.

My father, who worked a twelve-hour day in a luggage factory (plus half a day on Saturday and occasionally a few hours on Sunday), loved to lounge in the bathtub and read mystery magazines. *Manhunt* was his favorite. He looked at me sternly. He wanted to be in the bathtub with Bill Gault.

"Why?" my thin mother asked.

"I don't know."

"Why do you hate Manny?" asked my mother, trying to make sense of this bizarre behavior of her much-loved frail son, who looked so much like her.

"I don't," I said.

My mother looked at my father for help.

"What were you going to do with this?" my father asked.

I shrugged.

"Just hide it?" he tried.

I shrugged again.

"I don't understand," my mother said.

At that point I could see that she feared for the sanity and future of her son.

My family was rather unusual for a nearly impoverished Jewish family. My mother had graduated from high school. My father had not. The circumstances of his failure to graduate with only a few weeks to go intrigued me. I had thought about writing a story explaining it. My father's story was that in a moment of rage he had cut off the tie of the principal of Harrison High School and was immediately booted out. My father was given to outbursts of temper, but he never laid a finger on my sister or me, and I never saw him touch another person in anger. I had several good ideas for tales about his sudden departure from high school. My mother had no version of my father's story. She never confirmed nor denied his tale of rebellion. She was never a rebel in deed or thought.

So, I stood there before my parents, contrite, happy that I had written neither about our boarder nor my father's failure to graduate from high school.

Whatever the history, my parents had no aspirations regarding my future. I was not pushed to become a doctor, a lawyer, anything. I was not pushed to excel at school. I was on my own. Four years after this confrontation, I would announce to my parents that I planned to quit high school and join the Navy. I was serious. They didn't object. They did ask if I thought I'd be happy in the Navy. I decided not to join the Navy.

"Will you promise not to do this again?" my mother said, nodding at the crumpled pages.

"Not to write?"

"Not this kind of thing," she said.

I wanted to say, "What kind of thing?," but I didn't. I lied or partially lied. I said I wouldn't do this kind of thing again. If "this kind of thing" meant writing about Manny and Mitzi or anybody I knew, I wasn't lying. From that point on, I vowed to write only about people who did not exist, in situations drawn from comic books, television, radio, novels, movies, and my imagination.

My father destroyed the dreaded tale of Manny and Mitzi. My mother kissed me on the head. At least I think she did. I like to remember it that way. She forgave me for creating fiction.

Jump ahead decade upon decade to the present. My father is long dead. My mother is eighty-five years old. She lives alone, reads three or four novels a week, and reminds me frequently to send her copies of my books.

She doesn't read my books. She did try a few times.

When I have asked her why this is so, her answers are flexible.

"Too many names," she'll say.

"The stories are confusing."

"I don't like things with violence."

"Mom," I have tried. "I have very little violence in my books."

"You have violence," she says.

"Okay, what other reasons are there for not reading my books?"

"I really don't like mysteries," she says with a shrug not dissimilar to the one I gave many years ago when asked about that first short story.

At this point I give up. I know I can press her into trying one of my books again, but I don't like anyone, especially my mother, reading my books because they have to.

I think I can trace my unwillingness to write anything autobiographical to the discovery of that story in the leg of the sofa. I don't want to be discovered. Why? I don't know. This memoir, in fact, is the first attempt I have ever made at dealing with my life and that of my family, particularly my mother, in print.

My mom worked all her life. She had nine brothers and sisters and grew up on a farm on the South Side of Chicago. Yes, my grandfather's farm was well within the city limits. My grandfather, a small, black-bearded and black-clad religious zealot, crept into one of my novels, *Red Chameleon*. He dies in a bathtub early in the book just as my grandfather did. The difference is that in reality my seventy-two-year-old grandfather's mistress was with him at the time. At least that was and is the family tale. My mother never read *Red Chameleon*. I counted on that.

My mother and father married immediately after high school, and I was born less than a year later. My father drove delivery trucks, was a short-order cook, worked in that luggage factory, worked in a grocery store, and ended his career as a clerk in a cleaning store.

My mother was a saleswoman in various department stores. The central trauma in her life came during a race riot when she was working at the Lerner Shop on Madison Street. The neighborhood was almost entirely black. That never bothered my mother.

Her coworkers were black. My mother thought nothing of it and liked her job. Till the day of that riot. Black coworkers hid her in a bathroom and lied to the rioters. They saved her life.

When my mother emerged from that bathroom, she was in serious emotional trouble. Her coworkers comforted her and got her safely home. Result: My mother's lifelong fear of black people. She readily acknowledged that black friends had saved her, but the trauma could no more be dealt with logically than could her later refusal to read the novels or short stories of her son.

I'd like to capture my mother's feelings and life in fiction, but it would elude me. On this singular issue in her life, she never expressed a racist comment. She never used the dreaded "N" word or any other racist epithet, never. She would never have considered it. The fear was deep, involuntary, and deeper than simple prejudice. Her fear became "they," the other, the brown and black faces.

Years later, during the O.J. Simpson trial, when Mark Fuhrman said that he had never used the "N" word, my mother believed him. Since I, who was brought up in a ghetto surrounded by black neighborhoods, had never used the "N" word, it didn't strike me as impossible. My father did, from time to time, use the Yiddish derogatory word "shvartze," but never in anger. His use of the word was always one of condescension. My mother never condescended. She never, even in her moments of greatest panic and fear, used any term of derision or hate when referring to the Poles, Mexicans, or Slavs who lived nearby.

I used to think, when I was young and quite stupid, that I would become just the opposite of what my parents were. Superficially I did. I am educated, well spoken, and a lot of other things that seem to distance me from my parents, but I have learned, as most of us do, that I have not escaped. Neither have I embraced.

My mother remains, in many ways, an enigma to me. I think she is an enigma to herself.

My mother has always been there for me, a warm, loving enigma.

Rewind. Back to the time I was nine and my sister a baby. My parents went out to a New Year's Eve party. They almost never went out. There was an accident, a collision. My father was slightly bruised. My mother's nose was smashed to pulp.

They wouldn't let me look at her for about three days after she came home from the hospital, and when I did, her face was purple and her nose covered.

I held her hand and told her about the book I was reading. I told her the story of *Dick Donnelly, Paratrooper* that, I said, was even better than *The Army Boys in French Trenches*. She held my hand tightly, and I told her stories. From time to time, she smiled or dozed. I don't think she heard a word I said, but I realized that I loved to tell stories.

I changed the tales in the books I told her about. I knew my mother would never read them. I added characters. Taken by the madness of invention, I created Lupo Gantz, who was afraid of nothing and had a wild laugh. I also created Baron Tanaka, ruthless, without emotion, built like a brick. Lupo appeared from nowhere to save Dick Donnelly, the Army Boys, and The Hardy Boys from Baron Tanaka. I changed their names from book to book, but it was always Lupo Gantz and Baron Tanaka.

I went to bed thinking of Lupo Gantz adventures.

When my mother improved and went through several bouts of plastic surgery, which we couldn't afford, I began making up stories in my head. Unfortunately, I made them up in school. I was a terrible student, except in English. My mother, when she recovered sufficiently, spent many an hour at the

Roswell B. Mason Elementary School listening to the problems of my inattention.

Later, the same thing would happen in high school, where a science teacher once, in class, announced that I was the most stupid student he had ever had. Considering that Marshall High was one of the city's toughest inner-city schools, that was quite an achievement.

When I lied my way out of my second year of high school by feigning illness, my mother supported me, believed me. I was torn by guilt, but I have not, till this moment, confessed the lie to her. If she reads this, she will finally know.

In that year of cutting school, I read and read and read. I got a better education that year by missing school than I would have had had I gone. My mother, with the sole exception of that discovered Manny and Mitzi story, was always confident that I was (a) a good boy, (b) smart, and (c) that I would be all right if I were left alone.

She was right. When I went back to school after the year I had missed, I was transformed. Part of the reason was my discovery of soccer. I played, became team captain, made the all-Illinois team, went on to play at the University of Illinois and then for a semiprofessional team.

Neither of my parents ever saw me play. Not one game. It was very much like my mother not reading my novels. I don't think they ever even asked me whether my team had won or lost when I came home after a game. The odd part of this was that I grew to accept it. No, I didn't have to accept it. I never expected them at a game.

Nor did they respond with particular pride when I proved to be a remarkable student. It was as if I had been given a brain transplant. My mother saw nothing odd in her son suddenly becoming both an athlete and an honor student. When I went on to college, my parents were supportive but had neither pushed nor expected me to go on.

Now, writing about it, I recognize that my relationship to my parents, particularly my mother, was very odd. I was left alone. If I sought protection or help, they were there. It was clear my mother enjoyed my company and my presence. By the time I was eight, she was talking to me as she would an adult.

I remember one afternoon while she was cleaning the dining room, she asked me to sit at the table. She kept cleaning and told me that my Uncle Moe was dead. Moe was my mother's sister's husband. Moe was a milk truck driver. A quiet, gentle man, I had from time to time made the rounds with him and had all the chocolate milk I wanted to drink. A truck had struck Moe as he crossed a street to make a delivery. My mother told me that Moe had died that morning. She stopped dusting and looked at me.

"He's dead," she said.

I didn't know what to say. I was eight. I had no idea what death meant, though I knew it was a basic truth. My mother began to cry. She was not a crier. I got up, crossed the room, and hugged her. She hugged back and wept. I was not comfortable being the adult, but I realized at that moment that I would be considered an adult when my mother needed one. I also realized that my mother had a great secret fear of death. That fear never left her. She was later treated for depression stemming from this fear, which she passed on to me. I was treated for depression for years stemming from a fear of death, anger at death. Eventually, it passed for me. I came to terms. I know my mother never has. She knew and knows that I am there when the fear grows too great.

But there were pleasures at the age of eight and even earlier. One secret pleasure, the one I kept from my friends, was listening to the Metropolitan Opera on Saturday afternoons while my mother ironed. My mother loved opera, still does. Along with the fear of death, she gave me a love of opera.

Lilly Pons could do no wrong. Richard Tucker and Jan Pierce were nearly gods.

My mother knew the arias and sang along with the sopranos. Stop. That is not true. A false memory. I don't really remember my mother singing along with arias. I want to remember it, but I don't think it happened. I don't remember my mother ever singing. I don't know if my mother can even sing on key. But she did love the opera.

When my mother was eighty-two, my wife and I took her to her first live opera, *Madame Butterfly*, here in Sarasota, where we have an outstanding opera house and a wonderful opera company. She was lost in rapture and memories I couldn't penetrate. She didn't talk about the opera after it was over, but she smiled.

That reminds me. The first musical I ever saw, and this was shortly after the Manny-Mitzi story, was *Brigadoon*. I met my mother downtown. We had burgers at Wimpy's and then went to the theater. I don't know why my mother picked that show on that day.

It was the only time before the opera two years ago
that I went to a live performance with my mother. I
spent as much time looking at her as I did at the stage.
She was enraptured, smiling, taken.

My father's passion was mystery stories and
movies. My mother's was music. My father loved
Tarzan. My mother loved Lilly Pons. They met only at
the corner of Jeanette Macdonald and Nelson Eddy,
though my father was uncomfortable there.

Well, you might ask, what is the point of all this?
And I answer, I don't know. It's an exploration. When
you explore, you don't always know what you will
find, a buried trauma here, and a frozen truth there.

When she was a young woman, and even through
most of her adult life, my mother was anorexically
skinny. People were constantly pushing food at her.
She nibbled. And then, when my father died at the
age of sixty-three, my mother, who was a year older
than he, began to fall victim to her family's genetic
history. She gained weight. She grew heavy.

Her diet remained the same, but the quantity increased. She moved to California to be near one of her
sisters. She began going to a nearby movie theater
regularly. Her taste was and is a puzzle to me. She
hates "bad language," but gore movies are fine with
her. She won't see anything overtly sad. She doesn't
watch soap operas.

From Panorama City, she moved to Sacramento to
be near another sister. I visited her, and she seemed
content. Her passion for playing cards was being met.
She would proudly introduce me to friends saying,
"This is my son. I'm very proud of him."

She never said what she was proud of or told anyone that I was a university professor and an author. I was "a very good son." I never felt like a very good son, but that was what she saw or wanted to see, and I have done my best to play the role.

Eventually, as her older sisters died in their nineties, my mother moved back to Chicago, Rogers Park, the area where she and my father had lived much of their adult lives.

She lives in a high-rise building of small apartments managed by a Jewish agency. A good or creative psychiatrist might be able to tell me why I chose to use my mother's apartment building in my novel *Lieberman's Choice*. In the book, a renegade older cop murders his wife and her lover in the building and then barricades himself on the roof demanding that the man who he believes corrupted his wife come up to face him.

Much of the book takes place in the building. Death abounds. Terrorized tenants escape.

My mother is not in the book. Or is she?

Am I getting somewhere? Remarkable. In the past, I've had to pay for analysis and free association regarding my parents. For the first time, I'm getting paid for doing it.

When my mother was a girl, there was a Catholic Church near her home. Catholic children taunted her and my aunts, saying that they knew the Jew family was killing Christian babies as sacrifices. My bold aunt, Esther, younger than my mother by a year, took my mother's hand and dragged her to the church after a Mass. Esther, with my mother cowering behind her, confronted the priest and asked why he let such lies be spread. According to my mother, the priest was

confounded, then angry, and then defensive. Before
he could answer, my aunt led my mother away. The
confrontation was and still is meaningful to my
mother, though she doesn't know why.

When I was about five years old, an older boy
about ten slashed my hands with a razor. I don't
know why. I do remember the incident. The boy ran
away, and I came crying into our basement apartment, dripping blood on a yellow linoleum floor. I remember the floor vividly. I also remember my mother,
whose face turned as white as our refrigerator. She
did not weep. She did not rant. She did not go running. She was calm and reassuring. She was only
twenty-five years old and was dealing with her only
child, her curly-headed blond toddler with the sad
face. She cleaned, bandaged, taped, and led me to the
building next to ours where a young doctor lived. She
knocked at the door. The doctor's wife answered,
took us in, said her husband wouldn't be home for
hours. She treated my wounds and led me to a porch,
where she told me to sit while she talked to my
mother.

With a glass of milk in my hand, I looked around.
The walls were covered with books, not regular books
but the now-collectable Big Little Books. I couldn't
read, but I could look at the covers, at the cartoon pictures of Dan Dunn, Terry and the Pirates, Mickey
Mouse, Smilin' Jack. I forgot my wounds and carefully removed book after book to look at the covers
and return them to the shelves. I wanted a library like
that. I wanted, for the first time, to learn how to read.
When my mother took me home, she sat me in front
of the radio with a tuna sandwich and went in search

of the child who had injured me. Five minutes later I heard screaming. It was my mother. She was screaming at Bobby's mother in anger. I had never heard her scream in anger, had never really seen her angry. I would never hear her like that again. There was something magic and wonderful in that voice of rage. She outshouted the other woman, Bobby's mother. I heard none of the words. When she returned, she was calm.

"Bobby is moving," she said as she cleaned my plate and glass. "You'll never see him again."

Since I had decided never again to leave the apartment because of Bobby, I was in awe. My mother had been moved to fury. She had bullied a neighbor into moving. She was more than there for me. She was out there for me.

It happened only that one time.

My mother's name is Dorothy. I doubt if more than those with whom she worked ever called her Dorothy. She was Dot as a girl and became Aunt Dot as she grew older and for more than two decades has been Mimi to us all. The name was bestowed by her youngest grandchild and stuck. I think the operatic connection has always secretly appealed to her. I call her Mom. My sister calls her Mom. The rest of the rather large family knows her only as Mimi. I wonder if her seven grandchildren and five great-grandchildren even know her name is Dorothy.

Connection. Light bulb. Freud leans over and looks me in the eye.

"Dumbkopf," he says.

The Wizard of Oz is one of my three favorite movies. I know every line in the movie. It is the story of

Dorothy, who dreams of being somewhere else, somewhere magical, a bit dangerous, colorful, surrounded by loyal friends. But Dorothy longs to return to her family and does. She is content to remember a magical world but to live in a real one.

One more story. When I was about fourteen, my mother wanted to learn how to drive. My father tried to teach her, but he had little patience. He had tried to teach me. He had given up after ten minutes, handed me the keys, and said, "Teach yourself." I did.

My mother relied on me to help her, though I was a year away from that ten minutes of training from my father. She went around the block slowly, slowly, dozens of times, stomping on the brakes when a car approached from in front or behind.

Her refrain was, "I can't do this."

Mine was, "Sure you can. If Aunt Esther can drive, anyone can drive." With two days behind the wheel, my father told her that he was working late, and if she wanted to go to her sister's, she would have to drive. I sat beside her. She had no license, no confidence.

I guided her on a one-hour trip that should have taken twenty minutes. She thwarted traffic, made odd sounds, and came close to destruction at least eleven times.

We arrived on the street where my aunt lived. My uncle and two cousins were outside waiting for us, watching as I coached my mother into a parking space. She had one more small move to make, and we would be in. She hit the gas instead of the brake, and we rammed into the car behind us, rammed hard. My mother opened the door, left the keys in the ignition, and never drove again.

Why did I consider this my failure? Why do I remember the entire trip and the feeling that we were about to win together, mother and son? We had never done anything like this before, and we failed.

God, I grow dour when I think about my mother.

When I give workshops, I warn would-be writers not to try to capture those too close to them in works of fiction. I warn them that their mothers, father, spouses, children, and friends won't cooperate on the printed page.

The truth is that I don't want to bring my mother into a fictional world. I don't want to control her. I don't want her to be afraid even in a world that doesn't exist. She is an enigma to me. She should remain that way. My wife says that I am doomed like a tragic Greek figure. I can't understand anyone close to me, but I am amazingly insightful about people I barely know or friends who are not too close.

Leap back to that day when my mother and father discovered that first story of mine hidden in the sofa leg. Why does she look so sad? Does she fear her dreamy son is showing the first signs of inevitable madness? Or is she trying to understand what I am and will be?

I think I'll call my mother tonight.

Note: My mother is now living in Sarasota. She entered a nursing home here last week, I see her every day. Her reading has diminished, but she still reads large-print books—though she still doesn't read my books, large or small print. Some things do not change.

Marilyn Reynolds
with Matthew Reynolds

∞∞∞

Burritos and Beaches

*Matt and Marilyn Reynolds in Cancun,
August 1992.*

MARILYN: I keep thinking about Matt, the youngest, our son. During his coming winter break he will return to California from New York, to join us in our family holiday gatherings. Mid-January, before he goes back to the University of Rochester, we will celebrate his thirtieth birthday.

As scenes from our lives together wash over me, I picture us stretched out on Matt's bed in the old Altadena house, reading Dr. Seuss, or, later, *Grimm's Fairy Tales*. And there was all that time in my VW bug, driving to and from school, and soccer, and Little League. There were the long, hot, torturous drives to Arkansas that we made every few summers, Matt and I, my brother and his daughter, and assorted others, depending on whomever else we could convince that Arkansas in the summertime was a great vacation plan, and that visiting our ancient aunts and uncles was more fun than a cruise. All of these places and events helped define who Matt and I would be together, as mother and son.

Other building blocks in the foundation of our life-long bond were formed, one after another, during our weekly dinners, the two of us, at Ernie Jr.'s Taco House.

MATT: The ritual had been around as long as I can remember, but probably started when I was about eight. One night a week, Mom and I would go out to dinner, usually on Thursday when my dad was at choir rehearsal.

It was always to Ernie's for Mexican food, and always just the two of us. I would be doing my homework, or more likely watching TV, when Mom would get home from her teaching day. Within a few minutes we would be back in her car and on the way to Ernie's.

We lived in Altadena, which was about ten miles north of Los Angeles proper—a suburb, but all of L.A. was essentially suburban. My parents moved to Altadena when I was three. I think it offered them the things they wanted in a home and a community. Altadena had a rich history, character, and was ethnically and culturally diverse. My friends as a kid were black, white, Asian, Mexican-American, and I think my mom and dad appreciated this mix of cultures.

The drive from home to Pasadena, where we had our weekly dinners, was through a rougher part of town. The Jackie Robinson housing projects and West Altadena, right before the border of Pasadena, was a place where life was visibly different. The houses and apartment buildings and storefronts along Fair Oaks were run-down. There were bars on the windows, wrought-iron fences, paint-chipped facades. Somehow on smoggy days the air even seemed more polluted along this strip.

It was dusk. Mom and I were on Fair Oaks Boulevard. I was eleven. We were in her '63 Volkswagen bug—even then almost twenty years old. I remember the car. And the horn. It was faint and hardly made any noise when you pressed the skinny metal bar that ran along the radius of the steering wheel.

Before we got to the freeway overpass, Mom jerked the car to the side of the road and began pounding on the tinny horn and yelling out her window. I looked across the street to see three young men beating up another man. They could have been teenagers, but they looked huge. The man was lying near the curb, apparently unconscious. The others, above him, kicked him as he lay on the ground, no longer struggling against them.

My mom continued to scream, yelling at them to stop, honking her horn. Fair Oaks was a heavily trafficked road, but cars drove around us, slowed, and kept going.

It felt safe in the car, but I can remember wanting to leave, immediately, knowing that safety was the thinnest of illusions. I kept saying, "Let's go. . . . Please, Mom, let's go . . . keep driving," as this person was being beaten, what looked like, to death.

At one point I thought she was going to get out of the car. Even as a boy, I felt the need to protect my forty-five-year-old mother. If she got out of the car, though, there would be no way for me to protect her. The sight of such violence, the endless stream of blows this guy absorbed, filled me with a sense of sympathy and fear. Because she was calling attention to it, the force of that violence could be directed at my mother, at me, at us.

Then, abruptly, the attack stopped. The men ran off. Someone else appeared on the scene to call the police and tend to the beaten man. My mom and I drove on, over the freeway, and went to our dinner.

I can't remember what we talked about as we ate, although I'm certain we talked about what we saw, and that Mom tried to make sense of it. I'm sure she addressed the close proximity of untamed violence.

I thought my mother incredibly brave for even pulling her car over in the first place. To an eleven-year-old, it's a heroic act when a person who is, in reality, powerless to change a situation, nevertheless tries to do so. And I think I felt bad, cowardly, that I wanted so much for us to keep driving.

I have no idea what happened to the person lying on the corner of Fair Oaks and Orange Grove. How do you know what happens to such a person in a big city? Random acts of violence happen all the time. What should a person do in such a situation?

MARILYN: My memory of that event is nearly an exact replica of Matt's. I didn't feel brave, though, I felt helpless. And I remember that as soon as we got to Ernie's, I called the police and was assured that officers had already been dispatched to the scene.

Later in the evening, at home, after Matt was sleeping safely in his bed, I called the hospital. Of course, I could get no information on the condition of the beaten man, but, through a series of persistent questions, I *did* learn that no one brought into the emergency section that evening had been either fatally or critically beaten.

I agree with Matt, that we undoubtedly talked about "untamed" violence. I'm sure we talked about risk, and responsibility, and the general precariousness of life. Often our dinners at Ernie's were light-hearted, but this one, I'm certain, was not.

Now, at my computer in northern California, the table we sat at that night, the glow of yellowish light reflected on faux cracked walls, the taste of cheese-laden refried beans, is as real to me as the desk on which I rest my arms.

At Ernie Jr.'s Taco House, week after week, year after year, the same food would be placed before us, without our asking, by Juadi, a waiter who seemed to anticipate our dinners almost as eagerly as we did. As soon as we took a seat at one of his tables, Juadi brought a large order of guacamole and chips, plus a Coke for Matt and a glass of Chablis for me. When we finished the guacamole, he would bring Matt a bean and cheese burrito with sauce on the top. For me, he would bring *chili relleno* with beans and rice. Halfway through the meal, Juadi would bring another Coke for Matt, another glass of wine for me.

It was as if Ernie's, in some sweet way, opened the door of conversation for my usually reticent son, and we would talk and laugh our way through long, leisurely dinners, Juadi smiling gently at us each time he passed our table.

When Matt went away to college, and I occasionally went alone to Ernie's, Juadi's first question to me would be, "Where's the boy?" When, on Christmas break, Matt and I would steal time for an Ernie's din-ner, Juadi's eyes would light up when he caught sight of us. No matter how long the time between visits, Juadi always remembered our order. I long ago switched from Chablis to chardonnay, but I never had the heart to ask Juadi to change my order. Long after the taste of Chablis had become sweet and cloying on my tongue, I continued to drink it at Ernie's, because Juadi brought it. Perhaps I didn't want to tamper in the least with those dinners that had, unplanned, become the setting for some of our deepest and most enjoyable talks, and also that had helped keep our bond intact, through occasional difficult times. Whatever values I've managed to transmit to Matt have probably, mostly, come through bean and cheese burritos, though Matt remembers other methods, too.

MATT: Driving through the desert heat of New Mexico. Dale, my mom's brother, was at the wheel. I was ten.

I was beginning to take an interest in music, and my first rock-and-roll hero was Elvis Presley. Before he died, I had been obsessed with Elvis. When the concert from Hawaii was shown on television, when I was seven, I cried because he didn't sing "Hound Dog," my favorite song up to that point.

The radio was playing that day in the car, and Dale said that it was Elvis singing, coming over the New Mexico airwaves.

I was incredulous. It couldn't be. This song was a country song. Elvis's voice was unrecognizable, as far as I was concerned. I doubted my uncle's musical authority, but he insisted.

It wasn't Elvis. I knew.

"Wanna bet?" he asked.

Bets were serious. Even at ten the words "Wanna bet?" were ones I had heard from my mom's mouth a thousand times already. They scared me because she was a good gambler. She didn't bet unless she was pretty sure she was going to win. And if *she* had learned that skill from her father, then I was confident Dale had probably learned some valuable gambling lessons along the way, too.

I couldn't remember the last time I had won a bet from my mom. I also knew that there was something unusual about a mother betting money with her son, a son still young enough to be easily taken advantage of by someone older and wiser.

I paused a long time at the question, wondering if I were only going to enter into an insignificant wager or if I were about to learn a life lesson.

"Wanna bet?" Dale asked again. "Five dollars says it's the King."

"Okay. Five dollars."

When the DJ came on informing us that we had been listening to Elvis Presley sing "Green, Green Grass of Home," Dale didn't rub it in. He was a gracious winner. He just gave me a look that said more "pay up" than "I told you so."

I made a big stink about it. I think I claimed that he had cheated, that he didn't deserve to win because I was Elvis's biggest fan, and that I wasn't going to pay him. This last statement stopped the conversation cold in the car. My mom told me I had to pay him, that I was nothing if I couldn't live up to my word. The vividness with which this lesson was imparted to me on that day, during that drive, is still fresh. I never heard her say "My daddy taught me," or "A Dodson never reneges on a bet," but I knew she was serious. I knew this was imparted from her father. I knew that she was summoning the family ghosts and that they were now looking down on me at this crucial point. It was only a bet, but whether or not I paid the money to my uncle would say a lot about what kind of a person I was, what kind of person I would become. I can't remember paying him.

It's snowing in Rochester. As April approaches without any signs of spring, I drift back to those times when warmth was abundant. The smoggy days of southern California and the desert heat of the Southwest on long drives to Texas and Arkansas momentarily erase the reality of ice-covered windows and the bitter cold mornings in the Northeast.

I'm tempted to make nostalgia out of my past. I've learned so much from my mother and have cherished the humor and respect that has existed between us. But now the moments that stand out for me are the mistakes I've made; the times I thought I'd known her, or a given situation or setting, or even myself, only to find out I'd done something wrong or not really understood anything at all.

MARILYN: This surprises me, that Matt is focused on shortcomings and misunderstandings, rather than on his strengths and my knowledge of the pure goodness of his soul. If only he weren't clear across the country in the frozen East, if only we could meet for dinner at Ernie's . . . Over that artery-clogging *chili relleno*, with the cloying sweet wine, I would tell him of my sense that, though he may not always know all the details, he knows my heart, and that my experiences with his brief misunderstandings have been that they are simply that—brief. I have faith in his basic honesty as I did so long ago, at another of our regular Ernie's dinners.

Matt was fourteen. Earlier in the week, Mike and I had received a letter from LaSalle High School stating that marijuana had been found in the locker of one of Matt's friends. All of the circle of friends were questioned, and Matt had admitted to trying marijuana. The letter went on to talk of the seriousness of the situation, and to predict possible expulsion if there were reason to believe Matt was in any way involved in drugs on campus.

As high school teachers, we were not naive. As parents, though, we were shocked. We'd talked with Matt about the incident. We worried about him being led astray. He accepted full responsibility and did not place any blame on his friends.

At our next evening at Ernie's, I was hoping to extract a promise from Matt that his pot smoking days were over.

"I'd never do anything like that at school," he assured me.

"Did you like it?" I asked.

"Not too much."

"I hope you'll leave it alone," I told him. "I know it's not physically addictive, but I've seen too many kids lose themselves to it anyway."

"I can't say for sure I'll never try it again."

"I want you to stay away from it," I said.

"I know," he told me, not belligerently, but honestly.

My strongest impulse was to *demand* that Matt promise he would never again use marijuana. On the other hand, as much as I wanted a promise, I didn't want it at the expense of a lie. I knew from earlier experiences the sorrow of dishonesty, of lost trust, and I didn't want it with Matt. We shared our guacamole in silence for a few moments, then went on to a lighter topic. No false promise stood between us.

MATT: When I was little, and I'd get scared in the middle of the night, I used to get in bed with my parents.

MARILYN: I slept on the side closest to the door, and Matt would come in, in the middle of the night, and stand beside me, waiting for me to stir. It took only the slightest movement, and he would crawl over me to squirm and burrow between me and Mike. We would joke that we were a sandwich. Mike and I were the bread, and Matt was the baloney. The last time Matt crawled into our bed, he was seventeen.

MATT: The day had been typical of midsummer Los Angeles living. The valleys were smoggy and unbearably hot, and the days were slow and long. Even though I enjoyed the time off, it was hard not to occasionally be overwhelmed by boredom. I had talked with friends earlier in the week about going out to the beach. The coast was a reprieve from the inland areas. It was cool, the water was cold and crisp, and on a weekday, like this one, the sand was never overcrowded with people baking in the sun and basking in the water.

Mom was teaching summer school that day. Dad had gone to Paris to take some time to himself and see parts of Europe he hadn't seen before. Mom and I were to meet him later, in Germany. My sister, Cindi, was living with her husband in Germany, where he was stationed, and the trip was an excuse to visit them and see parts of Europe at the same time. Travel had been a part of my existence with my parents, and now, at seventeen, this figured to be my last big trip with Mom and Dad before I went off to college and left the safety and security of their home, their laughter, and their pocketbooks.

But our part of the trip was two weeks off still. As a southern California teenager, the beach sounded ideal.

I picked up my friends Donald and Mark around nine a.m. We were headed for Laguna Beach, one of the more scenic coastal cities in the area. We had a friend whose family had a beach house there, and he had introduced us to a smaller, more secluded cove where locals congregated. For us, the appeal was that this particular beach offered interesting and often challenging swims because of the effects on the tide produced by the geological formations near the shore. If you walked out far enough past the tide pools and out to the edge of the rocks away from the beach, there was also what the locals called a "blow hole." The incoming tide had worn away a kind of underwater bridge that you could swim through without much trouble. Even though the brief plunge was easy, it appeared to have the potential for danger because the lifeguards would come out and tell you to stop if they saw you. But on the weekdays, the lifeguards weren't on duty at the smaller beaches in Laguna, and so we decided to head there.

The day was perfect. Maybe it wasn't really. Maybe

it's the way the day ended that makes me want to remember it that way; the wondrousness of the day
contrasted with the harshness of what happened next.
But when I picture it in my mind, I had never seen the
sky so blue, or the water so clear. We were all
teenagers and on the verge of adulthood (at least
physically) and preoccupied with sex and girls and
making comments about how funny looking people
were, or how stupid, or what was happening at
school. But somehow the day was like a temporary return to childhood.

We spent the majority of our time in the water, and
we were less preoccupied with ourselves and how we
looked and trying to act cool than we usually were.

Around four or five we started to think about getting some food. And we also talked about how great it
would be to get something to drink and watch the
sunset. Drinking alcohol was a ritual in high school. I
think we all enjoyed drinking and probably took
more chances than we needed to while under its influence. But I know we also believed that the sunset,
the day, the camaraderie we felt would be more
meaningful if it was accompanied by a little intoxica-
tion.

We got a few slices of pizza and then headed to the
local liquor store up the street from the beach where
we had spent our time. None of us was old enough to
buy booze, so we stood outside the liquor store, asking people on their way in to buy us something, and
then give it to us once they got out. One of the first
people we asked agreed to buy us booze, and we got
a four-pack of wine coolers. It wasn't so much about
getting drunk. Even though there had been times

when I had taken risks driving under the influence and knew it was generally a stupid thing to do, I also realized it would be idiotic to drive the hour and ten minutes on the busy freeways back home with a buzz, or feeling groggy.

We took the wine coolers to a cliff that overlooked the water, and our plan proceeded without a hitch. We drank and talked and felt good about our day, about what we would do later that night, maybe even about our lives in general.

None of us saw the beach patrol cop come up from behind. When it was too late, we all tried to ditch our bottles in the bushes, simultaneously trying not to spill anything, in case he hadn't seen us drinking. Of course, he had seen us. He pulled us up to the street and began writing tickets for violating the community laws against liquor on the beach. He wrote a ticket for me both for being a minor and littering. Donald was getting a ticket for illegal consumption of alcohol on the beach. And Mark had finished his bottle before the patrolman had surprised us.

After he had written the tickets, a squad car pulled up and the beach patrolman went over to the other side of the car to talk to the officer. The cop came around and told me they would have to place me under arrest; I was a minor and it was policy to arrest minors in possession. Neither Donald nor Mark was arrested.

I don't remember making any fuss over it. I was completely scared, and pissed off. I wasn't drunk, as if that made a difference. And it seemed like such a waste of time to haul me into jail on something that, of course, was against the law, but was fairly innocent in the scheme of teenage life in and around Los Angeles.

The officer handcuffed me and put me in the back of the squad car and drove me to jail. The cuffs pinched my wrists, and the seat was uncomfortable. It was made of cheap, hard plastic, which probably made it easier to clean if someone was bleeding or got sick after being arrested.

I knew they would call Mom. And I knew she would be incredibly angry. And I knew she would probably be worried, too. It took about five minutes for the cops to drive me to the station. They took me in, booked me, took my fingerprints, and led me into a holding cell. I was the only one there.

My mom was a high school teacher at a continuation school in Alhambra, California. She taught the teenagers who had been kicked out of the "normal" high schools. I admired her for this. There was and is something noble about being the last best hope for some people, about being the branch on the cliff that sticks out and catches you before you fall all the way. Not to romanticize her calling, or to say that all of her students were on the verge of destroying themselves. But these were gang kids, problem teens, the pregnant girls, or the students who got busted with drugs. Her students were largely Hispanic, the marginal and the marginalized. I think she talked honestly with them. And openly. And treated them fairly. And, for the most part, respected them. And I think she reached a lot of them and made a difference in their lives and ultimately, what more can you ask of a career or a life?

But sitting in a jail cell, I wondered how my mom would react to getting a phone call that put me in a place similar to where so many of her students had come from or were going.

MARILYN: I'd read student journals until about eleven, then went to bed. I kept wishing to hear the sound of Matt's car rounding the corner and pulling into our driveway. I knew I couldn't demand that he, at seventeen, be home every night at ten, but ten was the time I began to fear for his safety if he wasn't home. I fought the irrationality of it, but the fear was there, anyway.

I'd been teaching at Century High School since 1972, when Matt was only three. Every single year, from 1972 until my retirement five years ago, news would come of a Century student's violent death. Some years there would be more than one. But in all that time, not a school year passed without the violent death of one I'd known at least from a distance. Or it may have been one I'd played Scrabble with, Friday after Friday, or taught to read. Once it was a student whose journal writings were so tender, it hurt to read them. Automobile accidents, drownings, gang violence, Russian roulette, drug overdoses, suicide, it was all there, year after year. I could not help being aware of how tenuous life is, particularly for teens.

Even after being in bed for over an hour that night, I was not wholly asleep when the phone rang. It was the same midnight ring that told me Cindi was in the hospital. It told me my father was dead. It was that ring.

"This is Officer Kennedy, Laguna Beach Police."

In that moment I envisioned all the worst of the fears I'd tried to hold at bay. Matt was dead. Drowned.

Killed on the highway. Fallen off a cliff onto the jagged rocks of Laguna Beach. I pictured him bloody, mangled, lifeless.

"We're holding your son. We arrested him for drinking on the beach."

I exhaled the relief that flooded through me, knowing Matt was alive, whole, safe, then inhaled the heat of anger over his stupidity for drinking on the beach, anger over having to drag myself out of bed and drive to Laguna, anger that Mike was off in *Paris* while I was home *working*, and that I was the parent who would have to go take responsibility. I'd be lucky to get home before four, then have to get up at six-thirty for school.

To top it all off, Matt had given his keys to Donald and Mark so they could drive home in his car—the car that he had promised to never let anyone else drive. So there, he'd committed the ultimate sin of breaking his word. Where was his head? Had he lost all integrity? Was he on a downhill slide that would leave him with no hope for the future? What kind of *idiot* had I spawned?

MATT: About an hour after I was locked in the cell, an officer from the station came in and told me he had called my mother. I had given him the number when I was first booked and remembered some strange questions about why my father was out of town, as if they thought my drinking had something to do with familial trouble. They told me she was coming to get me. I knew it would be a long drive for her and that as the distance between home and Laguna diminished, her anger would build.

My mom and I were close. I respected her, laughed with her, felt like I could talk to her. At least I realized I could say more to her about my life than my other teenage friends could say to their parents. She listened in a motherly way, but also in a way which showed her to be genuinely fascinated by the person I was becoming.

Of course we had our differences. I hated the way she made a big fuss about wearing a condom. Her warnings always came at the times when it would be most embarrassing for me, too. On the way out with a group of friends, when a girl I might be seeing would come over, in front of other family members, the words "Wear a condom!" would be the last thing ringing in my ears as I would walk out the door. And she was stubborn in a way that could be so annoying when it came to things like curfews and the times when I wanted to assert my own independence.

I hadn't seen Mom mad that often. My dad had more of a temper. When he got mad, he wouldn't yell or scream or throw or strike, but he was verbal about his emotions and it wasn't hard to tell when he was angry. Mom showed it in a different way. She got silent. She wouldn't talk. Just seethe. And that was worse because it was difficult to tell exactly what she was thinking or how mad she was, which made me worry even more.

Sitting in the sterile holding cell in the Laguna Beach Police Station, I worried about her growing anger, how getting arrested would change our relationship, if in fact I was worthy of the "another troublemaking adolescent" look I was getting from the cops when they brought me into the station.

It's funny, or weird, or stupid, or profound the way people pop into your head when you do bad things (or when you're about to). It's those thoughts, those people who keep you in check, who you live for, who you work for, who you want to please, and who guide you, even when they're an hour and a half, or a conti-nent, or a world, or a lifetime away. Mom was sud-denly all I could think of, and I realized that I had been thinking about her since I got busted throwing a wine cooler bottle into the bushes.

A short time after the cop came in to tell me he had called my mom, he came back. My friends were in the station and wanted to know if they were going to re-lease me and, if not, could they have the keys to my car so they could drive home. I think when my par-ents found out Donald and Mark had asked for the keys, they thought it was a lousy thing to do. I don't think they were impressed that I gave them the car, ei-ther, but I understood. If I were in my friends' spot, I, too, would have done anything to avoid an uncom-fortable drive back with a silent, infuriated mother.

MARILYN: Of course my first response to anger was si-lence! Who wants to be caught *saying* all the crap I was thinking? But once past Monrovia, on the way to Laguna, my anger subsided and other thoughts emerged. Matt wasn't the only stupid teenager I could hold for reference.

There was the time my high school friend Bobbie and I, anxious for spring break at Laguna, had left my house at one in the morning, instead of waiting until nine, as planned. We had left a note for my parents saying we decided to leave "a little early," and had picked up a couple of hitchhiking sailors on the way. At their suggestion, we stopped at a bar, where we each had a beer and they had several, before we went on to Laguna, and our appointed rendezvous with friends.

Anything could have happened. How could I be so angry with my son over something no more risky or wrong than any number of things I'd done as a teenager?

By San Dimas, I was angry again. I'd been raised by drinkers in an environment of benign neglect. The one time I'd had too much to drink as a teenager, my parents had offered me "a hair of the dog that bit you" as a remedy. But *Matt*, damn it, *Matt* had had more enlightened guidance.

By Diamond Bar I knew the situation had been all Donald's fault. Whenever Matt had been in any kind of trouble, Donald had been there. This was the second time Matt had been arrested when he was out with Donald, and both times Donald walked away free and unscathed. And now Donald had Matt's car, which, of course, was *our* legal responsibility, and how could Matt have possibly turned his keys over to Criminal Donald. So . . . mad again.

I stayed mad until I entered the quiet, cold space of the Laguna Beach Police Station. I waited for what felt like much too long for Officer Kennedy to bring Matt out from the cell. The cell. Matt was not waiting for me in the staff coffee room. My precious son was in a cell.

Growing up, I'd learned that the policeman was my friend. If I was lost, a policeman would help me. If a stranger tried to get me into his car, I was to run to a policeman. I held those beliefs until the bombardment of film from civil rights demonstrations, and from Vietnam War protests, and from a Chicago Democratic convention, persuaded me that things might be otherwise. When I began teaching a group of kids that was often targeted by police as troublemakers, my disillusionment grew. One day I saw an arresting officer slap handcuffs on a student in a such a brutal manner that the student's wrist broke with a snap. Broken bones, killer choke holds, beatings—these, I knew, were facts of some arrests.

Maybe Matt was back beyond the double doors, in pain. Maybe they'd put him in a cell with someone crazed on PCP. Maybe Matt had been beaten to death in his cell, and they were back there now, trying to come up with a story.

"Mrs. Reynolds?"

It was Officer Kennedy again, this time with Matt, who was whole and apparently unharmed. I signed the necessary papers, picked up information about the hearing Matt and one of his parents (Mike, damn it!) would have to attend.

We walked to the car, guarded, not looking at one another. So much I wanted to say, but I was afraid to start, afraid I'd say things I didn't really mean and that they'd be lodged forever in Matt's brain. I did ask why Matt gave his keys to Donald. He said they needed a way home and it seemed like the right thing to do at the time. I asked how much they'd been drinking, and the details of the arrest, and why Donald and Mark got off, but I shut up when I felt the anger rise. Matt went to sleep. Sure. Great. He wasn't the one who had to get up at six-thirty in the morning to go to work.

MATT: I can remember nothing about when she picked me up. I can't remember the look on her face, probably because I didn't want to look her in the eye. And I don't remember what she said to me. I could sense her anger. And she didn't say much.

What I remember the most is how much longer the drive home had seemed. It was a drive I had made with my mom, and with both of my parents, a thousand times. When I was really young, we would come back from the same beach, and I would lie down in the backseat and go to sleep; when we would get home, my dad would take me in the house and put me to bed. Mom wasn't talking. I wanted to sleep then, as I had as a child.

When we got home, we both went to bed. I knew the talking would come tomorrow and that I'd have to explain. I also knew that we'd have to call Dad and I'd have to explain to him, too.

I don't know at what point it was, but at some point during the night, I got out of bed and crawled in with my mom. I know that sounds weird for a seventeen-year-old to get in bed with his mother. But I also knew it was the right thing to do. I knew it was a gesture that my mom appreciated. It didn't make her any less angry. It didn't mean I wouldn't have to stand trial. And I'm not sure exactly what I said, exactly what that gesture meant. I think it meant that I was still her son and that I knew I messed up and I knew I still wanted her to mother me, even though I had been unintentionally initiated into adulthood by a ritual people spend their lives trying to avoid.

MARILYN: He stood, for a moment, at my side of the bed, as he had so many times as a child. I moved over and made room for him. If I had been of the ilk of my Arkansas aunts, I would have followed my impulse to put my arms around him and pull him close. But I was too well versed in Freudian principles to do that. Instead, I rested my arm beside his, barely touching, but touching, and we slept side by side until sometime before my alarm, when Matt went back to his own bed.

In the light of day, I knew we would talk calmly when I got home from school, and I was glad I hadn't spewed out my anger over his being an idiot, because he wasn't, and he didn't need to hear that from me. Matt was on his way to college in September. He'd worked since he was a little over fifteen. Except for his stubbornness about not holding to a curfew, and this one arrest, my life with Matt had been a delight.

I knew we would talk, again, about risks, and how tentative life is, and how necessary it is to respect that. I might remind Matt that he must follow his own light, not Donald's, or Mark's, or mine for that matter. Later we would call Mike at his hotel, and Matt would tell him the story. And although in the night I felt that Mike was totally irresponsible for being away when Matt was arrested, by daylight I knew that it could as easily have happened at a time when I was the one who was away. Mike would go to court with Matt. No one had to be left out.

* * *

It is only two days now until Matt will be home. Wherever "home" is and whatever it means, we are still using the word for his visit to our new place, near Sacramento. As we decorate the tree and talk of Matt's coming birthday, memory continues to intrude on practical affairs. I see the new baby, the kindergartner, the boy at his eighth-grade graduation dance. I remember his tears over a dying kitten, his laughter over the antics of our ever-entertaining mongrel dog. What a wrench of separation we felt as we waved good-bye to Matt, his car loaded down for the move to a college dorm four hundred miles north.

In no time, we were celebrating Matt's graduation, then following by sporadic postcards his travels through Europe. Finally, Matt returned home for a period of teaching before he headed north again, this time to pursue a master's degree in film. Now, in a doctoral program at the University of Rochester, he has surpassed us, both in years of education and intellectual capacity.

I wonder about the parts of his life that haven't included me, the places and events that also formed him—the times in between the postcards, and phone calls, and college degrees. These are the things that are also part of him, the adult Matt, whose life I share at long distance, by bits and pieces.

In early spring of 1998, Matt and I had what we didn't know at the time was our last Ernie's meal, on the last plate Juadi would ever deliver to us. By summer, I'd heard that Ernie's had closed and an upscale kitchen shop had moved into their building. I was glad we'd left town before we had to witness such sacrilege.

What I know, though, from the vantage point of sixty-three years, is that certain things stay, lodged at the core of one's being—the taste of my grandmother's potato salad, my father's scent of Old Spice and Schlitz and Camels, the laughter in the midst of iced tea and mosquitoes on Aunt Ruth's front porch. And I know dinners at Ernie's, the years in our Altadena home, the road trips, those times and places will live within us, enhance our lives, as long as we register life. And when I cease to register life, much of what has been me will show itself to Matt, through a laugh, a taste, the sight of a '63 VW bug, an ad for condoms. For good or ill, I will be there, barely below the surface, rising to consciousness in the most predictable and surprising of times.

This day, admiring the tree and anticipating the season, I fast-forward to mid-January, and Matt's birthday celebration. I can hardly wait for the party, to say again to the assembled crowd, how happy I am that Matt was the unique and complex soul that came down the chute on that long-ago day back in 1969.

MATT: There were so many times when I thought I knew what she was thinking. There were so many times when she was with me, even though she was physically far away. Nevertheless, there is an elusiveness to our relationship. It's strange to think that we were once one person, the same person. It's strange for me to realize that I was once a part of her but that now and always there are parts of her that I will never know. I'm saddened by this (and eternally grateful for those private spaces that are so necessarily solitary). And it excites me to know that there is still more to her that I can and will discover.

I know there are more stories about her past that will be told in my presence. I know there are more books for her to write. I know there will be conversations, and trips, and celebrations, and even deaths and mourning and loss. And I await all of those times and the possibility of discovery they contain. We are on the move, progressing together as individuals and as mother and son. And I am grateful.

Peter Straub

∞∞∞

Looking Back

Peter Straub, aged approximately two, on North Forty-fourth Street.

Elvena Nilsestuen, graduating from Mount Sinai, Milwaukee's School of Nursing, 1931.

My mother, Elvena, the third of five children, four of them daughters, born to Julius and Clara Nilsestuen, was raised on the family farm in what is called the "coulee country" of western Wisconsin. Halfway down the length of a country road, across a wide plain, and up a winding stretch over a steep, mountainous hill from a small town named Arcadia, not far from the bustling metropolis of LaCrosse, my grandparents' farm consisted of a hundred and fifty acres embedded within a context so comprehensively populated by the descendants of Norwegian immigrants that it was called "Norway Valley." Obviously in another time, that of the twentieth century's second decade, it might also have been in another country.

My mother's parents, grandparents, aunts, uncles, and all of the adults she encountered spoke Norwegian as well as English, and she and her siblings learned Norwegian side by side with English. My mother retained the traces of a Norwegian accent all her life. Her family's values, diet, and mores were those of mid-nineteenth-century, rural Norway. (The name Nilsestuen means "Nils's little house," so deeply back-country that modern Norwegians grin when they hear it.) In winter, they traveled by horse-drawn sleigh, complete with sleigh bells. Christmas began with a monumental housecleaning and universal baths on Christmas eve, an hour of bell-tolling from the Lutheran church down the valley, the arrival of relatives in chiming sleighs, gift-giving and a reading from a Norwegian translation of Luke, then a Norwegian-language service the next day, and it continued until New Year's. They ate lutefisk, fried pork with cream gravy, bread with sour cream and sorghum, and, as a special treat, lefse, a flat, circular, pancake-like bread concocted on a wood-burning stove, then smeared with butter, sprinkled with sugar, and rolled up. (Lefse was meltingly delicious, I remember from childhood visits to the farm, but unless it is made on a wood-burning stove, forget it, it's not the real thing; you might as well be eating cardboard.)

Despite the evocative bell-tolling, the religion passed along to my mother and her siblings was merciless, unforgiving, and apocalyptic. My uncle Gerhard, generally known as "Swede," wrote in his contribution to a collection of family reminiscences that "The Norwegian Lutheran God was not exactly a God of Love as I remember it." Sermons tended to focus on the Last Times, always terrifyingly close at hand. Swede felt that his Sunday school teacher, one Rönhovde, a forbidding character otherwise called "the Klökker," relished describing the horrors consequent upon the end of the world because he had intuited his pupil's fear before the prospect of the event. My mother now and again dreamed of a great fire spreading across the sky, and she knew these dreams originated in the sermons she had heard in her childhood. (Nightly, her brother used to pray for the arrival of dawn. She probably did, too.)

I allude to this background because every part of it was crucial to my relationship with my mother. Rural and small-town Midwestern Lutherans of Norwegian descent tend to share traits as distinctive, in their own way as piquant, as those of second- and third-generation Italians raised in lower Manhattan or Brooklyn, but no Norwegian-American counterpart of Francis Ford Coppola or Martin Scorsese ever came along to dramatize those traits. Instead, Garrison Keillor began to deliver lengthy, improvised-seeming monologues, funny, rhapsodic, and surreal in about equal measure, during weekly radio broadcasts of his own devise called "A Prairie Home Companion." Keillor's extended riffs depict Norwegian-American Lutherans under the unsparing but affectionate lens of close observation, and the ripe comedy of his reports is a direct product of their accuracy. "A Prairie Home Companion" demonstrates at least two great principles every time it is aired: that responsive human beings are capable of feeling tenderness and hostility for the same object at the same time; and that comedy is rooted in anger.

Like the residents of Lake Woebegon, nonfictional Lutheran Norwegian-Americans avoid complaint, lamentation, rebellion, and displays of sullenness in favor of steady, ongoing acceptance, because they do not believe anyone but a fool ever imagined that life was supposed to be easy. They avoid introspection and self-analysis because they believe that kind of thing can only make you feel worse instead of better. They do not believe that anyone should ever suppose himself or herself superior to anyone else, because sooner or later someone else is going to notice, and then you'll look stuck-up. They believe conversation to be a tricky business, riddled with booby traps and other opportunities to make yourself look foolish, and therefore should be confined to the weather, gossip, stoic accounts of recent ailments, tales of the grand-children. They distrust any display of emotion. You know how you feel, so the last thing you ought to do is talk about it or, even worse, act like you're a big deal and put it on display. Act nice, be a good neigh-bor, do your job without grousing about it, don't ex-pect too much, be grateful for whatever you have. Remember that the world doesn't owe you a living, that God barely knows you exist, that life is a grim struggle from beginning to end, and you'll be all right.

This point of view sounds far worse than it turns out to be in practice and, in fact, embodies a great deal of common sense. I don't see why people shouldn't be polite to each other, do what they are supposed to do without grousing, and know enough to avoid putting on airs. Snobs and whiners really are second-rate human beings, unless of course they possess enough wit to irradiate their snobbishness with brilliant self-awareness and whine with gorgeous, luxuriant elo-quence. No matter what your job is, composing minimalist string quartets, fielding grounders and making the throw to first, putting on an eye patch and singing Wotan in *Ring* cycles, winning stock-car races, delivering one-liners in comedy clubs, or delivering *pizzas*, the values taken for granted by the average Norwegian-Lutheran farmer would tend to elevate

your standards of performance. One thing I learned
from my mother was that if you didn't work hard
enough to do your job better than you thought you
could, you had already failed.

Nothing I have said negates the presence of ordi-
nary happiness. The collection of family reminiscences I mentioned earlier refers again and again to
the pleasures and satisfactions my mother and her
siblings experienced during their childhoods. (Being
Norwegian-Americans, one and all they eventually
mutter something like, "It had its bad side, too, if you
know what I mean, but I won't go into that.") They
lived intensely, out there on that farm. They formed
internecine alliances, ran through the woods, told stories, sang, played games and endless pranks, climbed
trees, skied down a homemade ski jump, and mar-
veled at the stiff collars and dress shirts of relatives
visiting from LaCrosse. (Ruth, the baby of the family,
wrote, "I could never understand why Shevlin liked
coming to the farm so much. To me it seemed that
anyone would surely rather be in a glamorous city
with stores and sidewalks and ice cream parlors."
Ruth eventually took off for Seattle.) My mother
emerges from the family memoirs as an active, even
adventurous child, the sort of girl that used to be
called, as she was, a "tomboy." She loved riding and
was in "seventh heaven" when a neighbor asked her
and her brother, to whom she was devoted, to halter
break a number of Shetland ponies. Later on, she and
Swede saved up enough money to order McLelland
saddles from the Montgomery Ward catalog. My
mother liked to remember the wild fun of dashing
around bareback on an unbroken pony, also the differ-

ent kind of pleasure afforded by saddling one of the
farm horses, climbing aboard, and coaxing the enor-
mous animal into a gallop.

Another time, she described the transcendent moment when, running, she felt the gears mesh as never
before and realized that she had just learned really
how to *run*. My brother John inherited this capacity
from her—John could run like an antelope. Me, I
hated running, and instead of transcendent moments,
I got stitches in my side, but I did eventually learn to
walk without falling down or holding on to the furniture. After I discovered jazz and began spending
every cent I had on records, my mother confided that
at roughly my current age, thirteen, she, too, had been
intensely interested in music: though she could not
quite explain how it happened, she had decided to become an opera singer, like Jenny Lind or Nellie Melba.
This ambition must have come from some source
other than the strictly musical, because her family did
not own a Victrola, and although Atwater-Kent radios
had appeared in neighboring farmhouses, her father
refused to buy one on the grounds that he couldn't
stand all the racket. Undaunted by never having
heard a single aria, my mother invented her own and
sang them to the receptive cows and horses until
some more demanding listener, probably one of her
sisters, informed her that she couldn't carry a tune
and had a voice like a crow. It was the truth, and she
knew it—her operatic career evaporated on the spot.

John may have inherited running, but I am proud
to say that my mother's musical talent came down to
me in undiminished form. In grade school, our music

teacher told me to move my lips along with the other kids, but not to make any actual noise.

I stumbled into an appreciation of Benjamin Britten and Peter Pears while working in a record store during my last two years of college, but began filling the air with Wagner, Richard Strauss, Verdi, *Lulu*, *Béatrice et Bénédict*, *A Village Romeo and Juliet*, *Péleas et Mélisande*, and *Cleofide* only after I turned forty, by which time my mother had entered into the vanishing act that was the last stage of her life and endured, becoming more and more horrific as it went along, until 1990. One Sunday afternoon in 1993, my wife and I went to a recital by the great mezzo-soprano Christa Ludwig at Alice Tully Hall. Although I had loved Christa Ludwig's singing for years, I had not consciously taken in her resemblance to my mother until she strode smiling onstage, halted three feet north of James Levine's keyboard, opened her mouth, and floated, in plangent voice, into her first song.

"Does she remind you of anybody?" Susie whispered, but I was already in tears. There she was, doing what she had wished to do, gloriously.

For her last two years of high school, my mother moved into an apartment in Arcadia with Swede and Ruth. She began nurse's training at Lutheran Hospital in LaCrosse. Then she summoned all her courage and took the train to Milwaukee to earn a degree from Mount Sinai Hospital. In Milwaukee, a fellow student named Kathleen Marie Straub introduced Elvena, by then known as "Nels," to her brother Gordon, a good-looking athlete unlike anyone she had ever known, and after that everything changed.

*   *   *

Nels and Gordon, "Gordy," a Catholic from the all-
but-surreal hamlet of Lone Rock and a creature im-
bued with more passion, fantasy, and recklessness
than anyone from Norway Valley had ever imagined
possible, flirted, dated, fell in love, married. They became Gordy and Nels, a lifelong couple. Gordy roistered, dreamed, and ranted, translating every inch of
life into his own point of view. Nels earned her R.N.
and went to work. Spinning fantasies at every step,
Gordy worked at this and that, tried and failed to en-
list in the Army (varicose veins), became a salesman, a
"manufacturer's rep," a job for which he was ideally
suited. Nels starched her nurse's cap, ironed her uniform, and reported for eight-hour shifts at Mount
Sinai. After meandering from one shabby apartment
to another, they moved into the ground floor of a du-
plex on North Forty-fourth Street near Sherman
Boulevard on Milwaukee's west side, then a Jewish
neighborhood. According to my father, they never
wasted any time thinking about children, but children
came along anyhow, three of them, all boys, the first
of them me.

Nels never stopped working, and Gordy never
stopped being himself. Neither one of them had any
choice. My father hatched schemes, moved from job
to job, and roistered; my mother held things together.
Caroline and Rhoda, younger cousins of hers happy
to escape the family farms, moved into the house on
Forty-fourth Street to baby-sit while she was on duty
at the hospital. I loved Caroline and Rhoda, they
seemed like unusually playful adults to the three-
year-old, four-year-old me. Both of them adored my

parents, in their eyes as sophisticated as William Powell and Myrna Loy. Never less than charming to younger women, my father dazzled Caroline and Rhoda. Now and then, I hope, he took the girls out and showed them off to his friends. He brought me with him a couple of times, and I remember the laughter, the bobbing faces, the haze of cigarette smoke above my perch on the bar. My father had no problem including his children in situations where he knew he was going to have a good time. Gordon Straub, that remarkable piece of work, is not the focus here, but he cannot be ignored, because his combination of impulsivity, loyalty, sentimentality, wild outbursts of anger, outright irrationality, emotional violence, and whimsical invention played so large a role in my relationship with my mother.

The children of nurses grow up in an atmosphere responsive to illness but not especially sympathetic to it, and they learn not to expect much slack. Sniffles, headaches, low-grade fevers, minor aches and pains mean nothing. You go to school anyhow. When your fever reaches 101, you can stay home, but your mother won't be there, because she has a job to do. Measles, chicken pox, whooping cough, influenza, diseases that leave you limp as a dishrag, soaked with sweat, and prone to hallucinations, she has seen a thousand times before, in versions a thousand times worse than yours, so lie down, drink lots of fluids, and enjoy your day off, because tomorrow you're going back to school. Experience has taught nurses to regard most doctors with a cold, cold eye, so their children spend little time in pediatrician's offices.

There were periods during my childhood when I nearly wished I were in the hospital, so I could receive the attentive care my mother bestowed upon her patients. However, because I was not in the hospital, I could listen to her tales of what went on there when she got home to change out of her uniform, pour a drink, drop into a chair, and light up a Kent. These tales were both comic and irate.

She was one kind of person at work, another kind at home. The tomboy, the breaker of ponies and builder of ski jumps, had disappeared. My mother sailed through her workday with professional expertise, and when she came home turned into a nervous wreck. Life had stranded her with three sons, a demanding occupation, and a colorful husband whose mother had taken care of every sort of household obligation and expected her to do the same. The sons charged squalling around the house, the husband was liable to come home late, come home in a raging sulk caused by something he had overheard or imagined overhearing, come home blasted along with a couple of friends who were also blasted, and in the meantime she had to make dinner and do the laundry. She was a resentful cook, and her meals showed it, a matter my father never quite took in. As long as it was food, it was fine with him. His mind was entirely elsewhere, generally off in contemplation of that topic of unfailing satisfaction, his own splendor.

It is true that when my father was not tormented by self-doubt or undergoing one of his spells of illumination, he really did like to contemplate his all-round splendor, but I must add here that my mother loved him. Gordon Straub astonished her in a thousand ways. He made life funny, heartbreaking, dramatic. Boredom was not a problem. My mother learned how to deal with his multiple vagaries; he kept her on her toes, alert for the next wave of fantasy, ire, or ambition. What undermined her was the sheer, hard, unrecognized labor of holding down a job and doing all the housework for a family of four inconsiderate males. Also, she had been raised with three sisters, and she missed the company of women. My mother always regretted that she never had a daughter. We were nothing but a noisy bunch of boys, my father included, and none of us understood anything, we were not at all like girls. In the familial chaos, my mother represented the single voice of reason, groundedness, useful common sense. Besides that, she was often the voice of pure grievance. During the nineteen-fifties, suburban wives and mothers, even those with full-time jobs, were unpaid domestic servants, except for the slovens among them. My mother was not a sloven, she was a Norwegian. She did all the cleaning, dusting, and vacuuming, all the laundry, the bed-making, the straightening and picking up, and 95 percent of the shopping. My father's excursions through the grocery store tended to result in a great many bags crammed with peanut brittle, cookies, cocktail olives, doughnuts, and buttermilk. About once a week, he decided to give her a break and wash up after dinner, and once a month or so it occurred to him that my brothers and I were tall enough to reach into the sink. When ordered, we washed the dishes, but with sullen lack of grace. It wasn't our job, after all.

The voice of grievance was the sound of my mother

talking to herself, *sotto voce,* as she hauled bundles of laundry back and forth from the basement, mopped the kitchen floor, or pushed the vacuum cleaner around the house. In a stage whisper, she talked to herself nonstop, unreeling her complaints in an endless sentence devoid of punctuation or even breaks between the individual words.

WhatdotheythinkIamtheirservantwellI'mnottheirservant andIamsickandtiredofbeingtreatedlikeoneit'shigh- timeTHEYdidsomeofthisworkoronedayI'mwalkingoutand nevercomingback. . . .

You could hear it from two rooms away. You could practically hear it from the other side of the house. Even when you couldn't hear it, you knew it was going on, that endless, steaming sentence, looping around the house and trailing up and down the basement stairs following my mother's resentful progress like a great ribbon. Her bitterness was too much for us, too scary. We didn't know how to cope with it, so we turned to stone and hoped it would pass. The stage-whisper monologue frightened us less than her rare outbursts, when she went over the edge and railed at us face-to-face. *I am sick and tired of being treated like your SERVANT! All I do is go around cleaning up your MESSES! Listen to me, I've had it up to HERE!* Certain stock phrases emerged over and over again: "one iota," as in, "I never get one iota of help from you ungrateful little shits," and, a great favorite, "twenty-seven times," as in, "Peter, I've told you twenty-seven times to hang up your shirts instead of throwing them on the floor, but do you pay one iota of attention?" I heard that so often that I began paying at least half a dozen iotas of attention, and now I hang up my shirts and trousers before going to bed even on nights when I'm operating on remote control. Once when we were all fairly small, therefore particularly nauseating, she actually did make good on her threat and tossed some clothes into a suitcase, tore out of the house, and drove off. (*You can take care of yourselves from now on, because I am SICK AND TIRED of doing it for you!*) Stunned, we crawled into various corners and pretended to be statues for an hour or two, after which she returned. For the next couple of days, we barely opened our mouths. Then we reverted to being ungrateful little shits, our natural condition.

The voice of reason, groundedness, and useful common sense was both more pervasive and more personal. My father's volatility and self-absorption, not to mention his unshakable assumption that disagreement equaled defiance, made our relationship difficult, but I always felt that my mother understood me, valued me for myself, and took pride in my accomplishments. There were times when she seemed able nearly to read my mind, which was enormously reassuring. In the dynamic of family life, she was my ally. Without an ally, I would have been lost. My father had been an athlete, and like most former athletes saw participation in sports as a crucial element in the development of character. He had played football and basketball in high school, been a football player in college, and played semi-professionally afterward. That he had always loved reading and had an instinctive gift for narrative, qualities I undoubtedly inherited from him, was merely personal, of no significance in his value-world. Reading and story-telling were essential to him but weightless when measured against sports. Somewhere inside him, I am sure, within a chamber he entered as seldom as possible, he imagined that these activities were tainted, suspect . . . effeminate.

Right from the start, from the moment I opened my eyes and took in the presence of billboards, road signs, labels, and headlines, I hungered for the written word. One of my clearest memories from early childhood is of an overwhelming desire to understand print. I taught myself to read by memorizing comic books and "reading" them to other kids until the words locked into place, and after that I was off, I was insatiable. After an encounter with a moving automobile in my seventh year led to a couple of operations and a year out of school, I turned to reading even more intensely. Because my father had been addicted to Tom Swift and Edgar Rice Burroughs in his boyhood, he was happy to drive me weekly to the local libraries and let me check out the maximum number of books, six. I was a terrific student, and he liked that; it reflected well on him, it gave him something to brag about. Yet he did not think it was enough, especially for a son destined to play for the Green Bay Packers. In summers, I was supposed to charge outside and play games, not just sit around and read novels. He didn't get it. I was missing the boat, and I didn't seem to care.

My father feared that there was something wrong with me, some characterological flaw that would lead me deeply astray, if not ruin my life. My mother worried, too, but she always trusted me to work things out in the end. Unlike my father, she knew that my

encounter with the automobile and its lengthy after-
math had contributed an extra degree of darkness, of
suppressed anger and unacknowledged fear, to my
personality, and at my worst moments she suspended
judgment and, as thoroughly as she could, mutely
shared my suffering, which was also mute.

For Norwegian Lutherans of her generation, as for
her parents' generation, physical demonstrations of
love took place in private, behind a closed door. After
my brothers and I advanced out of babyhood, we
were never hugged or kissed, except for the brief period when our father used to kiss us good night. (He
told me later that kissing boys made him feel creepy.)
The only times I remember being hugged by my
mother took place when I had alarmed her by doing
something extraordinarily stupid. She was stiff, awk-
ward, uncomfortable, twig-like. It was like being
hugged by a maiden aunt who on the whole would
rather not, like being hugged by a frightened bird. My
father sizzled away in the background, waiting to get
rid of me.

The grounded, sane, never less than necessary voice
of reasonable common sense emerged on those rare
occasions when no one else was in the room. She had
been saving up some comment or bit of advice, and
she looked you in the eye and got it off her chest. At
those moments, the things she said could put to rest a
dozen different worries, problems, and fears. She was
giving you the real deal, and you knew it. This happened over and over, and I hardly remember anything my mother said at those times. What I do
remember is the sense of becoming acquainted again
with the real world, in which people's motives led to

actual consequences. A haze of illusion and conjecture had been blown away. When I was fourteen or fifteen, she said to me, "Even if you don't like most of the people you meet, you should pretend you do, because after a while you will, and your whole life will be better." She was right—I started acting as though I liked other people, quickly discovered that I really did, and my life improved. She worked the same earth-mother magic on my brothers. John once told me that at nine or ten he had begun to imagine that he was a Martian and everyone knew but him, and when he mentioned this to our mother, she instantly dispelled his fears by saying, "No, John, that's crazy."

The things about me that infuriated my father—my total disinterest in business; my sense that literature, music, and art were essential to a civilized life; my adolescent intellectual pretensions; my assumption that somewhere there existed a world beyond Milwaukee and my father's circle of concerns, and that this larger, more generous world was not only of tremendous interest to me, but also necessary to my psychic survival—appealed to my mother as much or more than they aroused her concern. Long after I had found my place in the world, my father, on a visit to New York, sat down in my living room, where he was surrounded by paintings, and said, "You know, I hate art. I don't know why, I just hate it." (I know why, though—because he didn't know anything about art, he thought it diminished him.) My mother would have said, "I don't know much about art, but Peter knows what he likes." She believed that what was important to me would eventually let me find my path;

she trusted me to find the *way out* that was also the *way in*.

In 1977, when Susie and I were coming to the end of our long residence in London, my father's letters began to report disturbing news. My mother was having peculiar medical problems her doctors could not diagnose. One night after dinner, she had collapsed outside a restaurant. There were periods when she seemed unable to remember what she had been doing or saying. My father put an optimistic gloss on these matters. He could not disguise his worry, but he assumed everything would turn out fine in the end.

That summer, my parents spent a week at our house on Hillfield Avenue, N8, and for the most part my mother did appear to be fine. She rejoiced in Susie's pregnancy, she planted a ring of pansies around the rose bush in our small front yard, she regarded her husband's occasional flights into outer space with her by then customary mixture of wariness and amusement. After serving for more than a decade as alderman in Brookfield, our suburb, my father had run for mayor and lost, a failure which led him to brood about taking a powder somewhere not populated by knaves. We drove through the Sussex countryside and lingered in pubs. My father teetered around the house on his troublesome knees and bare feet, sometimes getting confused about which floor the living room was on—"I'm looking for that room with the big, square furniture," he said—now and then letting a freshly made drink drop from his hand to detonate on the tiles of the ground-floor hall. He seemed more disturbed than my mother.

One night when she and I sat up late in the kitchen, she said, "I'll never forget the first time I was sent out to spend a night in a patient's house. I was fresh out of nursing school, and the patient was an old woman who had been released from the hospital that day. She had a box of chocolates in her refrigerator." During the night, the old woman died. My mother was told to do nothing until morning. Unable to sleep, she ate all the chocolates. It was an interesting story. Five minutes later, my mother smiled and said, "I'll never forget the first time I was sent out to spend a night in a patient's house," and told me the whole story all over again. She perspired more than I had ever seen her do before. By early afternoon, a flushed red band crossed her face from cheek to cheek. There were times when she forgot what she had been talking about and fell silent. I had no idea what to make of these lapses, or even if they were lapses. They became significant only in retrospect.

The following summer, Susie and I paid a visit to Wisconsin with our infant son, Benjamin, and the damage could no longer be dismissed as a temporary aberration. Whatever was happening to my mother had accelerated to the point where its outward manifestations presented a persistent state of confusion and anxiety. The mother I remembered surfaced only intermittently.

My father had abandoned traitorous Brookfield to relocate himself and his wife in a small, "contemporary" house on Lake Halley, northwest of Milwaukee and close to Eau Claire. In the coulee country, Eau Claire was home to Rhoda and her sister Germaine, both of whom came for dinner on the second night of our visit to Lake Halley. Before we got there, I didn't know what to expect: my parents' letters had described a placid existence enlivened chiefly by the sightings of exotic waterfowl. According to them, their new life was working out perfectly well. It might have looked that way, too, if you were an expert in the psychological mechanism known as denial. Surrounded by trees, the little house was attractive, clean, functional, a sort of combination of a hunting lodge and a "hospitality suite" in a modern hotel. The backyard led to the water's edge and a short, sturdy pier where my parents liked to sit in the evenings.

Yet my mother seemed to exist in a mild but unassuageable panic without specific referent. Sitting down, she jittered, preoccupied with her own unease. Something had been left undone, an essential domestic task had been neglected, and the world was under the threat of ever-increasing disorder until the neglected task had been answered. Finally, her sense of responsibility pulled her from her chair and sent her pacing through the house in search of the overlooked duty, the thing undone, the forgotten. The kitchen offered a wrinkled dishcloth and a couple of used napkins, the bedroom a single pair of socks my father had dropped into the hamper an hour before. My mother gathered up these few objects and, intent on taking care of business, hurried washing machinewards. By our second day in the new house, I understood that she did this all the time. She trotted from one room to another, collected socks and dishcloths, and washed them in the washing machine, usually one by one. It was like watching a dog in a dog run.

At other times the compulsion to re-enact the rituals which once had evoked the voice of grievance abated, leaving a vaguer, more distracted but recognizable version of her old self. Infant Ben delighted her—everything he did gave her pleasure. I will never cease to be grateful for that. During our stay, my mother prepared meals, conversed, joked, described her adaptation to Lake Halley. She knew why Gordy had sold up and moved out, and that they had landed near most of her relatives eased the grief of having lost the house in Brookfield.

This grief was real, and the loss was profound. My mother may have filled that house with her endless sentence, but she had lived there for better than two decades, and she both loved and missed it. My brothers and I, along with our wives, spent about a year attributing Nels's problems to the shock of having been abruptly torn from her familiar surroundings: clearly, she would have preferred to remain in Brookfield and, but for her husband's wounded narcissism, would have done so for the rest of her life. Instead, she had been uprooted, drastically. In the absence of any other explanation, this one looked pretty good.

Rhoda and Germaine, my mother's younger cousins, arrived for dinner on the second night of our visit and yakked away in a manner I found wonderfully familiar, spinning off jokes and pungent comments on everything in sight. They were Gilbertsons, from my grandmother's side of the family, women blessed with a raucous wit, a lively capacity for enjoyment, unflagging warmth, and a sturdy sense of loyalty. Both of my parents meant a great deal to them, and before and after dinner, they took in their cousin's lapses into vagueness, her deposits of single dish towels into the washing machine, without breaking stride. During a private moment later on in the evening, Rhoda and Germaine expressed their concern for my mother, whose deterioration they, too, supposed a product of the almost brutally abrupt removal from Brookfield. This, of course, was not an opinion that could be aired in Gordy's presence. No one had any idea of what was actually going on. In any case, my father had chosen to ignore all signs to the contrary and act as though nothing, at least nothing of any significance, was wrong with his wife. He would maintain this position, which I am tempted to call a facade, for years to come. He surrendered to reality only when the inexorable progress of my mother's disease gave him no other choice.

Susie, baby Ben, and I went back to London and began the process of disentangling ourselves from England. My father wrote that disagreements with a neighbor had soured him on Lake Halley, too bad but nothing serious, he and my mother were moving to a town house development in the village of Hartland, closer to Milwaukee. (The "disagreements," I learned later, had been the product of Gordy's response to the neighbor's observation that Nels seemed to be losing her marbles.) In June of 1979, Susie and I swanned back to the United States on the *QE2*, for some reason rented a house in Westport, Connecticut, and, in a step even deeper into delusion, bought a big, lovely Victorian, just up from Burying Hill Beach on Beachside Avenue, known locally as "the Gold Coast." (Should you be wondering about the use of the word "delusion" in the previous sentence, a reading of

Floating Dragon, a book I wrote on the third floor of that house, will clear things up.) My parents came through Westport twice, and both times my father's capacity for denial had expanded to meet the increasing challenge to it posed by his wife.

That they were traveling at all, much less covering hundreds of miles every day on their journey from point to point, was remarkable in light of my mother's condition. She no longer knew quite what to do with silverware, so he cut up her food and brought it to her mouth with his own knife and fork. Because she was incapable of selecting her wardrobe for the day, he chose it for her, which meant that she wore sweatshirts and sweatpants, as he did. She conversed in fragments, and the fragments usually drifted off into benign silence. Startling, unexpected obscenities peppered her speech: in the old days, she had called us "ungrateful little shits" only when pushed over the border of propriety by stress and frustration; by the early nineteen-eighties, the border no longer existed, and she cut loose whenever she felt like it. However, being in my house made her happy. Her grandchildren, now including our daughter, Emma, born in 1980, thrilled her. She still had a grasp of who she was and what her life had been like, and if now and then she felt impelled to say, "Gordon, I don't give a shit about changing my goddamned socks," "Gordon, to hell with you, I want to sit out here a while longer," or something earthier, the worst part of what was happening to her seemed to be a relentless withdrawal into a distracted but essentially passive remoteness.

The withdrawal was baffling, disturbing, painful, horrible to behold. It was like seeing her being subjected, inch by inch, to an inexorable erasure. Medical professionals still had not identified the causes for the erasure, but it progressed. My father's sister, a former professor of nursing at Catholic University and long since metamorphosed from Kathleen Marie Straub to Dr. K. Mary Straub, diagnosed the central pathology as the failure of sufficient oxygen to reach the brain and recommended an operation. Unable to admit the gravity of the problem, her brother went on as before. I think he *couldn't* admit it, I think any such recognition would have blasted his world to pieces. Going on as before, whatever the emotional cost, was all he knew how to do.

He also knew that the retreat from the external world, the core of his wife's symptoms, brought with it others that were far from passive. Her obscenities emerged from a helpless rage that erupted only in private. A few years later, after bitter reality had claimed us all, my father told me that my mother had often stormed inconsolable and furious through their apartment, railing. She wanted out. To keep her from escaping, he piled furniture in front of the front door, and when she tried to toss it aside, they battled. One night while they were "vacationing" in Florida and my father was asleep, my mother managed to unlock the door of their motel room and vanish into the streets, to be found only after hours of desperate search in the rented car. Her incontinence had almost driven him crazy. The stress became unbearable. My parents drove to Rochester, Minnesota, and there, at least seven years after its onset, my mother's illness was finally given a name in the Mayo Clinic.

Most readers of this memoir were probably able to

identify the illness the moment my mother repeated her story of the dead patient and the chocolate box, but in 1983 Alzheimer's disease had not yet come into anything like general public awareness. I'd never heard of it before I learned of my mother's diagnosis at Mayo, and neither had anyone else I knew. Until I saw the name in print, I thought it was spelled "Aylzheimer's."

For the following eight years, Alzheimer's disease greedily devoured the remains of my mother's life, character, and self, turning brain cells into tangles of filament and swallowing trace after trace of humanity until the body it at last murdered had been reduced to a withered, fetal husk. These years were enormously, cruelly, even—I want to say—exquisitely painful for all of us. My father soldiered on until, realizing that he was about to snap, he placed Nels in the nursing home, or "elder care," wing of an old hospital in Trempeleau County, where the staff's unfamiliarity with Alzheimer's resulted in inadequate, sometimes ignorant treatment. The one time I visited my mother there, a shrunken, stick-like wraith on the verge of death came shuffling down a gloomy corridor, looked at me with red eyes instantly blazing forth love and recognition, and my heart folded in half with shock. My father quickly transferred her to a far more modern and humane facility in tiny West Salem, just outside LaCrosse, and moved into an apartment down the street. For the rest of her life, he visited her twice every day, gabbed at her for hours on end, joked, washed her hair, cut her nails, escorted her on walks, fed her, insured that she was getting the best possible care. Under his ministrations, she put on weight and, to the extent this was possible, flourished. My father prolonged her life for many years, lovingly and self-lessly. Attending to my mother amounted to an extended repayment for decades of what he perceived as less than stellar treatment, the years in which he had been, as he announced in a West Salem bar on a night when both of us had too much to drink, "a son of a bitch bastard."

I felt like one myself, because the combination of misery, terror, and sheer horror aroused in me by my mother's Alzheimer's made it extremely difficult for me to visit her. The shuffling, red-eyed wraith had all but paralyzed me, and although I knew that she had come a long way back from the lip of the grave, I feared to stand in her presence. My mother's deterioration surrounded me like an invisible, toxic atmosphere; since what she was enduring was truly unthinkable, I thought of it constantly, at one level beneath consciousness. It was as though I were gazing into the absolute darkness gathering about her, and the idea of that darkness unstrung me. I often wished that I could face the darkness in her place, take it on for her and set her free. Mistakenly, I imagined that death must be preferable to that cruel imprisonment—I mean, that I would experience her death as a release. Susie and I flew to LaCrosse once or twice a year, and every time we drove to West Salem, picked up my father, went the next eighth of a mile down Garland Street, and turned into the drive leading to the nursing home, my anxiety doubled and redoubled, increasing exponentially. By the time we pulled up before the entrance, I half expected to be killed by my own emotions a second after we walked inside.

What kept me from returning to West Salem more than once or twice a year was grief of such power and magnitude that my existence as a working, rational being seemed to depend on keeping it at arm's length. Like most great emotional misjudgments, this feeling was entirely unconscious. Though I was doing nothing of the kind, if anyone had asked I would have said that I was dealing with my sorrow about as well as I could. Inevitably, the unconscious took its revenge: shortly after Valentine's Day, 1990, my father called to say that my mother was fading fast; the next day, a few hours after her death-in-life had slipped into straightforward death, we arrived in Wisconsin and joined the extended family of Straubs and Nilsestuens in a cycle of funeral parlor visitations, reunions, meals, marathon conversations, reminiscences and condolences which culminated in a memorial service in the same Tamarack Lutheran Church where Rönhovde, "the Klökker," had sown terror; we flew back to New York—and my accumulated grief and sorrow, no longer to be held at bay, swarmed up, blew the hinges off the gate, and flattened me. For that, too, I shall always be grateful.

After the gate flew open, I learned the most important lessons of my life. I learned that grief is precisely equivalent to love, and that the terrible grief felt after the loss of a person one has loved deeply is a necessary consequence of that love and represents its survival in another form. However bitterly, grief is an honor. I learned that grief universally saturates and enriches our world, for sooner or later loss of an almost unimaginable order transforms everyone. Parents die, spouses and siblings die, even children die, and these deaths create irreparable wounds that shrink over time but never heal. They are not supposed to heal. On all sides, tears lie just beneath the surface. The emotion that gives rise to those tears is a connective tissue extending far, far down into our common humanity and our individual beings, and in those depths it becomes indistinguishable from joy.

ABOUT THE AUTHORS

Lawrence Block's fiction ranges from the urban noir of Matthew Scudder to the urbane effervescence of Bernie Rhodenbarr. He has published forty-plus novels, as well as four books for writers and five collections of short stories. A Mystery Writers of America Grand Master, he has won that organization's Edgar Allan Poe Award four times, and is a multiple winner as well of the Shamus and Maltese Falcon awards. Born in Buffalo in 1938, Block has lived most of his adult life in New York City, where the greater portion of his fiction is set. The father of three daughters from his first marriage, he has been married since 1983 to Lynne Wood. When they are not busy being avid and intrepid world travelers, the two share an apartment in Greenwich Village.

Eric Jerome Dickey is the *New York Times* bestselling author of the #1 Blackboard bestsellers, *Cheaters, Milk in My Coffee, Friends and Lovers,* and *Sister, Sister,* all available in paperback from Signet. Originally from Memphis, Tennessee, he is a former computer programmer, middle school teacher, actor, and stand-up comic. He attended Carver High School and graduated from Memphis State University (okay, the University of Memphis, but MSU is what it was called back in the day) with a B.S. in computer systems technology, and also attended UCLA's creative writing program on a SEED scholarship sponsored by the International Black Writers and Artists/Los Angeles chapter. His first screenplay, *Cappuccino*, was directed and produced by Craig Ross, Jr. Dickey currently resides in Los Angeles. His new novel, *Liar's Game*, was published in hardcover by Dutton.

Eileen Dreyer has published five medical suspense novels and eight short stories under her own name and twenty-one romances under the pseudonym Kathleen Dreyer. She has also written stories for the collections *Mothers & Daughters* and *Fathers & Daughters*. A retired trauma nurse, she lives in St. Louis with her husband of twenty-five years, Rick, and her two children. Kevin Dreyer, or "World War II" to his grandmother, is twenty-one and a junior in college where he's studying business. He is currently putting much of his considerable energy and talent into his co-ownership of a successful DJ company, and still spends most weekends muddying up his mother's floor. With her blessings.

Diana Gabaldon is the author of the *New York Times* bestselling *Outlander* novels—stories which, as her own editor says, "have to be word-of-mouth books, because they're too weird to describe to anyone!" She has also written pieces for the collections *Mothers & Daughters* and *Fathers & Daughters*. Trained as a scientist, Dr. Gabaldon has assorted degrees in arcane subjects (zoology, marine biology, behavioral ecology), and worked as a university professor for twelve years before retiring to cast spells full time. "People always ask me," she says, "how I got from being a scientist to being a novelist. I tell them it was easy—all you do is write a book, and bing! There you are. Sort of like being a mother—you don't need a license to do it; you just learn on the job." Gabaldon and her husband, Doug Watkins, have three children: Laura (17), Samuel (15), and Jennifer (13).

Eileen Goudge is the *New York Times* bestselling author of *Garden of Lies, Such Devoted Sisters, Blessings in Disguise, Trail of Secrets, Thorns of Truth,* and *One Last Dance,* all available in paperback from Signet. She has also written stories for the collections *Mothers & Daughters* and *Fathers & Daughters,* and is an editorial board member and frequent contributor to *The Writer* magazine. Goudge shares an 1850s Manhattan carriage house with her husband, Sandy Kenyon, a renowned broadcaster whom she met over the phone while being interviewed on the radio. Her son, Michael, a video game designer, lives on the West Coast. Her daughter, Mary, recently graduated from Bryn Mawr and is living abroad. Goudge describes her life as a single mom as, "Unpredictable and exhausting, but ultimately rewarding. There is no paint-by-numbers diagram for raising children; it's strictly do-it-yourself. You know you've done a pretty good job when you're able to look back and laugh (or cringe!), and see that it wasn't all perfect." Her latest novel, *The Second Silence,* will be available in paperback from Signet in May 2001. Look for her new hard-cover, *Stranger in Paradise*, available in June from Viking Books.

Stuart M. Kaminsky is the author of more than fifty books, most of them novels. He has also written more than forty published short stories and has had five of his screenplays produced. A book in his successful Porfiry Petrovich Rostnikov series set in contemporary Russia won the Edgar Allan Poe Award, and two others have received Edgar nominations. He also writes the Toby Peters series of nostalgic private detective novels set in the 1940s, the Abe Lieberman series about a Jewish and an Irish detective in the Chicago Police Department, the Rockford Files novels based on the popular television series, and the new Lew Fonesca series about a process server in Sarasota, Florida. Two Fonesca stories have been nominated for Edgar awards and a Macavity Reader's Choice Award. Kaminsky holds a B.S. in journalism and an M.A. in English literature from the University of Illinois, and a Ph.D. in speech from Northwestern University. He taught for sixteen years at Northwestern and at Florida State University for six years. Kaminsky lives in Sarasota with his wife and family.

Faye Kellerman is the award-winning author of numerous short stories and thirteen books, including the *New York Times* bestselling Peter Decker/Rina Lazarus thriller series. The first novel in the series, *Ritual Bath*, won the Macavity Award for best first novel. Her other books include *The Quality of Mercy, Moon Music, Sacred and Profane, Milk and Honey, Day of Atonement,*

False Prophet, Grievous Sin, Sanctuary, Justice, Prayers for the Dead, and *Serpent's Tooth.* She has also written pieces for the collections *Mothers & Daughters* and *Fathers & Daughters,* and her most recent novel, *Jupiter's Bones,* was published by Morrow. Kellerman was born in St. Louis, Missouri, and grew up in Sherman Oaks, California. She and her husband, the novelist and wonderful guy, Jonathan Kellerman, have four mind-boggling children, three intransigent dogs, one amazing bird who refuses to die, and fish too numerous to count. She lives in Los Angeles and loves her city.

Joe R. Lansdale is the author of thirteen novels and over two hundred short pieces (including fiction, non-fiction, essays, and reviews), and has edited or co-edited four fiction anthologies, one anthology of collected graphic works, and two non-fiction books. He has written for *Batman, The Animated Series* and *Superman, The Animated Series,* sold several screenplays, and even had his own comic book series, Joe R. Lansdale's *By Bizarre Hands* from Dark Horse Comics. Lansdale grew up in Gladewater, Texas, and surrounding areas, and now makes his home in Nacogdoches, Texas, with his lovely wife, Karen, and their two children, Keith and Kasey. Together they have three dogs, eleven gerbils, one guinea pig, and two cats. Lansdale is the founder of Shen Chuan, Martial Science, and operates Lansdale's Self-Defense Systems. For more information on Joe R. Lansdale, visit his website at www.joerlansdale.com.

Marcus Major's first novel, *Good Peoples,* was published by Dutton in March 2000. He dedicated the book to his mother. Major was born in Fort Bragg, North Carolina. The son of a career military man, he grew up in various parts of the United States—a childhood that was both transient and enriching. He attended Richard Stockton College, where he received a degree in literature. Major taught middle school in New Jersey before turning to writing full-time. He currently resides in south Jersey.

Jill Morgan is the author of sixteen novels, including the ecological thriller Eden trilogy: *Desert Eden*, *Beyond Eden*, and *Future Eden*. Morgan is the editor or co-editor of six major anthologies, including *Mothers & Daughters* and *Fathers & Daughters*, for which she also contributed a short story. She was born in Texas, where many of her novels are set, but now lives in southern California with her husband, John, a high school science teacher. They are the parents of two grown sons and a daughter, who make them very proud.

Maxine O'Callaghan's novels of mystery and dark suspense include a series that features Orange County PI Delilah West, credited by many critics as the first of the new female private investigators. She was also a contributor to the collection *Fathers & Daughters*. O'Callaghan's work has been nominated for the Anthony and Shamus awards in the mystery field and for the Bram Stoker Award for horror. In 1999, she received the Lifetime Achievement Award from Private Eye Writers of America for her contribution to the private eye genre. She also makes short films with her son, John. Born in rural Tennessee, she now lives in Southern California. O'Callaghan has two children and a grandson, and shares a close relationship with her family, including her children's spouses.

Marilyn Reynolds's latest book, *If You Loved Me*, was released last June and is the seventh in the popular and critically acclaimed teen fiction series, "True-to-Life from Hamilton High." Reynolds received an Emmy nomination for her work on the *ABC After-school Special* adaptation of her novel *Too Soon for Jeff*. Her essays and short stories have appeared in major national newspapers, anthologies, and literary magazines. She was also a contributor to the collection *Fathers & Daughters*. Reynolds and her husband, Mike, have recently moved from the Los Angeles area to northern California, causing all three of their adult children, but especially Matt, to rethink the idea of "home." **Matthew Reynolds** is currently doing graduate work toward a Ph.D. in visual and cultural studies at the University of Rochester in New York, and his writing has appeared in numerous publications.

Peter Straub was born in Milwaukee, Wisconsin, in 1943, and is the author of many bestselling novels, including *Ghost Story*, *Shadowland*, *Koko*, *Mystery*, *The Throat*, *The Hellfire Club*, and the recent *New York Times* bestseller, *Mr. X*. He has won a Bram Stoker Award, a British Fantasy award, two World Fantasy awards, an International Horror Guild Award, and in 1998 was elected Grand Master at the World Horror convention. Peter and Susan Straub, married for thirty-two years, live half a block from Central Park in a brownstone on the Upper West Side of Manhattan. Their two children, Benjamin and Emma, are in college.

Penguin Putnam Inc.
Online

Your Internet gateway to a virtual environment with
hundreds of entertaining and enlightening books
from Penguin Putnam Inc.

*While you're there, get the latest buzz on
the best authors and books around—*

Tom Clancy, Patricia Cornwell, W.E.B. Griffin,
Nora Roberts, William Gibson, Robin Cook,
Brian Jacques, Catherine Coulter, Stephen King,
Jacquelyn Mitchard, and many more!

**Penguin Putnam Online is located at
http://www.penguinputnam.com**

PENGUIN PUTNAM NEWS

Every month you'll get an inside look at our upcom-
ing books and new features on our site. This is an
ongoing effort to provide you with the most
up-to-date information about
our books and authors.

**Subscribe to Penguin Putnam News at
http://www.penguinputnam.com/ClubPPI**